外國名著愛情描寫一百段

100 LOVE DESCRIPTIONS FROM GREAT NOVELS

一百叢書

英漢對照 English-Chinese

符力群譯　張國楨　主編

外國名著
愛情描寫一百段

100
LOVE
DESCRIPTIONS
FROM
GREAT NOVELS

台灣日報叢書發行

《一百叢書》總序

本館出版英漢(或漢英)對照《一百叢書》的目的,是希望憑藉着英、漢兩種語言的對譯,把中國和世界各類著名作品的精華部分介紹給中外讀者。

本叢書的涉及面很廣。題材包括了寓言、詩歌、散文、短篇小説、書信、演説、語錄、神話故事、聖經故事、成語故事、名著選段等等。

顧名思義,《一百叢書》中的每一種都由一百個單元組成。以一百為單位,主要是讓編譯者在浩瀚的名著的海洋中作挑選時有一個取捨的最低和最高限額。至於取捨的標準,則是見仁見智,各有心得。

由於各種書中被選用的篇章節段,都是以原文或已被認定的範本作藍本,而譯文又經專家學者們精雕細琢,千錘百煉,故本叢書除可作為各種題材的精選讀本外,也是研習英漢兩種語言對譯的理想參考書,部分更可用作朗誦教材。外國學者如要研習漢語,本書亦不失為理想工具。

商務印書館(香港)有限公司

編輯部

前　言

　　很難想像有哪一部小說不涉及愛情。不少作品實際就是膾炙人口的愛情故事，如哈代的《無名的裘德》、小仲馬的《茶花女》、米切爾的《飄》等。愛情成為文學作品中一個永恒的主題，也是最富詩意的題材。愛情是人類的天性，使人類世世代代延續。人們栽培愛情，作家歌頌愛情，視之為人類最聖潔美好的一種感情。

　　文學作品中的愛情描寫基於現實，而又超乎現實。海明威的幾部作品都基於他在戰爭中的親身經歷。《戰地鐘聲》中的羅伯特和《永別了，武器》中的凱瑟琳都是由於戰爭而早逝。作者譴責了戰爭和侵掠對人類的摧殘，同時謳歌了在戰火中形成的純真感情，相信愛情可以超越死亡。高爾斯華綏的《福爾賽世家》、德萊塞的《美國悲劇》、菲茨杰拉德的《大亨小傳》等作品的不少情節都有現實根據。其中所描繪的不幸愛情揭露了拜金主義社會的殘酷無情。

　　《外國名著愛情描寫一百段》旨在讓讀者能在一本書中欣賞多位名家多部著作，不僅獲得美感和啟迪，產生共鳴，也在提高英語方面有所得益。

　　我們從古今中外浩如煙海的文學作品中選擇了全世界

廣為流傳的名家小說。三分之二的作品屬英美文學，而其餘的三分之一屬法國文學和俄國文學。絕大多數選材是十九世紀和二十世紀初期的經典名著，涉及作者二十九人，作品四十七部。從這些名著中，我們再選出描繪愛情及戀愛人物的心理和行為的精彩段落。

　　書中人物有不同的社會背景、職業、年齡和性格。他們在愛情生活上的經驗，反映出的個性和心情，都活現於各選段內，使本書成為一個個戀愛人物栩栩如生的劇照，把讀者帶入戀人的內心世界。

　　全書一百篇選段分九個題目，即邂逅、愛慕、戀愛、失戀、求婚、結婚、愛情之果、離別和重逢。各篇按作者出生年代先後順序排列。注釋用於提示情節、人物簡介、文化背景，以及一些語言難點。出於學習語言的目的，本書的漢譯文，在保持漢語通順的條件下，盡量貼近原文。

　　譙德鄰女士曾協助選材，郭瑞清先生對譯文作了潤飾，並負責全書電腦文字處理，特向他們表示誠摯的謝意。

　　本書在編寫和翻譯方面遠非盡善盡美，懇請讀者批評指教。

賀　方

一九九八年七月

PREFACE

It is hard to think of a novel that is not in some way about love. Quite a few novels are in fact love stories which enjoy great popularity—among others, *Jude the Obscure* by· Hardy, *La Dame aux Camélias* by Dumas fils and *Gone with the Wind* by Mitchell. Love becomes an ageless theme in works of literature and it is the most poetical topic. Love is one of the original instincts of human beings. It makes the world go round. People nurture love. Writers sing praises of love. They see it as one of the best feelings of human beings.

The description of love in literary works is based on reality but transcends it. Some novels written by Hemingway are based on his personal experience in the wars. Robert in *For Whom the Bell Tolls* and Catherine in *A Farewell to Arms* suffered from the wars and died prematurely. While condemning wars for destroying human lives and humanity, the author eulogizes the sincere feelings developed in the conflagrations of war, believing that love survives death. Many things written about in Galsworthy's *The Forsyte Saga*, Dreiser's *An American Tragedy* and Fitzgerald's *The Great Gatsby* have happened in real life. The unfortunate love experiences described in these novels reveal the cruelty of a society of money worship.

100 Love Descriptions from Great Novels aims to enable readers to appreciate different works of different masters of letter within one volume. These works often evoke the empathy of the readers. In addition to gaining aesthetic delight and inspiration, the readers will benefit in improving their English language.

Among the innumerable literary works at different times and in different countries, we have selected great novels most popular in the world. Two thirds of the selected works belong to the literature of Great Britain and the literature of the United States, while the other third to French and Russian writings. The majority of the passages have been taken from the classics of the 19th and the early 20th centuries. This book includes 29 authors and their 47 works, from which have been selected splendid passages describing love and the psychology and behaviour of the characters in love.

The characters in this book are of different social background, walks of life, age and temperament. Their experiences in love, their individual personalities and different frames of mind in love are shown vividly in the selected passages. As a result, this book becomes a lifelike portrait gallery of the characters in love, and it takes the readers on a journey into the minds of these characters.

The 100 passages are classified under nine subjects: Encounter, Affection, In Love, Disappointment, Proposal, Marriage, Fruit of Love, Separation and Reunion. Within each subject, the passages are in chronological order of the years of birth of the authors. Explanatory notes provide cues for the plots, brief information about the characters, cultural background and some language points. To answer the purpose of language learning, the Chinese translation has been made close to the English original without damaging fluency in Chinese.

I am grateful to Mrs Qiao Delin for her help in selecting materials and Mr Guo Ruiqing for his work of polishing the Chinese translations and typing the whole book on the computer.

Readers' comments or suggestions for improvement are appreciated.

He Fang
July, 1998

目　錄

CONTENTS

AFFECTION 愛慕

IN LOVE　戀愛

xiii

DISAPPOINTMENT 失戀

xiv

xvi

Encounter

邂逅

Painting by Antoine Watteau (1684-1721)

1 What Her Fancy Had Drawn

... She[1] had raised herself from the ground, but her foot had been twisted in the fall, and she was scarcely able to stand. The gentleman[2] offered his services, and perceiving that her modesty declined what her situation rendered necessary, took her up in his arms without further delay and carried her down the hill. ...

Elinor and her mother rose up in amazement at their entrance, and while the eyes of both were fixed on him with an evident wonder and a secret admiration which equally sprung from his appearance, he apologized for his intrusion by relating its cause in a manner so frank and so graceful, that his person, which was uncommonly handsome, received additional charms from his voice and expression. ...

... Marianne herself had seen less of his person than the rest, for the confusion which crimsoned over her face, on his lifting her up, had robbed her of the power of regarding him after their entering the house. But she had seen enough of

---

1. She：指 Marianne。三姐妹埃莉諾（Elinor）、瑪麗安（Marianne）和瑪格麗特（Margaret）中埃莉諾是理智的化身，瑪麗安是情感的化身。此篇中瑪麗安和瑪格麗特姐妹倆出外遊玩遇大雨，在跑下山坡時，瑪麗安不慎跌倒。

一　白馬王子

……她已經站起身來，可是她的一隻腳在跌倒時扭傷了，所以站穩腳跟十分勉強。這位紳士自告奮勇，雖然察覺她的情況需要幫助而她卻不好意思接受幫助，還是及時地把她抱起來，送下山去。……

埃莉諾和她母親看到他們進屋，驚訝地站起來。母女倆都注視着他，他的儀表顯然使她們驚嘆，暗暗讚賞。這時，他說明了唐突而來的緣由，並表示歉意，說得那麼坦誠，那麼風度翩翩，他的聲音和表情給他英俊的外貌更增添了魅力。……

……瑪麗安本人對他的外貌不如別人看得多，因為當他抱起她的時候，她心中慌亂，滿臉通紅，進屋以後也顧不上看看他了。可是她所見到的，還是足以使她能夠跟着

---

2. The gentleman：此紳士的名字是威洛比（Willoughby）。

3

him to join in all the admiration of the others, and with an energy which always adorned her praise. His person and air were equal to what her fancy had ever drawn for the hero of a favourite story; and in his carrying her into the house with so little previous formality, there was a rapidity of thought which particularly recommended the action to her. Every circumstance belonging to him was interesting. His name was good; his residence was in their favourite village; and she soon found out that of all manly dresses a shooting jacket was the most becoming. Her imagination was busy; her reflections were pleasant; and the pain of a sprained ankle was disregarded.

Jane Austen: <u>Sense and Sensibility</u>

大家對他讚賞，而且她談起來勁頭十足，使她的讚賞變得妙趣橫生。他的風姿神態，跟她愛讀的一本小説中她所幻想的白馬王子一模一樣。他抱着她送回家時，並沒有以前的繁文縟節，所以不假思索採取了有利於她的行動。有關他的情況都是頗為吸引人的。他的名字好聽，他的住處就在他們喜愛的村子裏，而且她很快發現，獵裝是最適合他的男士服裝。她的想像活躍起來，她的回憶是愉快的，腳踝傷痛也就不放在心上了。

（英）奧斯丁：《理智與情感》

2 An Object of His Interest

Occupied in observing Mr. Bingley's attentions to her sister, Elizabeth was far from suspecting that she was herself becoming an object of some interest in the eyes of his friend. Mr. Darcy had at first scarcely allowed her to be pretty; he had looked at her without admiration at the ball; and when they next met, he looked at her only to criticize. But no sooner had he made it clear to himself and his friends that she had hardly a good feature in her face, than he began to find it was rendered uncommonly intelligent by the beautiful expression of her dark eyes. ... Though he had detected with a critical eye more than one failure of perfect symmetry in her form, he was forced to acknowledge her figure to be light and pleasing; and in spite of his asserting that her manners were not those of the fashionable world, he was caught by their easy playfulness. Of this she was perfectly unaware; —to her he was only the man who made himself agreeable no where, and who had not thought her handsome enough to dance with.

Jane Austen: <u>Pride and Prejudice</u>

二　受到青睞

伊麗莎白全神貫注於賓格萊先生對她姐姐的追求，卻根本沒想到她自己受到賓格萊的朋友的青睞。達西先生起初未必認為她長得漂亮。在舞會上他並沒把她放在眼裏。難怪第二次他們相遇時，他用挑剔的眼光看着她。可是正當他使自己和他的朋友們相信她的相貌毫無可取之處的時候，轉眼之間，他開始發現她那烏黑動人的眼睛使她的面貌顯得異常聰慧。……儘管他以吹毛求疵的眼光發現她的體型多處缺乏勻稱，他還是不得不承認她的體態輕盈，討人喜歡。儘管他一再聲稱，她的言談舉止沒有上流社會的風度，他還是迷戀上她那輕鬆詼諧的情態。她對此絲毫沒有察覺，因為在她看來，他簡直是個難以討好的人，因她的長相不好而不屑和她跳舞的人。

(英) 奧斯丁：《傲慢與偏見》

3 What an Idiot!

... Myshkin[1] unbolted the door, opened it, and stepped
back in amazement, startled. Nastasya Filippovna stood
before him. He knew her at once from her photograph. There
was a gleam of annoyance in her eyes when she saw him.
She walked quickly into the hall, pushing him out of her
way, and said angrily, flinging off her fur coat:

"If you are too lazy to mend the bell, you might at least
be in the hall when people knock. Now he's dropped my
coat, the duffer!"

The coat was indeed lying on the floor. Nastasya
Filippovna, without waiting for him to help her off with it,
had flung it on his arm from behind without looking, but
Myshkin was not quick enough to catch it.

"They ought to turn you off. Go along and announce
me."

Myshkin was about to say something, but was so abashed
that he could not, and, carrying the coat which he had picked
up from the floor, he walked towards the drawing-room.

---

1. Myshkin：本書主人公梅詩金（Myshkin）腦受損傷，被人稱作"白
痴"，傾心於娜斯塔霞（Nastasya），後來與她結婚。

三　白痴

　　……梅詩金拉開門栓，開了門，嚇了一跳，驚恐地倒
退了一步。娜斯塔霞·菲立波夫娜站在他的面前。根據她
的照片，他一下子就認出她來了。她見到他時，眼中閃過
一絲厭煩的神情。她很快走進門廳，把他推到一邊，匆匆
地脫掉皮大衣，生氣地説：

　　"要是你懶得不願修好門鈴，有人敲門的時候，至少也
得待在門廳裏。看，這笨蛋又把我的大衣拖在地上啦！"

　　大衣真的拖拉在地上。娜斯塔霞·菲立波夫娜沒等他
幫着脫大衣，就從後面看也不看把大衣扔在他的手臂上
了。可是梅詩金行動太慢，沒接住。

　　"他們應該把你解僱。快去給我通報。"

　　梅詩金想要説些什麼，可是他十分尷尬，一句話也説
不出來，拿着從地上揀起來的大衣往客廳走去。

"Well, now he is taking my coat with him! Why are you carrying my coat away? Ha, ha, ha! Are you crazy?"

Myshkin went back and stared at her, as though he were petrified. When she laughed he smiled too, but still he could not speak. At the first moment when he opened the door to her, he was pale; now the colour rushed to his face.

"What an idiot!" Nastasya Filippovna cried out, stamping her foot in indignation. "Where are you going now? What name are you going to take in?"

"Nastasya Filippovna," muttered Myshkin.

"How do you know me?" she asked him quickly. "I've never seen you. Go along, take in my name. What's the shouting about in there?"

Fyodor Dostoyevsky: The Idiot

“唉，你看他又把我的大衣拿走了！你幹嗎把我的大衣帶着走？哈，哈，哈！你瘋了嗎？”

梅詩金走了回來，呆若木雞地盯着她看。她哈哈大笑的時候，他也報以微笑，不過還是說不出話來。當他為她開門的最初一剎那，臉色蒼白，可現在臉漲得通紅。

“簡直是個白痴！”娜斯塔霞·菲立波夫娜喊道，氣得直跺腳，“你現在上哪兒去？你通報什麼姓名？”

“娜斯塔霞·菲立波夫娜。”梅詩金輕聲含糊地説。

“你是怎麼認識我的？”她很快地問他，“我可從來沒見過你。去吧，去通報我的姓名。裏面吵吵鬧鬧的，怎麼回事？”

(俄)陀思妥耶夫斯基：《白痴》

4 When This Camellia Is a Different Colour

Imperceptibly, I had drawn closer to Marguerite[1], I had put my arms around her waist and could feel her supple body pressing lightly against my clasped hands.

"If you only knew how much I love you!" I whispered.

"Do you really mean it?"

"I swear it." ...

"But I warn you, I want to be free to do whatever I choose, without having to tell you anything about the life I lead. For a long time now, I've been looking for a young, easy-going lover, someone who would love me without asking questions, someone I could love without his feeling that he has any rights over me. I have never found one yet. ... If I decide to take a new lover now, I want him to have three very rare qualities: he must be trusting, submissive and discreet."

"Very well, I shall be everything you desire."

"We'll see."

"And when will we see?"

"Later."

---

1. Marguerite：貧家女瑪格麗特（Marguerite）淪為上流社會的玩物，
   藝名 "茶花女"。 她渴望真正的幸福，遇青年阿爾芒（Armand）後
   與他相愛。文中的 "我" 指阿爾芒。

四　一朵茶花

　　我不知不覺地挨近了瑪格麗特，摟着她的腰，可以感到她那柔軟的身軀輕盈地靠着我擁抱她的雙臂。

　　"你知道我是多麼愛你！"我小聲説。

　　"你是認真的？"

　　"我發誓。"……

　　"可是我要提醒你，我是不想受約束的，想幹什麼就幹什麼，不必把任何我的生活情況告訴你。長時間以來，我一直在尋找一位年輕的、合得來的情人。他能愛我，但是不盤問我，我能愛他，但不會令他感到可以支配我。這樣的人我還沒找到呢。……要是我決定要一位新的情人，我要求他具備三種很少有的品格：他必須是對人信任的、順從的、穩重的。"

　　"好極了，你的要求我都能做到。"

　　"我們看情況吧。"

　　"那麼什麼時候我們看呢？"

　　"過些時候。"

"Why?"

"Because," said Marguerite, slipping out of my arms and taking a single bloom from a large bunch of red camellias which had been delivered that morning and putting it in my buttonhole, "because you can't always implement treaties the day they are signed."

The meaning is plain.

"And when shall I see you again?" I said, taking her in my arms.

"When this camellia is a different colour."

"And when will it be a different colour?"

"Tomorrow, between eleven and midnight. Are you happy?"

"How can you ask?"

A. Dumas fils: La Dame aux Camélias

"為什麼？"

"因為，"瑪格麗特滑脫我的懷抱，從早上送來的大
束紅茶花中摘下一朵，插到我的衣紐孔裏，說道，"因為
我們總不能在協議簽訂的當天馬上就執行啊。"

這是不言而喻的。

"那麼我哪天再能見到你？"我把她抱到懷裏問道。

"當這朵茶花變顏色的時候。"

"那麼茶花什麼時候變顏色？"

"明天，晚上十一點到十二點之間。你高興嗎？"

"那還用問嗎？"

(法）小仲馬：《茶花女》

5 The Subdued Animation

Vronsky followed the guard to the carriage and had to stop at the entrance of the compartment to let a lady[1] pass out.

The trained insight of a Society man enabled Vronsky with a single glance to decide that she belonged to the best Society. He apologized for being in her way and was about to enter the carriage, but felt compelled to have another look at her, not because she was very beautiful nor because of the elegance and modest grace of her whole figure, but because he saw in her sweet face as she passed him something specially tender and kind. When he looked round she too turned her head. Her bright grey eyes which seemed dark because of their black lashes rested for a moment on his face as if recognizing him, and then turned to the passing crowd evidently in search of some one. In that short look Vronsky had time to notice the subdued animation that enlivened her face and seemed to flutter between her bright eyes and a scarcely perceptible smile which curved her rosy lips. It was

---

1. a lady：貴婦人 Anna 純潔善良，嫁給高官後，敢於反抗封建勢力，爭取愛情和自由。此篇描述她與伏倫斯基（Vronsky）相遇，四目交投的情形。

五 被壓抑的生氣

　　伏倫斯基隨列車員來到車廂，為了讓一位女士走出去，只得在包房門口站住。

　　伏倫斯基憑他上流社會磨練出來的眼光，一眼就看出來，她屬於上流社會的女子。他因為擋了道而向她道歉，正要走進車廂，但是感到非再看她一眼不可。這倒不是因為她很漂亮，也不是因為她整個體態雅致優美，恰到好處，而是因為當她走過身邊時，在她可愛的臉上，他看到了一種特別溫柔和藹的神情。他轉身看的時候，她也回過頭來。她那對明亮的灰眼睛因黑黑的眼睫毛而顯得深暗，她的目光在他臉上停留了一會兒，好像在辨認他是誰。然後她又轉向走過的乘客，顯然是在尋找一個人。伏倫斯基在這短促的一瞥中卻來得及發現了被壓抑的生氣，在她明亮的雙目間跳動，給她臉上帶來活潑的表情。他看到幾乎不能察覺的嫣然一笑，使她的玫瑰紅唇微微彎曲。她全身

as if an excess of vitality so filled her whole being that it betrayed itself against her will, now in her smile, now in the light of her eyes. She deliberately tried to extinguish that light in her eyes, but it shone despite of her in her faint smile.

Lev Tolstoy: <u>Anna Karenina</u>

好像洋溢着過剩的活力，違背着她的意願，一會兒在她的微笑中，一會兒在她的目光中，顯露出來。她特意設法熄滅眼中的光亮，可是這光亮不顧她的努力，還是在她淡淡的微笑中閃耀。

（俄）列夫·托爾斯泰：《安娜·卡列尼娜》

6　The Man from Paris

... They were walking slowly; and though it was too dark for much discovery of character from aspect, the gait of them showed that they were not workers on the heath. Eustacia[1] stepped a little out of the foot-track to let them pass. They were two women and a man; and the voices of the women were those of Mrs. Yeobright and Thomasin[2].

They went by her, and at the moment of passing appeared to discern her dusky form. There came to her ears in a masculine voice, "Good night!"

She murmured a reply, glided by them, and turned round. She could not, for a moment, believe that chance, unrequested, had brought into her presence the soul of the house she had gone to inspect[3], the man without whom her inspection would not have been thought of. ...

She could follow every word that the ramblers uttered. ... But it was not to the words that Eustacia listened; she

---

1. Eustacia（游苔莎）：熱情美貌，屬荒原的外來戶，在愛情上多經周折。
2. Mrs. Yeobright and Thomasin Yeobright（朵蓀·姚伯）：前者是克林（Clym）的母親，後者是他的堂妹。
3. the house...inspect：游苔莎（Eustacia）鍾情於克林（Clym），曾暗地裏去他的住處周圍察看過。

六　巴黎歸來人

　　……他們走得很慢。雖然天色已晚，從他們的外形不太看出是幹什麼的，但是他們走路的姿態表明，不是這兒荒原上的工人。游苔莎稍稍離開小路，讓他們走過。他們是兩個女的，一個男的。說話的兩個女人是姚伯夫人和朵蓀。

　　他們在她身邊走過。他們走過的那一會，好像看出了她在昏暗中的形體。　她聽到了男人的聲音："晚安！"

　　她低聲地回答了一句，悄悄地走過他們，又轉過身來。她一時不能相信，機緣竟不期而來，她想去察看的那幢房子的中心人物，沒有他就不會去察看的那個人，竟出現在她的面前。……

　　行路人說的每句話，她都聽得見。……但是游苔莎聽

could not even have recalled, a few minutes later, what the words were. It was to the alternating voice that gave out about one-tenth of them — the voice that had wished her good night. ... No event could have been more exciting. During the greater part of the afternoon she had been entrancing herself by imagining the fascination which must attend a man come direct from beautiful Paris — laden with its atmosphere, familiar with its charms. And this man had greeted her.

...Yeobright's son— for Clym[4] it was—startling as a sound? No: it was simply comprehensive. All emotional things were possible to the speaker of that "good night." Eustacia's imagination supplied the rest— ...

Thomas Hardy: The Return of the Native

---

4. Clym Yeobright（克林・姚伯）：荒原本地居民，曾到巴黎求學。

的不是説些什麼話，幾分鐘之後，她甚至記不起他們説些什麼了。她聽的是約佔談話十分之一的那人的應答聲 —— 剛才祝她晚安的那個説話聲。……再沒有更讓人興奮的事了。下午多半的時間，她想像着這個從美麗的巴黎直接回來的人所具有的魅力，他滿身都是巴黎味，對巴黎的美妙之處瞭如指掌。她想得出了神。就是這個人向她道了晚安。

　　……姚伯夫人的兒子 —— 。他就是克林 —— 的説話聲中有什麼驚人之處嗎？沒有，只不過是內容廣泛，無所不談罷了。在這個説晚安的人身上，感情方面的各種情況都可能發生。游苔莎的想像力提供了其他的一切 —— ……

　　　　　　　　　　　　　　（英）哈代：《還鄉》

7 A Daughter of Nature

For several days after Tess's[1] arrival Clare, sitting abstractedly reading from some book, periodical, or piece of music just come by post, hardly noticed that she was present at table. She talked so little, and the other maids talked so much, that the babble did not strike him as possessing a new note; and he was ever in the habit of neglecting the particulars of an outward scene for the general impression. ...

... The conversation at the table mixed in with his phantasmal orchestra, till he thought, "What a fluty voice one of those milkmaids has. I suppose it is the new one." Clare looked round upon her, seated with the others.

She was not looking towards him. Indeed, owing to his long silence his presence in the room was almost forgotten. ...

Clare continued to observe her. She soon finished her eating, and having a consciousness that Clare was regarding her began to trace imaginary patterns on the tablecloth with her forefinger, with the constraint of a domestic animal that perceives itself to be watched.

---

1. Tess's：苔絲（Tess）是窮苦的農村姑娘，在出外打工時被主人家的兒子亞歷克（Alec d'Urberville）誘姦，私生子又夭折。後遇牧師的兒子克萊（Angel Clare），產生愛情。

七 自然之女

　　苔絲來後的好幾天，克萊都坐在那兒出神地讀着郵差剛送來的書、雜誌，或樂譜，幾乎沒注意到她在飯桌上進餐。她說話說的那麼少，別的女工說的那麼多，在這嘮叨聲中他也就聽不出有新的嗓音了。何況他對外界事物從來只求有個總印象，而不注意細節。……

　　……飯桌上的談話聲一直混雜在他幻覺中的樂隊聲中，可現在他想：“擠奶工裏有個聲音多麼柔和清脆。我想一定是新來的。”克萊轉身看到她和大家坐在一起。

　　她沒朝他看。其實，由於他老不說話，大家幾乎忘了屋裏有他在那兒。……

　　克萊還注視着她。她很快吃完了飯，意識到克萊在看她，於是用食指在桌布上劃起虛構的圖案來，好像一頭家畜發現被人看着而感到局促不安一樣。

"What a fresh and virginal daughter of Nature that milkmaid is," he said to himself.

And then he seemed to discern in her something that was familiar, something which carried him back into a joyous and unforeseeing past, before the necessity of taking thought had made the Heavens grey. He concluded that he had beheld her before; where he could not tell. A casual encounter during some country ramble it certainly had been; and he was not greatly curious about it. But the circumstance was sufficient to lead him to select Tess in preference to the other pretty milkmaids when he wished to contemplate contiguous womankind.

Thomas Hardy: <u>Tess of the d'Urbervilles</u>

"這擠奶工是個多麼朝氣蓬勃、純潔無暇的自然之女啊！"他對自己説。

接着，他好像在她身上發現了一點熟悉的東西，這東西把他帶回到歡樂的、無遠慮的過去，那時還不必考慮那麼多以致使天堂也變得死氣沉沉。他斷定在什麼時候見到過她，但是説不準在什麼地方。一定是哪次鄉間閒逛時偶然遇見過。他對那次相遇並沒有很大的好奇心。但是現在，當他想對身邊的這些女人留意的時候，眼前的情況足以使他挑選苔絲，而別的漂亮擠奶工都不想看了。

（英）哈代：《德伯家的苔絲》

8　Her Magnetism

"... I don't know your name."

"Ah, no. Shall I tell it to you?"

"Do!"

"Arabella Donn. I'm living here."

"I must have known it if I had often come this way. But I mostly go straight along the high road."

"My father is a pig-breeder, and these girls are helping me wash the innards for black-puddings[1] and such like."

They talked a little more, and a little more, as they stood regarding each other and leaning against the hand-rail of the bridge. The unvoiced call of woman to man, which was uttered very distinctly by Arabella's personality, held Jude[2] to the spot against his intention — almost against his will, and in a way new to his experience. It is scarcely an exaggeration to say that till this moment Jude had never looked at a woman to consider her as such, but had vaguely regarded the sex as being outside his life and purposes. He gazed from her eyes

---

1. black-puddings：（用血、羊油、大麥等製成的）黑香腸。
2. Jude：《無名的裘德》描寫裘德（Jude）事業與愛情的矛盾，靈與肉的鬥爭。 他與艾拉白拉（Arabella）匆忙完婚是純肉體的結合，成為他終生的痛苦。

八　她的魅力

“……我不知道你叫什麼。”

“啊，是啊。要我告訴你嗎？”

“要！”

“我叫艾拉白拉·鄧。我就住在這兒。”

“要是過去我常走這條路，我一定早就認識了。可是我多半是一直地走大道。”

“我爸是養豬的，這幾個女孩子在幫我洗豬腸，好用來做豬血灌腸什麼的。”

他們站着，彼此看着對方，背靠着橋的欄杆，談了一會，又談一會。女性對男性無聲的呼喚，通過艾拉白拉的個性清楚地表現出來，使裘德違背原來的打算 —— 幾乎是違背意願 —— 站在那裏不走了，對他來説這是新的體驗。此刻之前，裘德看女人的時候從不想到那是個女人，而是模糊地把女性看作與他生活和目標無關的事情，這樣説並

to her mouth, thence to her bosom, and to her full round naked arms, wet, mottled with the chill of the water, and firm as marble.

"What a nice-looking girl you are!" he murmured, though the words had not been necessary to express his sense of her magnetism.

Thomas Hardy: <u>Jude the Obscure</u>

不誇張。他盯着她看，從眼睛看到嘴，從嘴看到胸，看到圓鼓鼓裸着的胳膊，濕漉漉的，因水涼變得紅一塊白一塊，堅實得像大理石。

"你真是個漂亮的姑娘！"他輕聲説，其實他對她魅力的感受，不説這句話也已經表達出來了。

（英）哈代：《無名的裘德》

9   The Crossmark

The broad street was silent, and almost deserted, although it was not late. He saw a figure on the other side, which turned out to be hers, and they both converged towards the crossmark[1] at the same moment. Before either had reached it, she called out to him:

"I am not going to meet you just there, for the first time in my life! Come further on."

The voice, though positive and silvery, had been tremulous. They walked on in parallel lines, and, waiting her pleasure, Jude[2] watched till she showed signs of closing in, ...

"I am sorry that I asked you to meet me, and didn't call," began Jude with the bashfulness of a lover. ...

"O—I don't mind that," she said with the freedom of a friend. "I have really no place to ask anybody in to. What I meant was that the place you chose was so horrid —I suppose I ought not to say horrid, —I mean gloomy and inauspicious in its associations. ... But isn't it funny to begin like this,

---

1. crossmark：路面中間石砌的十字形紀念碑，紀念兩位殉教烈士。裘德約她在十字碑處初次見面，她避開了這個地方，但她的命運並未逃脫"殉難"。

九 十字碑

　　雖然不是太晚，寬闊的街上靜悄悄的，幾乎看不見行人。他看到街對面有個人。這個人原來就是她。於是他倆齊頭並進，同時朝十字碑走去。不等誰走到那兒，她朝他喊起來：

　　"我第一次見你，不要在那兒見你！再往前走。"

　　她說話的聲音自信、清脆，不過是顫抖的。他倆一直是平行地各走各的道，在她表示有意靠近一起走之前，裘德觀察着，等着她什麼時候願意。……

　　"對不起，要你出來見我，我沒上門找你，"裘德以戀人的忸怩開口說。……

　　"哦 —— 我不在乎，"她說，像一個無拘無束的朋友，"我的確也沒地方可請客人進去的。我剛才想說的是，你選的地方太可怕 —— 我想不該說可怕 —— 我是說聯想到陰暗、不吉祥。……不過在我還不認識你的時候就

when I don't know you yet?" She looked him up and down curiously, though Jude did not look much at her.

"You seem to know me more than I know you," she added.

"Yes—I have seen you now and then."

"And you knew who I was, and didn't speak? And now I am going away."

"Yes. That's unfortunate . ...."

...

Though they had talked of nothing more than general subjects Jude[2] was surprised to find what a revelation of woman his cousin was to him. ... It was with heartsickness he perceived that, while her sentiments towards him were those of the frankest friendliness only, he loved her more than before becoming acquainted with her; and the gloom of the walk home lay not in the night overhead, but in the thought of her departure.

Thomas Hardy: Jude the Obscure

---

2. Jude：裘德對事業的追求，他對理想的愛情的追求是《無名的裘德》的兩條主要綫索。他對淑‧布萊德赫心靈相感相通。 此篇中的她指的就是淑。

這樣見面，不也很有意思嗎？"她好奇地上下打量着他，可是裘德沒有怎麼看她。

"你跟我好像比我跟你更熟一些。"她又說了一句。

"是啊 —— 我偶爾見過你幾次。"

"你早已認識我，可沒和我說過話，是嗎？可是我這就要離開這個地方了。"

"是啊。真不走運。……"

……

雖然他倆談的只是些普通話題，裘德卻驚奇地發現，這個表妹向他顯盡了一個女人的風采。……她對於他的感情只是最坦率的友誼，而他卻比認識她前更加鍾情了。他沮喪地覺察到這一點。他在歸家途中感到悶悶不樂，不是因為陰沉的夜色，而是因為她即將離去這件事縈懷心頭。

(英) 哈代：《無名的裘德》

10   Love Trap

I felt as if I were expanding in the sunshine. I was in love with everything: ... everything. I wanted to kiss something, no matter what: this was Love setting its trap for me.

...

I looked at her and she looked at me, but only now and then, ... After we had exchanged glances for some time I felt that we knew each other well enough to start a conversation. So I spoke to her and she replied. She was a sweet girl, there was no doubt about that, and she went straight to my head.

...

"Would you care to take a stroll with me, Mademoiselle?"

She gave me a quick sidelong glance, as if to size me up, and then, after hesitating for a moment, agreed. Soon we were walking side by side among the trees. ... We could hear birds singing everywhere. My companion began running and skipping, intoxicated by the fresh air and the country smells. And I ran after her, skipping and jumping in the same way.

...

Then we gazed into each other's eyes for a long time.

Oh, what power there is in a woman's eyes! ... How deep they seem, how full of infinite promise! People call that looking into each other's souls. What nonsense, Monsieur!

十 愛情陷阱

　　我沐浴在陽光裏，似乎感到熱情洋溢。我愛上了一切：……總之一切。我想吻一下什麼，不管是什麼。這時愛情在給我設陷阱。

　　……

　　我看看她，她看看我，不過只是不時地，……經過一陣眉來眼去，我感到彼此已經相識，可以交談了。我便跟她攀談起來，她也作出反應。她是個可愛的姑娘，這是無可懷疑的，她使我陶醉。

　　……

　　"小姐，你願意和我隨便走走嗎？"

　　她斜着目光迅速地看了我一眼，好像是在估量着我，接着猶豫了一下，便表示同意。不一會兒，我們肩並肩地在樹林中漫步了。……到處都聽得到鳥兒啼囀。我的同伴開始為新鮮空氣和鄉村氣息而陶醉，跑呀，跳呀。我也跑在她的後面，和她一樣蹦蹦跳跳。

　　……

　　後來我們面對面地互相看了好久。

　　啊，女人的眼睛有多麼大的威力！……這雙眼睛多麼深邃，充滿無限希望！人們說這是看到彼此的靈魂深處。

If we could really see into each other's souls we'd be much wiser than we are!

To cut a long story short, I was swept off my feet, mad with love. I tried to take her in my arms, but she cried: "Hands off!" So then I knelt down beside her and opened my heart to her, pouring out all the tenderness which was choking me. She seemed astonished at my change of manner and gave me a sidelong glance as if she were saying to herself: "So that's his little game, is it? Well, we shall see!"

In love, Monsieur, we men are always the innocents and women the tricksters.

Maupassant: <u>In the Spring</u>

先生哪，這是無稽之談！如果我們確能看到彼此的靈魂深
處，那我們比目前要聰明多了。

　　長話短説，我激動萬分，深深地愛上了她。我要把她
摟進懷裏，可是她叫了起來：“別碰我！”我便跪在她的
身邊，向她敞開心扉，把噎塞咽喉的綿綿情話一股腦地傾
吐出來。她看到我態度變化，好像很驚奇，用斜眼掃了我
一下，像是在自言自語：“這是他在耍花招吧？好吧，我
們瞧着吧！”

　　在愛情方面，先生哪，我們男人總是傻瓜，而女人總
是戲弄人的人。

　　　　　　　　　　　　　　　（法）莫泊桑：《春天》

11   Love with Just Our Souls

It was at the bottom of this garden that Maitre[1] Moreau's wife had given a rendezvous, for the first time, to Captain Sommerive, who had been paying attentions to her for a long time.

...

Now she was waiting for him, huddled against the wall, her heart pounding wildly, and starting at the slightest sound.

Suddenly she heard somebody clambering over the wall and she nearly ran away. What if it weren't the captain? What if it were a thief? But no—a voice called out softly: "Mathilde!" She replied: "Étienne!" And a man dropped on to the path with a clatter of metal.

It was he! And what a kiss they exchanged!

For a long time they remained clasped in each other's arms, their lips pressed together. ...

"Mathilde," he said, "my darling, my love, my sweet, my angel, let's go indoors. It's midnight; we have nothing to fear. Let's go inside, please."

"No, dearest," she replied. "I'm frightened. Who knows what might happen?"

---

1.   Maitre：用於對教授、律師等人的尊稱，莫羅（Moreau）是位公證人。

十一　只要心靈相愛

　　莫羅先生的妻子就是在這個花園的盡頭初次與索默里夫上尉約會的。上尉追求她已經很久了。

　　……

　　現在她正等着他，縮靠在圍牆邊上，心猛烈地怦怦跳着，稍有聲響就心驚膽戰。

　　突然，她聽見有人爬過牆來，她差點要逃走。要不是上尉呢？要是個小偷呢？還好不是，有人輕聲呼喚："馬蒂爾德！"她便回應："埃蒂安納！"於是一個男人跳落到小路上，發出金屬碰撞聲。

　　是他！他們吻了個夠！

　　他們緊緊擁抱，久久不放，嘴唇相貼。……

　　他說："馬蒂爾德，親愛的，我的心上人，寶貝，心肝，我們進屋去吧。現在是深更半夜，沒什麼好怕的。我們進屋去吧，求你了。"

　　她回答說："不行啊，親愛的。我害怕。誰知道會怎麼樣？"

But he held her tight in his arms and whispered in her ear: "Your servants' rooms are on the third floor, overlooking the square. Your room is on the first floor, looking on to the garden. Nobody will hear us. I love you, and I want to love you freely and completely, from head to foot." And he embraced her passionately, covering her face with kisses.

She still resisted him, frightened and even ashamed. But he put his arm round her waist, picked her up, and carried her off through the rain which was now pouring down.

...

Then she fell half-fainting into an armchair. He knelt down and slowly began undressing her, taking off her boots and stockings and kissing her feet.

"No, Étienne," she gasped, "please let me keep my virtue! I'd hate you for it afterwards! Besides, it's so crude and ugly! Why can't we love each other with just our souls?... Étienne!"

Maupassant: _The Matter with André_

可是他把她緊摟在懷裏，在她耳邊悄聲說："你們傭人的房間在四樓，對着廣場。你的房間在二樓，對着花園。誰也不會聽見我們。我愛你，我要自由自在地愛你，徹底地、從頭到腳地愛你。"他滿懷激情地擁抱着她，在她臉上狂吻不止。

她還是反抗着，又害怕，又害羞。可是他摟着她的腰，把她從地上抱起，走過了正下着的傾盆大雨。

……

接着她半醒半昏迷地倒在扶手椅上。而他跪在地上，開始慢慢地解開她的衣服，脫鞋脫襪，吻着她的雙腳。

她氣喘地說："埃蒂安納，別這樣，求求你，讓我保持清白！這樣做，將來我會恨你的！再說，這也太俗氣太不體面了！我們用心靈相愛不行嗎？……埃蒂安納！"

(法) 莫泊桑：《安德烈的毛病》

12　She Was an Enigma

... Mrs. Liversedge[1], with a sense of the fitness of things, had given a musical tea in his[2] honour. Late in the course of this function, which Soames, no musician, had regarded as an unmitigated bore, his eye had been caught by the face of a girl dressed in mourning, standing by herself. The lines of her tall, as yet rather thin, figure, showed through the wispy, clinging stuff of her black dress, her black-gloved hands were crossed in front of her, her lips slightly parted, and her large dark eyes wandered from face to face. ... And as Soames stood looking at her, the sensation that most men have felt at one time or another went stealing through him — a peculiar satisfaction of the senses, a peculiar certainty, which novelists and old ladies call love at first sight. Still stealthily watching her, he at once made his way to his hostess, and stood doggedly waiting for the music to cease.

"Who is that girl with yellow hair and dark eyes?" he asked.

"That—oh! Irene Heron. Her father, Professor Heron, died this year. She lives with her stepmother. She's a nice

---

1. Mrs. Liversedge：索米斯（Soames）老同學的夫人。
2. his：指索米斯，福爾賽家族（the Forsytes）的成員之一。

十二　她是個謎

　　……列佛賽基夫人頗識情理，專為他舉行了一個音樂茶會。索米斯不是音樂家，認為音樂茶會是極其乏味的活動。茶會進行到近尾聲時，他看見了一位戴孝的女郎獨自站在那裏。透過稀薄貼身的黑色衣裙，顯示出她高窈纖瘦的身材，戴着黑手套的一雙手在身前交叉着，嘴唇略微張開，褐色的大眼睛一會看看這個人的臉，一會看看那個人的臉。……當索米斯站着看她時，他身上出現了一股潛流，這是多數男人在不同時候都會感到的 —— 一種特殊的感官滿足，一種特殊的肯定，小説家和老年婦人稱之為一見鍾情。他仍舊偷偷地注視着她，同時立即走到女主人那裏，站着，耐心地等着音樂停下來。

　　"那個黃頭髮褐色眼睛的姑娘是誰？"他問道。

　　"那個 —— 噢！伊琳·海隆。她父親海隆教授今年去世的。她跟繼母住在一起。她是個好姑娘，人長得漂

girl, a pretty girl, but no money!"

"Introduce me, please," said Soames.

˙It was very little that he found to say, nor did he find her responsive to that little. But he went away with the resolution to see her again. He effected his object by chance, meeting her on the pier with her stepmother, who had the habit of walking there from twelve to one of a forenoon.

...

... Once after they were married he asked her, "What made you refuse me so often?" She had answered by a strange silence. An enigma to him from the day that he first saw her, she was an enigma to him still....

John Galsworthy: The Forsyte Saga

亮，可是沒錢！”

“請給我介紹一下。”索米斯説。

他找不到幾句話好説，即使對這不多的話也不見她有什麼反應。但是他離開時，決心還要見到她。他碰巧達到了他的目的，在碼頭那兒遇見她陪伴着她的繼母。她們有個習慣，中午十二點到一點總在那裏散步。

……

……他們結婚以後，有一次他問她：“你為什麼多次拒絕我的求婚？”她只是以古怪的沉默作為回答。從他第一次見到她以後，她對於他就是一個謎，她一直是個謎。……

（英）高爾斯華綏：《福爾賽世家》

13   He Was Captivated

But fortunately at this moment, the door opened and Bella[1] entered, accompanied by two girls such as Clyde would have assumed at once belonged to this world. How different to Rita and Zella[2] with whom his thought so recently had been disturbedly concerned. He did not know Bella, of course, until she proceeded most familiarly to address her family. But the others—one was Sondra Finchley, so frequently referred to by Bella and her mother—as smart and vain and sweet a girl as Clyde had ever laid his eyes upon—so different to any he had ever known and so superior. ... To Clyde's eyes she was the most adorable feminine thing he had seen in all his days. Indeed her effect on him was electric—thrilling—arousing in him a curiously stinging sense of what it was to want and not to have—to wish to win and yet to feel, almost agonizingly that he was destined not even to win a glance from her. It tortured and flustered him. At one moment he had a keen desire to close his eyes and shut her out—at another to look only at her constantly—so truly was he captivated.

...

---

1. Bella：貝拉，富商廠長的女兒。
2. Rita and Zella：克萊德（Clycle）結識的朋友。

十三 他被迷住了

　　可是幸運的是，就在這時門開了，貝拉走了進來，還有兩個姑娘陪伴着。克萊德立即就能看出，她們是屬於這上流社會的。她們跟他最近為之心神不定的麗達和澤拉相比，多麼不同啊。當然，他認識貝拉，只是在她開始很親密地對家人打招呼以後。但是另外兩個 —— 一個是桑德拉‧芬奇利，她就是貝拉和她母親經常提到的那個姑娘 —— 克萊德從未見到過像她這樣伶俐、自負、可愛的姑娘 —— 她跟他認識的那些姑娘是多麼不一樣，她真是鶴立雞群啊。……在克萊德眼裏，她是他有生以來最值得傾慕的女性了。她對於他的作用猶如一股電流 —— 使人震顫 —— 引起他一陣奇特的刺痛感，感到這正是他需要而又不具備的，企望贏得它，可是又感到，幾乎是痛苦地感到，他命中注定得不到哪怕是她的回首一盼。這種感覺折磨着他，使他坐立不安。有一會，他真想閉上眼睛不去看她 —— 又有一會想不停地看着她 —— 他確是被她迷住了。

　　……

Sondra nodded, pleased to note in the first instance that he was somewhat better-looking than Bella's brother, whom she did not like — next that he was obviously stricken with her, which was her due, as she invariably decided in connection with youths thus smitten with her. But having thus decided, and seeing that his glance was persistently and helplessly drawn to her, she concluded that she need pay no more attention to him, for the present anyway. He was too easy.

Theodore Dreiser: <u>An American Tragedy</u>[3]

---

3. *An American Tragedy*：《美國悲劇》描述窮苦青年 Clyde（克萊德）
   羨慕榮華富貴，為追求閣小姐 Sondra（桑德拉）而墮落為殺人犯，
   自己也成了美國之夢的受害者。

桑德拉點點頭，第一眼就看到他比貝拉的哥哥好看些，她並不喜歡貝拉的哥哥。接着她又發現，他明顯地被她迷住了。她對此受之無愧，正如她一貫認為小伙子都為她而神魂顛倒。但是她想到這裏，而且看到他的目光可憐地盯着她不放，她就決定不必再注意他了，至少這一會兒不必注意。他是很容易征服得了的。

（美）德萊塞：《美國悲劇》

14   A Girl on the Bank

He rounded a point studded with a clump of trees and bushes and covering a shallow where were scores of water lilies afloat, their large leaves resting flat upon the still water of the lake. And on the bank to the left was a girl standing and looking at them. ... She was very pretty, he thought, as he paused in his paddling to look at her. The sleeves of a pale blue waist came only to her elbows. And a darker blue skirt of flannel reconveyed to him the trimness of her figure. It wasn't Roberta[1]! It couldn't be! Yes, it was!

Almost before he had decided, he was quite beside her, some twenty feet from the shore, and was looking up at her, his face lit by the radiance of one who had suddenly, and beyond his belief, realized a dream. ... she in turn stood staring down at him, her lips unable to resist the wavy line of beauty that a happy mood always brought to them.

"My, Miss Alden! It is you, isn't it?" he called. "I was wondering whether it was. I couldn't be sure from out there."

---

1. Roberta：羅伯塔‧奧爾登（Roberta Alden）是克萊德（Clyde）同廠的女工。克萊德跟廠長有親屬關係，又在廠裏當個小頭頭，因而羅伯塔雖對他傾心，但有戒備。

十四　湖畔少女

　　他繞過一處密布着樹木和灌木叢的地方，樹叢掩蔽着一片淺水，水上漂浮着數十來朵睡蓮，睡蓮的大片葉子平躺在靜止的湖水面上。湖岸的左邊站着一位姑娘，觀賞着睡蓮。……他停下槳來看她，他想，她很美。淡藍色上身的袖子只到肘部，深一些的藍色法蘭絨裙子更向他顯示了亭亭玉立的身材。這不是羅伯塔嘛！這不可能！可是，就是她！

　　他幾乎還沒來得及考慮，就靠近她了，離岸約有二十英尺。他抬頭看着她，容光煥發，就像一個人的夢想突然變成了現實，還不敢相信那樣。……而她呢，站在那裏向下凝視着他，她的嘴唇不由得因高興而形成美麗的波浪綫條。

　　"天哪，奧爾登小姐！是你呀？"他叫道，"我還在想是不是你呢，剛才在那邊我拿不準。"

"Why, yes it is," she laughed, puzzled, and again just the least bit abashed by the reality of him. ... And yet here was her friend, Grace Marr. Would she want her to know of Clyde and her interest in him? She was troubled. And yet she could not resist smiling and looking at him in a frank and welcoming way. She had been thinking of him so much and wishing for him in some happy, secure, commendable way. And now here he was. And there could be nothing more innocent than his presence here—nor hers.

Theodore Dreiser: <u>An American Tragedy</u>

"可不就是我嗎，"她哈哈笑起來，感到窘迫，還因為真的見到他而感到有點羞怯。……可是她的女友格雷斯·瑪爾也在這兒。要不要讓她知道克萊德的事呢？讓她知道對他有意呢？羅伯塔感到為難了。可是她不由自主地微笑着，望着他，神情是坦率的，欣喜的。她對他朝思暮想，想找個妥當的機會，高興地見他一面。可現在他就在眼前。他在這裏出現是最自然不過的，她來到這裏，也同樣是最自然的。

　　　　　　　　　(美）德萊塞：《美國悲劇》

15   His Fate Was Coming

He[1] felt also a curious certainty about her[2], as if she were destined to him. It was to him a profound satisfaction that she was a foreigner.

A swift change had taken place on the earth for him, as if a new creation were fulfilled, in which he had real existence. ...

He dared scarcely think of the woman. He was afraid. Only all the time he was aware of her presence not far off, he lived in her. But he dared not know her, even acquaint himself with her by thinking of her.

One day he met her walking along the road with her little girl. It was a child with a face like a bud of apple-blossom.... The child clung jealously to her mother's side when he looked at her, staring with resentful black eyes. But the mother glanced at him again, almost vacantly. And the very vacancy of her look inflamed him. She had wide grey-brown eyes with very dark, fathomless pupils. He felt the fine flame running under his skin, as if all his veins had caught fire on the surface. ...

---

1. He：指湯姆・布朗溫（Tom Brangwen）。
2. her：指蘭斯基太太（Mrs. Lensky），蘭斯基醫生的遺孀。

十五　命運來了

　　他覺得對她有一種莫名其妙的確認，好像她就是為他而生的。她是外國人，對這一點他特別滿意。

　　世界對他發生了迅速的變化，好像有一件新事物出現了，他真實地存在於其中。……

　　他幾乎不敢去想這個女人。他害怕。只是時時刻刻他感到她就在近旁，他與她同呼吸，共命運。但是他不敢去認識她，即使在心中想念着認識也不敢。

　　一天，他遇見她正和她小女兒在路上走着。這孩子的臉像朵蘋果花，含苞待放，……當他看着她的時候，這孩子有戒心地緊緊依偎在她母親身邊，一對黑眼睛不滿地凝視着。這母親又對他茫然地看了一眼。正是這茫然的目光點燃了他的熱情。她長着一對灰褐色的大眼睛，黑黑的瞳孔深不可測。他感到一股純煉的火焰在表皮下流動，仿佛每根血管上都着了火。……

It was coming, he knew, his fate. The world was submitting to its transformation. He made no move: it would come, what would come.

When his sister Effie came to the Marsh for a week, he went with her for once to church. In the tiny place, with its mere dozen pews, he sat not far from the stranger. There was a fineness about her, a poignancy about the way she sat and held her head lifted. She was strange, from far off, yet so intimate. She was from far away, a presence, so close to his soul.

D. H. Lawrence: *The Rainbow*

他知道，他的命運來了。世界在變化。他一動也沒動，因為該來的自然會來。

　　他姐姐艾菲來馬施住了一個星期。他跟她去了一次教堂。裏面窄小，只有十二條長凳。他坐得離那陌生人不遠。她儀態端莊，抬着頭的坐姿給人以深刻印象。她是外地來的，很遙遠，可是又那麼親近。她來自遠方，可是她的存在離他的心靈卻近在咫尺。

　　　　　　　　　　　　　　（英）勞倫斯：《虹》

16 Rather He Took a Liberty

Rhett said frankly that the crêpe veil made her look like a crow and the black dresses[1] added ten years to her age. This ungallant statement sent her flying to the mirror to see if she really did look twenty-eight instead of eighteen.

...

One bright summer morning some weeks later, he reappeared with a brightly trimmed hatbox in his hand and, ...

"Put it on," said Rhett, smiling.

She flew across the room to the mirror and popped it on her head, pushing back her hair to show her earrings and tying the ribbon under her chin.

...

"Oh, dear," thought Scarlett, looking first at herself in the mirror and then at Rhett's unreadable face. "I simply can't tell him I won't accept it. It's too darling. I'd—I'd almost rather he took a liberty, if it was a very small one." Then she was horrified at herself for having such a thought and she turned pink.

...

---

1. ... the black dresses：斯卡雷特（Scarlett）先後與查爾斯和弗蘭克結婚，並無真正的愛情。他們死後，瑞得（Rhett）愛上了她，且設法贏得了她的愛。此篇描寫斯卡雷特新寡期間與瑞得一次會見時的心態。

十六　讓他放肆

　　瑞得直率地説過，帽子上的黑紗弄得她像隻烏鴉，黑衣服讓她老了十歲。她聽到這不客氣的話後就飛快地跑向鏡子，看看自己是不是真的不是十八歲，而是二十八歲了。

　　……

　　幾個星期以後，一個陽光燦爛的夏天早晨，他手提一個裝飾華麗的帽子盒又來了，……

　　"把它戴上。"瑞得笑着説。

　　她飛跑到鏡子前，迅速地把帽子戴到頭上，把頭髮推到腦後，露出耳環，在頦下繫好帽帶。

　　……

　　"啊，真棒，"斯卡雷特心裏想。她先照照鏡子，再看看瑞得那令人猜不透的臉。"我簡直沒法對他説我不收下這帽子。這帽子太惹人喜歡了。我寧可 —— 寧可讓他放肆一點，要是那是小小的放肆的話。"這時，她感到驚恐，怎麼會有這樣的想法，臉微微紅了起來。

　　……

His black eyes sought her face and travelled to her lips. Scarlett cast down her eyes, excitement filling her. Now, he was going to try to take liberties, ... He was going to kiss her, or try to kiss her, and she couldn't quite make up her flurried mind which it should be. If she refused, he might jerk the bonnet right off her head and give it to some other girl. On the other hand, if she permitted one chaste peck, he might bring her other lovely presents in the hope of getting another kiss. Men set such a store by[2] kisses, though Heaven alone knew why. And lots of times, after one kiss they fell completely in love with a girl. ... It would be so exciting to have Rhett Butler in love with her and admitting it and begging for a kiss or smile. Yes, she would let him kiss her.

Margaret Mitchell: <u>Gone with the Wind</u>

---

2. set such a store by：重視。

他那對黑眼珠在她臉上搜索，眼光移到了她的嘴唇上。斯卡雷特目光低垂，萬分激動。現在，他就要放肆了，……他要吻她了，或者說他要試圖吻她了。她心慌意亂，拿不定主意，不知道怎麼才好。要是她拒絕，他就可能一下子把帽子從她頭上摘下來，拿去給別的女孩子。反之，要是她讓他規矩地快吻一下，他就可能再給她帶來可愛的禮物，希望再吻她。男人這樣注重親吻，只有天知道為什麼。往往他們經過一次接吻，就完全愛上了一個女孩子……。讓瑞得‧巴特勒愛上她，而且他承認愛她，要求吻一下或者笑一笑，那是多麼帶勁啊。是啊，她願意讓他吻。

　　　　　　　　　　　　（美）米切爾：《飄》

Affection
愛慕

Painting by Pablo Picasso (1881-1973)

17　One Great Difference Between Us

When Jane and Elizabeth[1] were alone, the former, who had been cautious in her praise of Mr. Bingley before, expressed to her sister how very much she admired him.

"He is just what a young man ought to be," said she, "sensible, good humoured, lively; and I never saw such happy manners!—so much ease, with such perfect good breeding!"

"He is also handsome," replied Elizabeth, "which a young man ought likewise to be, if he possibly can. His character is thereby complete."

"I was very much flattered by his asking me to dance a second time. I did not expect such a compliment."

"Did not you? I did for you. But that is one great difference between us. Compliments always take you by surprise, and me never. What could be more natural than his asking you again? He could not help seeing that you were about five times as pretty as every other woman in the room. No thanks to his gallantry for that. Well, he certainly is very agreeable, and I give you leave[2] to like him. You have liked many a stupider person."

---

1. Jane and Elizabeth：珍妮（Jane）和伊麗莎白（Elizabeth）都在物色意中人。珍妮看中了賓格萊（Bingley），卻不表露。作者通過姐妹倆的談心，刻劃了伊麗莎白的獨特性格。
2. give you leave (to do sth.)：同意（某人做某事）。

十七　大不相同

　　珍妮對賓格萊先生的讚許一直保持緘默慎重的態度，只是和妹妹伊麗莎白在一起的時候，才向妹妹訴說她是多麼愛慕他。

　　"他正是個年輕人的樣子，"她説，"他通情達理，脾氣好，又活潑。我從來沒見到過這樣得體的舉止！—— 那麼瀟灑，又有完美的教養！"

　　"他長得儀表堂堂，"伊麗莎白回答道，"一個年輕人，只要做得到，就應該像這個樣子。所以他的品格夠完美的了。"

　　"他第二次來邀請我跳舞，我感到高興極了。這樣抬舉我，真沒想到。"

　　"你真沒想到？我倒是為你想到了。這恰好是你我兩人大不相同的地方。別人的恭維總是使你受寵若驚，而我，卻從來不這樣。他第二次邀請你跳舞，還有比這更自然的事嗎？他不能不看到你比起屋裏別的女人漂亮好幾倍。對他獻的殷勤何必感激。不過，他當然是很討人喜歡的。你喜歡他，我不反對。你喜歡過好多更蠢的人。"

"Dear Lizzy[3]!"

"Oh! you are a great deal too apt, you know, to like people in general. You never see a fault in anybody. All the world are good and agreeable in your eyes. I never heard you speak ill of a human being in my life."

Jane Austen: <u>Pride and Prejudice</u>

---

3. Lizzy：Elizabeth 的昵稱。

“麗莎！”

“哦！你知道，你總是太輕易對人產生好感了。你從來看不出任何人的短處。在你的眼裏，世上的人都是好人，都討人喜愛。我有生以來，從來沒聽你說過誰不好。”

（英）奧斯丁：《傲慢與偏見》

18   He Seemed Belong to Her

... She[1] heard enough to know that Mr. Weston was giving some information about his son: she heard the words "my son," and "Frank," and "my son," repeated several times over; and, from a few other half syllables, very much suspected that he was announcing an early visit from his son; but...the subject was so completely past, that any reviving question from her would have been awkward.

Now it so happened, that, in spite of Emma's resolution of never marrying, there was something in the name, in the idea, of Mr. Frank Churchill[2], which always interested her. She had frequently thought—especially since his father's marriage with Miss Taylor—that if she were to marry, he was the very person to suit her in age, character, and condition. He seemed, by this connection between the families, quite to belong to her. She could not but suppose it to be a match that everybody who knew them must think of. That Mr. and Mrs. Weston did think of it, she was very strongly persuaded; ...

---

1. She：指愛瑪（Emma）。她的家庭教師泰勒（Taylor）嫁給威斯頓（Weston）。這次愛瑪隨父親到威斯頓家作客，遇見了一些親友。
2. Frank Churchill（弗蘭克・邱吉爾）：威斯頓前妻生的兒子，住在外地舅母家。

十八　天生佳偶

　　……她從聽到的一些話中得知，威斯頓先生正在講他
兒子的消息。她聽到"我的兒子"、"弗蘭克"、"我的
兒子"這樣一些話，重複了好幾遍。她從一些其他片言隻
語裏可以猜到，他在宣布他兒子的一次及早的來訪。但
是……話題已經完全轉換了，她要是再提個問題來恢復這
個話題，就會讓人感到彆扭的。

　　現在發生了這樣的情況：愛瑪雖然決心永遠不結婚，
不過凡是提到弗蘭克・邱吉爾先生的名字，凡是想到他的
事，她都感興趣。她常常想——特別是弗蘭克父親和泰勒
小姐結婚以來——如果她結婚，那麼他在年齡、性格、處
境等方面，是最合適她的人選了。由於兩家的這種關係，
好像他就是屬於她的。她不能不認為，這是他們的熟人必
定想到的姻緣。威斯頓夫婦想到這件事，她是確信無疑

she had a great curiosity to see him, a decided intention of finding him pleasant, of being liked by him to a certain degree, and a sort of pleasure in the idea of their being coupled in their friends' imaginations.

Jane Austen: <u>*Emma*</u>

的。……她懷有極大的好奇心要見見他，決意要發現他是個討人喜歡的人，很想在一定程度上得到他的喜歡，一想到他們倆在親友的心目中是一對佳偶，就有一種欣喜感。

(英) 奧斯丁：《愛瑪》

19   Her Soul Was Led Astray

... Julien[1] covered the hand that had been left to him with passionate kisses, or at least so they seemed to Madame de Rênal. And yet the poor woman had had proof during that fateful day that the man she adored, without admitting it to herself, was in love with someone else! All during his absence she had been in the grip of intense unhappiness, and this had made her think seriously.

"What!" she said to herself. "Can I be in love? I, a married woman, in love? But I've never felt for my husband that dark passion which makes it impossible for me to take my mind off Julien. He's actually only a boy who's filled with respect for me! This madness will pass. What difference do my feelings for the young man make to my husband? Monsieur de Rênal would be bored by the conversations Julien and I have about things of the imagination. He thinks of nothing except his business. I'm not taking anything away from him to give to Julien."

---

1. Julien：于連在市長德・勒那爾先生（Monsieur de Rênal）家做家庭教師，為了考驗自己的意志力，他誘騙了善良的女主人（Madame de Rênal）的愛情。

十九　歧途

　　……于連在那隻沒抽回去的手上蓋滿了熱情的吻，至少德·勒那爾夫人覺得是熱情的。不過這可憐的女人在這倒霉的一天裏找到了證據，她所愛慕的、但自己並不承認愛慕的這個人正跟別人戀愛！在他不在的這段時間裏，她一直非常悶悶不樂，這使她認真地思索。

　　"怎麼！"她自言自語，"我會墮入情網？我，已婚的女人，墮入情網？這種使我不可能不想于連的隱秘的激情，我對於丈夫是從來沒有過的。他實際上不過是對我十分尊敬的孩子！這種瘋狂就會過去的。我對這個年輕人的感情會對我的丈夫有什麼影響呢？德·勒那爾先生對于連和我有關空想事物的談話會厭煩的。他想的只是他的業務。我並沒從他那裏奪取什麼去給于連。"

No hypocrisy soiled the purity of her guileless soul, led astray by a passion it had never known before. She was mistaken, although she did not know it, and yet a certain instinct of virtue in her had been alarmed. Such were the inner conflicts that had been troubling her when Julien appeared in the garden. ...

His passionate kisses, unlike any she had ever received before, suddenly made her forget that he was perhaps in love with another woman. Soon he was no longer guilty in her eyes. The cessation of her keen anguish, born of suspicion, and the presence of a happiness she had never even dreamed of, gave her intense surges of love and wild gaiety.

H. B. Stendhal: The Red and the Black

她的心靈是真誠的，它的純潔一點也沒有被虛偽玷污，卻被它從未感受過的激情引入了歧途。她錯了，儘管她並不知道這一點，可是她內心裏貞潔的本性已經受到驚嚇了。這就是于連在花園裏出現時困擾她的內心鬥爭。⋯⋯

他熱情的吻不像她以前接受過的吻，突然使她忘掉，說不定他還跟另外一個女人談戀愛。過不多久，在她眼裏，他不再有罪了。猜疑引起的劇痛已經停止，做夢也想不到的幸福感出現了，使她心裏激蕩着澎湃的愛情和狂喜。

(法) 司湯達：《紅與黑》

20　The Musketeer's Dreams

But what were the meditations which thus led him[1] from his way; contemplating, with successive sighs and smiles, the stars that glittered in the sky.

Alas! he was intent on Madame Bonancieux[2]. To an apprentice musketeer, the charms of that young person raised her almost into an ideal of love. Pretty, mysterious, and initiated into all the court secrets, which reflected so much charming seriousness over her seductive features, he supposed her, also, to be not wholly unimpassioned, which is an irresistible attraction to novices in these engagements of the heart. He felt, moreover, that he had delivered her from the hands of miscreants who wished to search and maltreat her; and this important service had prepossessed her with a sentiment of gratitude towards him, which might easily be made to take a character of greater tenderness.

So rapidly do our dreams travel on imagination's wings, that d'Artagnan already fancied himself accosted by some messenger from Madame Bonancieux, handing to him an

---

1. him：指達達尼昂（d'Artagnan），一個沒落貴族家庭出身的青年，最後成為火槍營副統領。
2. Madame Bonancieux（波那雪夫人）：王后的女侍，求助達達尼昂解救了王后的危機。

二十　火槍手的美夢

　　他在想些什麼以致走錯了路。他凝視着天空中閃爍的星星，接連不斷地微笑和嘆氣。

　　哎呀！他一心想的是波那雪夫人。這位年輕女子的美貌對於一個火槍手學徒來説，幾乎是愛情的最高理想了。她漂亮、神秘，知道宮廷裏的一切秘密，這使她誘人的容顏反映出迷人的莊嚴。他也認為她不是完全不動感情的，這對初涉情場的新手確是抵擋不住的誘惑。何況，他覺得，他把她從那些想搜捕虐待她的歹徒手中救了出來，而這項重要效勞足以使她對他懷有感激之情，而這種感情很容易帶有更多的柔情。

　　我們的美夢插着想像的翅膀飛行得很快，達達尼昂已經幻想着波那雪夫人的一位信差來到身邊，交給他一封約

appointment for an interview, or a diamond or a chain of gold. We have already intimated that the young cavaliers were not then ashamed of accepting presents from their king; and we may add, that, in those times of easy morality, they were not more scrupulous in respect of their mistresses, and that these latter almost always conferred upon them some precious and durable memorials, as though they were endeavouring to overcome the instability of their sentiments by the solidity of gifts.

Men did not then blush at owing their advancement to women; and we might refer to many amongst the heroes of that age of gallantry, who would neither have won their spurs[3] at first, nor their battles afterwards, but for the better or worse furnished purse which some mistress had suspended at their saddle-bow.

A. Dumas: *The Three Musketeers*

---

3. won their spurs：（古時）因功被封為武士；（喻）立功成名。

會的信，或者一顆鑽石，或者一條金鏈。我們已經提到過，那時候的年輕騎士接受他們國王的禮物是不感到羞愧的。我們還可以補充一句，在那個道德觀念寬鬆的時代，年輕騎士對於情人更是不拘小節了。 情人差不多總是贈送給他們珍貴的長久性紀念物品，仿佛想靠充實的禮物克服他們輕浮反覆的情感。

那時候，男人靠女人而飛黃騰達是不會臉紅的。我們可以指出騎士時代的許多英雄人物，要不是在馬鞍的前穹掛着一位情婦提供的或大或小的錢袋，是既不能建樹功勳，也不會打勝仗的。

（法）大仲馬：《三個火槍手》

21　A Look of Infinite Sweetness

... He leaned over the balustrade and called out, "Mademoiselle[1]!"

She was not beating her tambourine at that moment. She turned her head in the direction from which the call had come, saw Phoebus and stopped short. He beckoned to her. She continued to look at him, then blushed as if a flame had come up into her cheeks. Placing her tambourine under her arm, she walked past the gaping spectators toward the door of the Gondelaurier mansion, slowly, unsteadily and with the troubled look of a bird which has yielded to the fascination of a snake.

A moment later she appeared on the threshold, blushing, speechless, breathless, her large eyes cast down, not daring to take another step into the room. ...

"My dear girl," said Phoebus pompously, "I don't know if I have the extreme good fortune to be recognized by you ..."

She interrupted him with a smile and a look of infinite sweetness. "Oh, yes!" she said. ...

---

1. Mademoiselle：指愛斯美臘達（Esmeralda）。活潑、純潔、漂亮的愛斯美臘達見到年輕瀟灑、性格輕薄的御前侍衛弓手隊長費比斯（Phoebus），便產生了愛慕之情。

二十一　溫情脈脈

　　……他倚在陽台欄杆上喊了一聲："小姐！"

　　這時，她不在敲鈴鼓。她轉過頭朝喊叫的方向望去，看見了費比斯，突然停止了舞步。他招手要她過去。她還是看着他，接着兩頰緋紅，好像燃起了火焰。她把鈴鼓挾在腋下，穿過目瞪口呆的觀眾，朝貢得羅里埃府第的大門走去，腳步緩慢不穩。她的目光就像小鳥抵擋不住蛇的魅力時那樣慌亂失措。

　　不一會兒，她出現在門檻上，紅着臉，屏息無語，一雙大眼睛低垂，不敢往屋裏上前一步。……

　　"我親愛的姑娘，"費比斯裝腔作勢地説，"我不知道是不是極為榮幸被您認出來了……"

　　她嫣然一笑，目光裏充滿無限的柔情，打斷了他的話説："啊，是啊！"……

"You were certainly in a hurry to get away from me the other evening," said Phoebus. "Are you afraid of me?"

"Oh, no!" replied the gypsy girl.

There was something in the way she said this "Oh, no!" immediately after the "Oh, yes!"

...

Madame de Gondelaurier stood up and said irritably, "Well, now, if you're not going to entertain us, what are you doing in here?"

Without answering, the gypsy girl began to walk toward the door. But the closer she came to it the more slowly she walked. All at once she turned, looked at Phoebus with tearful eyes and stopped.

"Wait a minute!" cried the captain. "That's no way to leave. Come back and dance for us awhile. By the way, what's your name?"

"La Esmeralda," she said without taking her eyes off him.

Victor Hugo: The Hunchback of Notre Dame

"那天晚上您一定逃走得很匆忙，"費比斯說，"您怕我嗎？"

"噢，不！"吉卜賽姑娘說。

她說完"啊，是啊！"又馬上說"噢，不！"，說話的神態中有點值得注意的東西。

……

貢得羅里埃夫人站了起來，煩躁地說："好吧，要是你不打算讓我們得到娛樂，你在這兒還能幹些什麼呢？"

吉卜賽姑娘沒有回答，開始朝門走去。她離門愈近，走得愈慢。突然她轉過身來，眼淚汪汪地看着費比斯，又站住了。

"等一等！"衛隊長喊道，"您不能走。回來給我們跳一會兒舞。對了，您叫什麼名字？"

"愛斯美臘達。"她目不轉睛地看着他說。

（法）雨果：《巴黎聖母院》

22　Practice Makes Perfect

... Jem Wilson[1] said nothing, but loved on and on, ever more fondly; he hoped against hope[2]; he would not give up, for it seemed like giving up life to give up thought of Mary. He did not dare to look to any end of all this; the present, so that he saw her, touched the hem of her garment, was enough. Surely, in time, such deep love would beget love.

He would not relinquish hope, and yet her coldness of manner was enough to daunt any man; and it made Jem more despairing than he would acknowledge for a long time even to himself.

But one evening he came round by Barton's house, a willing messenger for his father, and opening the door saw Margaret[3] sitting asleep before the fire. She had come in to speak to Mary; and worn out by a long, working, watching night, she fell asleep in the genial warmth.

... and stepping gently up; he kissed Margaret with a friendly kiss.

---

1. Jem Wilson：《瑪麗‧巴頓》一書以十九世紀英國經濟蕭條時期為背景，棉紡廠老工人約翰‧巴頓在貧困綫上掙扎。機工杰姆‧威爾遜（Jem Wilson）鍾情於他的女兒瑪麗（Mary）。
2. hoped against hope：絕望中抱一綫希望。
3. Margaret：瑪麗的密友。

二十二　熟能生巧

　　……杰姆·威爾遜沒説什麼，只是不停地愛着，愈益執着。他還抱有一綫希望。他並不放棄，因為放棄思念瑪麗就像放棄生命。他不敢預料這一切會有什麼結果。現在，只要他能見到她，那怕只碰到她衣服的邊緣，這就夠了。這樣的深情最終一定會喚起對方的愛的。

　　他不放棄希望，不過她的冷淡態度足以使任何人灰心。杰姆也很失望，但很長時間甚至對自己還不承認。

　　有一天晚上，他自願為父親做送信人，來到巴頓的家。他開門的時候，看見瑪格萊特正坐在火爐旁瞌睡。她是來找瑪麗談事的，由於晚上長時間工作值夜，在溫暖宜人的爐火旁睡着了。

　　……他輕輕地走近瑪格萊特，像朋友那樣吻了她一下。

She awoke, and perfectly understanding the thing, she said, "For shame of yourself, Jem! What would Mary say?"

Lightly said, lightly answered.

"She'd nobbut[4] say, practice makes perfect." And they both laughed. But the words Margaret had said rankled in Jem's mind. Would Mary care? Would she care in the very least? They seemed to call for an answer by night and by day; and Jem felt that his heart told him Mary was quite indifferent to any action of his. Still he loved, on and on, ever more fondly.

Mrs. Gaskell: <u>Mary Barton</u>

---

4. nobbut：none but，only。

她醒了，很清楚是怎麽回事，便說：“杰姆，你多丢臉！看瑪麗會怎麽説？”

　　問得輕鬆，答得也好。

　　“她只不過會説，熟能生巧。”他們兩個人都笑了。可是瑪格萊特説的話刺痛了杰姆的心。瑪麗會在乎嗎？她會有一點在乎嗎？對這些問題無論晚上還是白天，好像要他作出回答。而杰姆覺得，他内心對自己説，他做些什麽，瑪麗絲毫也不關心。可他還是不停地愛着，愈益執着。

　　　　　　　　（英）蓋斯凱爾夫人：《瑪麗·巴頓》

23 An Abyss of Love

..."Where is Miss Dora[1]?" said Mr. Spenlow to the servant. "Dora!" I thought. "What a beautiful name!"

... I was a captive and a slave. I loved Dora Spenlow to distraction!

She was more than human to me. She was a Fairy, a Sylph[2], I don't know what she was: anything that no one ever saw, and everything that everybody ever wanted. I was swallowed up in an abyss of love in an instant. There was no pausing on the brink; no looking down, or looking back; I was gone, headlong, before I had sense to say a word to her. ...

The idea of dressing one's self, or doing anything in the way of action, in that state of love, was a little too ridiculous. I could only sit down before my fire, biting the key of my carpet-bag, and think of the captivating, girlish, bright-eyed lovely Dora. What a form she had, what a face she had, what a graceful, variable, enchanting manner! ...

I don't remember who was there, except Dora. I have not the least idea what we had for dinner, besides Dora. My

---

1. Dora：大衛‧科波菲爾（David Copperfield）在斯本羅（Spenlow）律師事務所當見習生，與律師女兒朵拉（Dora）一見鍾情。
2. Sylph：古代神話中空氣裏的女神，後借用來比喻美女。

二十三　愛情深淵

……"朵拉小姐在哪兒？"斯本羅先生問僕人。"朵拉！"我在想："多好聽的名字！"

……我是個俘虜，我是個奴隸。我愛朵拉·斯本羅愛得發狂了！

她對於我來說已經不是凡人了。她是仙女，她是空氣中的精靈。我說不清楚她是怎麼樣的一個人：是一個沒人看見過的人，是每個人需要的人。一瞬間，我被愛情的深淵吞噬了。在深淵的邊緣上沒停留，沒往下看，也沒回頭。我還沒來得及意識到該對她說句話，就一頭栽了進去。……

處於戀愛狀態下，要想打扮自己或做點什麼事情，不免有些可笑。我只能坐在火爐旁，咬着毯製的旅行包上的鑰匙，想着迷人的、女孩子氣的、眼睛明亮的、可愛的朵拉。她有多好的身材！多漂亮的臉龐！她的動作多麼優雅多變、嫵媚動人！……

除了朵拉，還有誰在座，我不記得了。除了朵拉，我們還吃了什麼，我毫無印象。我唯一的印象是：整個朵拉

impression is, that I dined off Dora, entirely, and sent away half-a-dozen plates untouched. I sat next to her. I talked to her. She had the most delightful little voice, the gayest little laugh, the pleasantest and most fascinating little ways, that ever led a lost youth into hopeless slavery. She was rather diminutive altogether. So much the more precious, I thought.

Charles Dickens: <u>David Copperfield</u>

秀色可餐，我把她飽餐了一頓，而半打的菜餚乾脆沒碰就撤走了。我挨着她坐。我跟她攀談。她細聲細氣的說話最悦耳，她低聲的微笑最歡快，他的小動作最討人喜歡、最迷人，能使一個迷茫的青年成為絕望的奴隸。她整個人全都是小巧的。我想，她也就更受珍愛了。

(英) 狄更斯：《大衛·科波菲爾》

24　You Are a Dog in the Manger

..."You are surely losing your reason. When have I[1] been harsh, tell me?"

"Yesterday," sobbed Isabella, "and now!"

"Yesterday!" said her sister-in-law. "On what occasion?"

"In our walk along the moor; you told me to ramble where I pleased, while you sauntered on with Mr. Heathcliff!"

"And that's your notion of harshness!" said Catherine, laughing. "It was no hint that your company was superfluous; we didn't care whether you kept with us or not; I merely thought Heathcliff's talk would have nothing entertaining for your ears."

"Oh, no," wept the young lady. "you wished me away, because you knew I liked to be there!"

... "I'll repeat our conversation, word for word, Isabella; and you point out any charm it could have had for you."

"I don't mind the conversation," she answered: "I wanted to be with—"

---

1. I：指呼嘯山莊的凱瑟琳（Catherine）。她雖然嫁給了畫眉田莊的埃德加・林頓（Edgar Linton），卻跟希斯克利夫（Heathcliff）的舊情藕斷絲連。 希斯克利夫騙取了埃德加的妹妹伊莎貝拉（Isabella）的愛情，最後與她結了婚。

二十四　損人不利己

　　……"你一定是神經失常了。我什麼時候對你厲害
了？你説呀。"

　　"昨天，"伊莎貝拉抽噎地説，"還有現在！"

　　"昨天！"她嫂嫂説，"哪件事上？"

　　"我們在荒野散步的時候。你叫我隨便上哪兒去都行，
而你呢，還繼續和希斯克利夫先生一起閒逛！"

　　"啊，這就是你認為的厲害？"凱瑟琳大笑説，"這不
説明我們嫌你跟我們在一起。你在不在，我們不在乎。我
只是想，希斯克利夫的談話你聽了不會有興趣。"

　　"噢，不是這樣，"姑娘哭着説，"你要我走開，是因
為你知道我願意在那兒。"

　　……"我可以把我們的談話一句一句地給你再説一
遍，伊莎貝拉，你就指出來，有哪句話你是感興趣的。"

　　"你們談些什麼，我不在意，"她回答説，"我是要跟
───"

"Well!" said Catherine, perceiving her hesitate to complete the sentence.

"With him; and I won't be always sent off!" she continued, kindling up. "You are a dog in the manger[2], Cathy, and desire no one to be loved but yourself!"

"You are an impertinent little monkey!" exclaimed Mrs. Linton, in surprise. "But I'll not believe this idiocy! It is impossible that you can covet the admiration of Heathcliff—that you can consider him an agreeable person! I hope I have misunderstood you, Isabella?"

"No, you have not," said the infatuated girl. " I love him more than ever you loved Edgar; and he might love me if you would let him!"

Emily Brontë: <u>Wuthering Heights</u>

---

2. a dog in the manger：源自《伊索寓言》，喻自己不能享用，又不讓給別人者。

"説呀！"凱瑟琳説，發現她遲疑着沒把話説完。

"跟他，我不會總是讓人打發走的！"她接着説下去，變得激動起來，"你是佔馬槽的狗，卡瑟，只想人愛你，不讓人愛別人！"

"你是個瞎胡鬧的小猢猻！"林頓夫人驚叫道，"我不會相信這樣的蠢事！你妄想希斯克利夫愛慕你，你要把他當作可愛的人，這是做不到的！我希望我誤會了你的意思，伊莎貝拉，是嗎？"

"不，你沒誤會，"這個迷了心竅的姑娘説，"我愛他比你愛埃德加還要深。只要你允許他，他可能愛我的！"

（英）艾米莉·勃朗特：《呼嘯山莊》

25 The Dangerous Intimacy

... Not a day passed, in that dangerous intimacy of teacher and pupil, in which my hand was not close to Miss Fairlie's; my cheek, as we bent together over her sketchbook, almost touching hers. The more attentively she watched every movement of my brush, the more closely I was breathing the perfume of her hair, and the warm fragrance of her breath. ...

The evenings which followed the sketching excursions of the afternoon, varied, rather than checked, these innocent, these inevitable familiarities. My natural fondness for the music which she played with such tender feeling, such delicate womanly taste, and her natural enjoyment of giving me back, by the practice of her art, the pleasure which I had offered to her by the practice of mine, only wove another tie which drew us closer and closer to one another. ...

... I should have asked why any room in the house was better than home to me when she entered it, and barren as a desert when she went out again—why I always noticed and remembered the little changes in her dress that I had noticed and remembered in no other woman's before—why I saw her, heard her, and touched her (when we shook hands at night and morning) as I had never seen, heard, and touched any other woman in my life? I should have looked into my

二十五　危險的親密

　　……我和費爾利小姐處於這種師生間危險的親密狀態中。我的手沒有一天不緊靠她的手。我們俯身一起看她的寫生簿的時候，我的臉頰幾乎碰到了她的臉頰。她看着我畫筆的每一個動作，她愈是專心，我愈是靠近她的頭，聞到頭髮的香味，也聞到她溫馨的呼吸。……

　　下午出外寫生以後的夜晚並沒有停止這種純真的、不可避免的親密關係，只是變換了形式罷了。她彈奏的音樂是那麼委婉纏綿，富於女性的嬌柔，對於這樣的音樂我出自內心地愛聽。她以彈奏音樂回報了我教她繪畫的樂趣，對於這樣的回報她也出自內心地高興。這樣又編織了新的紐帶，把我們聯繫得更加緊密。……

　　……那時我該問問自己為什麼每當她進來的時候，我覺得這幢房子裏的任何房間都比我的家還好？而每當她走出房間的時候，為什麼就像沙漠一樣荒涼？為什麼對於她穿戴的微小變化，我總是關注，而且也記在心裏？而以前我是從不關注，也不記得別的女人的穿戴變化的。每當我看到她，聽到她說話，（早上和晚上握手問好）觸碰到她的時候，為什麼不像我有生以來看到、聽到、觸碰到別的女人那樣呢？那時我該查看一下我的內心世界，發現新的苗

own heart, and found this new growth springing up there, and plucked it out while it was young. Why was this easiest, simplest work of self-culture always too much for me? The explanation has been written already in the three words that were many enough, and plain enough, for my confession. I loved her.

W. W. Collins: The Woman in White

頭，就在萌芽狀態中把它拔除。為什麼連這樣最容易、最簡單自我修養的事情我總辦不到呢？我寫的三個字已經可以說明了。我的表白只需三個字就夠，而且也夠清楚的：我愛她。

（英）科林斯：《白衣女人》

26 Seeing Her As One Sees the Sun

At four o'clock that afternoon Levin[1], conscious that his heart was beating rapidly, got out of the hired sleoge at the Zoological Gardens and went down the path leading to the ice-hills[2] and skating lake, sure of finding Kitty there, for he had noticed the Shcherbatsky's[3] carriage at the entrance.

He walked along the path leading to the skating lake, and kept repeating to himself: "I must not be excited. I must be quiet! ... What are you doing? What's the matter? Be quiet, stupid!" he said to his heart. But the more he tried to be calm, the more laboured grew his breath. He met an acquaintance who called to him, but Levin did not even notice who it was. ... A few more steps brought him to the skating lake, and among all the skaters he at once recognized her. He knew she was there by the joy and terror that took possession of his heart. She stood talking to a lady at the other end of the lake. There seemed to be nothing striking in her dress or attitude, but it was as easy for Levin to recognize her in that

---

1. Levin：列文；他懷着對吉蒂(Kitty)愛慕之情，從家鄉特意趕到莫斯科與她會面。
2. ice-hills：有冰道的小山坡，用於滑雪橇運動。
3. Shcherbatsky：謝爾巴茨基，吉蒂家族的姓。

二十六　她像太陽

　　那天下午四時，列文感到心跳得很快，在動物園門前走下出租雪橇，順着小路走去，小路通向滑雪橇小山坡和湖面冰場。他相信一定能在那裏找到吉蒂，因為他看到謝爾巴茨基家的馬車已經停在入口處。

　　他順着通向湖面冰場的小路走去，不斷地對自己說："我不應該激動。我應該鎮靜！……你在幹什麼？你怎麼啦？鎮靜，傻瓜！"他心裏這麼說着。可是他愈是要鎮靜，呼吸愈是困難。列文遇到一位熟人叫他，但他甚至沒注意到這是誰。……他再走幾步，來到了湖面冰場。他在滑冰人群裏立刻認出了她。他驚喜交加的心情說明，他知道她就在那兒。她站在湖的另一端跟一位女士交談着。她的衣著和姿態看起來並無特別之處，但是列文在人群中認

crowd as to find a rose among nettles. Everything was lit up by her. She was the smile that brightened everything around.

"Can I really step down on to the ice, and go up to her?" he thought. The spot where she stood seemed to him an unapproachable sanctuary, and there was a moment when he nearly went away, he was so filled with awe. He had to make an effort and reason with himself that all sorts of people were passing near her and he himself might have come just to skate. He stepped down, avoiding any long look at her as one avoids long looks at the sun, but seeing her as one sees the sun, without looking.

Lev Tolstoy: <u>Anna Karenina</u>

出了她，就像在蕁麻叢中找到一朵玫瑰花那樣容易。一切都因為有了她而生輝。她是照亮周圍一切的微笑。

"我真的能踏上冰場，走到她身邊去嗎？"他想。他覺得她站着的地方是可望不可及的聖殿。有一瞬間，他幾乎想走開了，因為他滿懷敬畏。他不得不竭力為自己找到理由，既然各種各樣的人都從她身邊走過，他也未嘗不可來滑冰。他走了過去，不對她多看，就像人們不多看太陽那樣，但是能看到她，就像人們即使不看着太陽，也能看到太陽。

(俄) 列夫·托爾斯泰：《安娜·卡列尼娜》

27 Something to Tell You

"Boris, come here," said she[1] with a sly and significant look. "I have something to tell you. Here, here!" ...

"What is the *something*?" asked he.

She grew confused, glanced round, and seeing the doll she had thrown down on one of the tubs, picked it up.

"Kiss the doll," said she.

Boris looked attentively and kindly at her eager face, but did not reply.

"Don't you want to? Well then, come here," said she, and went further in among the plants and threw down the doll. "Closer, closer!" she whispered.

She caught the young officer by his cuffs, and a look of solemnity and fear appeared on her flushed face.

"And me? Would you like to kiss me?" she whispered almost inaudibly, glancing up at him from under her brows, smiling, and almost crying from excitement.

Boris blushed.

"How funny you are!" he said, bending down to her and blushing still more, but he waited and did nothing.

---

1. she：指娜塔莎（Natasha）。此篇裏的娜塔莎當時只有十二歲。

二十七 愛的承諾

"鮑里斯，過來。"她說，神情是頑皮而意味深長的，"我有事對你說。這兒來，來。"……

"什麼事？"他問。

她發起窘來，看看四周，看見她扔在一個花桶上的布娃娃，便把布娃娃拾起來。"親親這布娃娃吧。"她說。

鮑里斯專注而和藹地看着她那熱切的臉，卻沒回答。

"您不想親親它嗎？那麼，到這兒來。"她說，走到花叢的深處，扔掉了布娃娃。"走近點，近點！"她低聲說。

她抓住年輕軍官的兩隻袖口，泛紅的臉蛋兒上露出一副莊嚴、害怕的神情。

"我呢？您願意親親我嗎？"她說，聲音低得幾乎聽不到，眼睛從眉毛下面往上看着他，微笑着，激動得差點哭出來了。

鮑里斯臉紅了。

"你真好玩！"他說，對她俯下身來，臉更紅了，可是等待着，一動也不動。

Suddenly she jumped up onto a tub to be higher than he, embraced him so that both her slender bare arms clasped him above his neck, and tossing back her hair, kissed him full on the lips.

Then she slipped down among the flower pots on the other side of the tubs and stood, hanging her head.

"Natasha," he said, "you know that I love you, but..."

"You are in love with me?" Natasha broke in.

"Yes, I am, but please don't let us do like that... In another four years... then I will ask for your hand."

Natasha considered.

"Thirteen, fourteen, fifteen, sixteen," she counted on her slender little fingers. "All right! Then it's settled?"

A smile of joy and satisfaction lit up her eager face.

Lev Tolstoy: War and Peace

突然，她跳上一個花桶，站得比他高些，用那雙裸露的細小的胳膊摟住他的脖子，把頭髮甩向腦後，在他的嘴唇上不偏不倚地吻了一下。

然後她穿過一些花盆，溜到花桶的另一邊，低頭站在那裏。

"娜塔莎，"他說，"您知道我愛您，可是……"

"您愛上我了嗎？"娜塔莎插嘴說。

"是啊，我愛上您了，可是求您，我們別這樣……再過四年……到那時我會向您求婚。"

娜塔莎思量着。

"十三，十四，十五，十六，"她用纖細的小指頭數着。"好吧！就這麼說定了？"

欣喜和滿意的笑容為她帶着熱切神情的臉龐平添光彩。

（俄）列夫·托爾斯泰：《戰爭與和平》

28　The Insoluble Question

... Behind her sat Anatole, and conscious of his proximity she experienced a frightened sense of expectancy.

...

... Anatole asked Natasha for a valse and as they danced he pressed her waist and hand and told her she was bewitching and that he loved her. During the Écossaise[1], which she also danced with him, Anatole said nothing when they happened to be by themselves, but merely gazed at her. Natasha lifted her frightend eyes to him, but there was such confident tenderness in his affectionate look and smile that she could not, whilst looking at him, say what she had to say. She lowered her eyes.

"Don't say such things to me. I am betrothed and love another," she said rapidly. ... She glanced at him.

Anatole was not upset or pained by what she had said.

"Don't speak to me of that! What can I do?" said he. "I tell you I am madly, madly, in love with you! Is it my fault that you are enchanting? ... It's our turn to begin."

1.　Écossaise：（法文）蘇格蘭舞。

二十八　究竟愛誰

……她後面坐的是阿納托爾。她意識到他就在近旁，因而有一種期待着什麼的惶恐不安的感覺。

……

……阿納托爾邀請了娜塔莎跳華爾茲舞。跳舞的時候，他摟着她的腰，捏着她的手，對她説她很迷人，他愛她。她還和他跳了蘇格蘭舞。在這過程中，只有他們兩個人在一起的時候，阿納托爾一句話也沒説，只是望着她。娜塔莎抬頭以驚恐的眼光看看他，可是在他情意綿綿的眼神和笑容裏充滿着那樣自信的表情，她面對着他看的時候，連該説的話也説不出來了。她雙目低垂。

"別對我説這樣的話。我已經訂婚，愛着別人了。"她急忙説，……看了他一眼。

阿納托爾並沒有因為她説的話而不高興，也不痛苦。

"不用對我説這些！我有什麼辦法？"他説，"我告訴你，我深深地，深深地愛上了你！你這樣迷人能怨我嗎？……該我們跳了。"

Natasha animated and excited, looked about her with wide-open frightened eyes and seemed merrier than usual. She understood hardly anything that went on that evening....

...

After reaching home Natasha did not sleep all night. She was tormented by the insoluble question whether she loved Anatole or Prince Andrew.... "...What am I to do if I love him and the other one too?" she asked herself, unable to find an answer to these terrible questions.

Lev Tolstoy: War and Peace

娜塔莎興奮、激動，張大着驚恐的眼睛，朝四周看看，好像比平時高興。她對這天晚上發生的事情迷惑不解。……

　　　　……

　　娜塔莎回家後，整夜不能入眠。一個解決不了的難題折磨着她：究竟她愛阿納托爾，還是愛安德烈公爵？……“……我愛他，也愛另一個，我該怎麼辦呢？”她自言自語，而對這些可怕的問題找不到答案。

　　　　（俄）列夫·托爾斯泰：《戰爭與和平》

29 He Grew Very Sad

From that moment relations between Nekhlyudov[1] and Katusha were changed and the sort of connexion was established which often exists between an innocent young man and an equally innocent young girl, who are attracted to one another.

The instant Katya[2] entered the room, or if he saw her white apron from a distance, it was as if the sun had come out: everything seemed more interesting, gayer, and life held more meaning and was happier. And she felt the same. But it was not only Katusha's presence or the fact that she was near that had this effect on Nekhlyudov: the mere thought that Katusha existed, and for her that Nekhlyudov existed, produced the same effect. If Nekhlyudov received an unpleasant letter from his mother, or could not get on with his thesis, or if he felt sad for no reason, the way young people do—he had only to think that there was a Katusha and he would be seeing her, and all his troubles would vanish.

---

1. Nekhlyudov：貴族大學生聶赫留朵夫（Nekhlyudov）在姑媽家度暑假，遇侍女卡秋莎（Katusha）。
2. Katya（卡佳）：卡秋莎的另一稱呼。

二十九　無限惆悵

　　從那時起，聶赫留朵夫和卡秋莎兩人間的關係起了變化。這是天真單純的青年和同樣天真單純的少女互相吸引時，常有的一種聯繫。

　　每當卡秋莎走進房間，或者他從老遠看見她的白圍裙的時候，一瞬間好像陽光燦爛，一切顯得更有趣，更快活，生活更有意義，更加幸福。她的感覺也是一樣。不過這不僅僅是因為卡秋莎在場，或者她在近旁，才對聶赫留朵夫有這種作用的。只要他想到卡秋莎存在，而且他為她存在，也會產生同樣的效果。如果聶赫留朵夫收到母親的一封使人不高興的信，或者論文寫不下去，或者像青年人常有的那樣無端憂愁，他只需想想有個卡秋莎，他就要見到她，這時，他的一切煩惱也就煙消雲散了。

... And it was these talks in Matriona Pavlovna's[3] presence which were the most enjoyable. When they were alone it was worse. Their eyes at once began to say something very different and far more important than what their lips were saying; their mouths seemed shuttered, and a strange unaccountable fear made them part hurriedly.

... and so he left, still unaware of his love for Katusha.

He was sure that his feeling for Katusha was simply one of the manifestations of the joy of life that filled his whole being and was shared by that sweet, light-hearted girl. Yet for all that, when he was going away and Katusha, standing on the porch with his aunts, saw him off with her black eyes that had a slight cast full of tears, he was conscious of leaving behind him something beautiful and precious, which could never be repeated. And he grew very sad.

"Good-bye, Dmitri Ivanovich[4]," she said in her agreeable, caressing voice, and, keeping back the tears which filled her eyes, ran into the hall, where she could cry her fill.

Lev Tolstoy: Resurrection

---

3. Matriona Pavlovna（瑪特寥娜・帕夫洛夫娜）：老女僕。
4. Dmitri Ivanovich（德米特里・伊凡內奇）：聶赫留朵夫的名字。

……瑪特寥娜‧帕夫洛夫娜在場的時候，他們談起話來，興致勃勃。只有他們兩人獨處的時候，談話就不那麼輕鬆愉快了。他們眼睛表示的比起嘴説的，很不相同，而且重要得多。他們的嘴好像被封上了，一種莫名其妙的恐懼使他們匆匆分手。

　　……所以他還是沒意識到他已經愛上了卡秋莎，就離開了姑媽的家。

　　他滿以為，他對卡秋莎的感情只不過是他全身洋溢着人生喜悦的一種表現罷了，而這種喜悦也是這位無憂無慮的溫柔姑娘同樣感受到的。儘管是這樣，他走的那天，卡秋莎跟着他姑媽一起站在門口，她那雙烏黑的眼睛熱淚盈眶，略微斜倪，目送着他，這時他意識到，他失去一種美麗及珍貴的東西，它一去不復返了。於是，他感到無限惆悵。

　　“再見，德米特里‧伊凡內奇！”她説，嗓音悦耳，充滿撫愛。她忍住滿溢的淚水，跑進門廊，在那裏好哭個夠。

　　　　　　(俄) 列夫‧托爾斯泰：《復活》

30 A Private Enjoyment

The only superiority in women that is tolerable to the rival sex is, as a rule, that of the unconscious kind; but a superiority which recognizes itself may sometimes please by suggesting possibilities of capture to the subordinated man.

This well-favoured and comely girl[1] soon made appreciable inroads upon the emotional constitution of young Farmer Oak.

... every morning Oak's feelings were as sensitive as the money-market in calculations upon his chances. His dog waited for his meals in a way so like that in which Oak waited for the girl's presence that the farmer was quite struck with the resemblance, felt it lowering, and would not look at the dog. However, he continued to watch through the hedge for her regular coming, and thus his sentiments towards her were deepened without any corresponding effect being produced upon herself. ...

By making inquiries he found that the girl's name was Bathsheba Everdene, and that the cow would go dry in about seven days. He dreaded the eighth day.

---

1. This...girl：指巴絲謝芭（Bathsheba）。好幾個人追求着她。這些追求者改變了她原來的生活秩序。她擺脫不了這樣的 madding crowd（狂亂的人群）。書名《Far from the Madding Crowd》頗具諷刺意味。

三十 自得其樂

　　女人身上唯一能使異性容忍的優勢，通常是一種不自覺的優勢，但是優勢一旦自覺，卻會向願從屬於她的男人暗示她可能屈服，這往往就能討得對方的喜歡。

　　這個清秀可人的姑娘過不多久就顯而易見地闖入了年輕農民奧克的感情世界。

　　……每天早晨奧克的感情就像金融市場那樣敏感，盤算着他的機緣。奧克的那隻狗等着主人吃飯，很像他等着那姑娘出現，這種相似使他深有感觸。他感到這貶低自己，於是不去看狗了。儘管如此，他還是繼續透過樹籬觀看等着她按時來到，這樣，他對她的感情加深了，而在她身上卻沒有造成任何相應的反應。……

　　他經過打聽，得知這姑娘的姓名是巴絲謝芭·埃弗登。他還了解到那頭奶牛再過七天左右就沒奶了。他擔心着第八天。

At last the eighth day came. The cow had ceased to give milk for that year, and Bathsheba Everdene came up the hill no more. Gabriel[2] had reached a pitch of existence he never could have anticipated a short time before. He liked saying "Bathsheba" as a private enjoyment instead of whistling; turned over his taste to black hair, though he had sworn by brown ever since he was a boy; isolated himself till the space he filled in the public eye was contemptibly small. ... and said to himself, "I'll make her my wife, or upon my soul I shall be good for nothing!"

Thomas Hardy: <u>Far from the Madding Crowd</u>

---

2. Gabriel：奧克（Oak）的名字。

第八天還是到了。這頭奶牛這年不再產奶了。巴絲謝芭·埃弗登再也不上山來了。奧克活得這麼有勁，就在不久以前，他還沒料想到。他不吹口哨而喜歡念叨着"巴絲謝芭"，暗暗地自得其樂。雖然他自幼就鄭重表示過喜歡褐色頭髮，現在他卻變得喜歡黑頭髮了。他不與人來往，使他在大家眼裏所佔的位置已經小到讓人不屑一顧了。……他對自己説："我要娶她，要不我敢發誓我是個窩囊廢！"

(英) 哈代：《遠離塵囂》

31 Such Dreams Are Not for You

The next day was windy—so windy that walking in the garden she picked up a portion of the draft of a letter on business in Donald Farfrae's writing, which had flown over the wall from the office. The useless scrap she took indoors, and began to copy the calligraphy, which she much admired. The letter began "Dear Sir," and presently writing on a loose slip "Elizabeth-Jane," she laid the latter over "Sir," making the phrase "Dear Elizabeth-Jane." When she saw the effect a quick red ran up her face and warmed her through, though nobody was there to see what she had done. She quickly tore up the slip, and threw it away. After this she grew cool and laughed at herself, walked about the room and laughed again; not joyfully, but distressfully rather. ...

Her heart fluttered when she heard of this step of Donald's, proving that he meant to remain—and yet—would a man who cared one little bit for her have endangered his suit by setting up a business in opposition to Mr. Henchard's? Surely not; and it must have been a passing impulse only which had led him to address her so softly.

To solve the problem whether her appearance on the evening of the dance were such as to inspire a fleeting love at first sight, she dressed herself up exactly as she had dressed

三十一　少女的心事

　　第二天是個颱風天。風那麼大,她在花園走的時候,拾到一張業務信函的部分草稿,是從辦公室吹過牆來的,是唐納·法爾弗雷的筆迹。她把這作廢的信紙碎片拿進屋裏,照着信上寫的字臨摹起來,信上寫的字她很欣賞。信的開頭是"親愛的先生"。現在她在稀薄的紙條上寫了"伊麗莎白·珍妮",再把寫好的紙條蓋住"先生",變成短語"親愛的伊麗莎白·珍妮"。她看到這個效果時,雖然沒人在那看到她做的事,她臉上還是立即泛起了紅暈,全身發熱。於是她很快把寫的字條撕毀扔掉了。隨後她冷靜下來,對自己笑笑,在房間裏來回走着,又笑了一陣,不是高興地笑,而是有點苦惱。……

　　當她得知唐納的這一步計劃時,她的心一陣亂跳。這計劃說明唐納要留下來不走了 —— 可是 —— 對她稍稍有意的人怎麼會開一家與亨查德對峙的商號來危害他的求婚呢?肯定是不會的;這必定只是一時的衝動,才對她說了一些溫柔的話。

　　那天晚間舞會上,她的外貌是否一下子就能激起別人瞬間的愛慕?為了解答這個問題,她又照那天晚上的穿着

then—the muslin, the spencer, the sandals, the parasol—and looked in the mirror. The picture glassed back was, in her opinion, precisely of such a kind as to inspire that fleeting regard, and no more;—"just enough to make him silly, and not enough to keep him so," she said luminously; and Elizabeth thought, in a much lower key[1], that by this time he had discovered how plain and homely was the informing spirit of that pretty outside.

Hence, when she felt her heart going out to him she would say to herself with a mock pleasantry that carried an ache with it, "No, no, Elizabeth-Jane—such dreams are not for you!" She tried to prevent herself from seeing him, and thinking of him; succeeding fairly well in the former attempt, in the latter not so completely.

Thomas Hardy: The Mayor of Casterbridge

---

1. in a low key：用低沉的聲調。

一模一樣地打扮起來 —— 薄紗衫、短上衣、涼鞋、陽傘
—— 對着鏡子看。依她的想法，鏡子裏照出來的確實是一
種能夠激起瞬間愛慕的模樣，僅此而已；——"只夠蒙
混，不夠持久。"她說得明白易懂。伊麗莎白又以克制的
心情想，這時他已經發現，這漂亮的外表展示的精神卻是
平庸的、普通的。

　　從此以後，每當她的心飛向法爾弗雷時，她總是痛苦
地對自己開玩笑說："不，不，伊麗莎白·珍妮 —— 這樣
的夢不是該你做的！"她竭力不讓自己見到法爾弗雷，也
不想他。不見他，做得相當好，而不想他卻不能完全做到
了。

　　　　　　　　　（英）哈代：《卡斯特橋市長》

32　He Was Stronger and Higher

"I say," said Hurstwood[1], as they came up the theatre lobby, "we are exceedingly charming this evening."

Carrie fluttered under his approving glance.

"Did you ever see Jefferson?" he questioned, as he leaned toward Carrie in the box.

"I never did," she returned.

"He's delightful, delightful," he went on, giving the commonplace rendition of approval which such men know. He sent Drouet after a programme, and then discoursed to Carrie concerning Jefferson as he had heard of him. The former was pleased beyond expression, and was really hypnotised by the environment, the trappings of the box, the elegance of her companion. Several times their eyes accidentally met, and then there poured into hers such a flood of feeling as she had never before experienced. She could not for the moment explain it, for in the next glance or the next move of the hand there was seeming indifference, mingled only with the kindest attention.

1.　Hurstwood：上流酒吧經理赫斯特伍德（Hurstwood）邀請德魯埃（Drouet）和嘉莉（Carrie）看劇。

三十二　更強更高

　　"我説，"當他們走到劇場門廳時，赫斯特伍德説，"今晚我們都非常的楚楚動人。"

　　嘉莉在他的讚賞目光下微覺不安。

　　"你看過杰斐遜的劇嗎？"他在包廂裏俯身對着嘉莉問道。

　　"我從來沒看過。"她回答説。

　　"他演得很好，不俗。"他接着説，説着這種人常用的一般讚美語言。他讓德魯埃去拿節目表，便跟嘉莉談論起他聽説杰斐遜的有關情況。嘉莉高興得無法形容。周圍的環境、包廂的裝飾和這位同伴的雅致風度使她着了迷。他們的目光好幾次偶爾相遇，這時有一股感情熱流注入她的眼睛，這是她從未感受過的熱流。她對這個一時也説不清楚，因為下一次的目光或手勢裏又是表面上的冷淡，只不過夾雜着最親切的關心。

Drouet shared in the conversation, but he was almost dull in comparison. Hurstwood entertained them both, and now it was driven into Carrie's mind that here was the superior man. She instinctively felt that he was stronger and higher, and yet withal so simple. By the end of the third act she was sure that Drouet was only a kindly soul, but otherwise defective. He sank every moment in her estimation by the strong comparison.

"I have had such a nice time," said Carrie, when it was all over and they were coming out.

"Yes, indeed," added Drouet, who was not in the least aware that a battle had been fought and his defences weakened. He was like the Emperor of China, who sat glorying in himself, unaware that his fairest provinces were being wrested from him.

"Well, you have saved me a dreary evening," returned Hurstwood. "Good-night."

He took Carrie's little hand, and a current of feeling swept from one to the other.

Theodore Dreiser: <u>Sister Carrie</u>

德魯埃也參與談話，不過相比之下，他幾乎是遲鈍乏味的。赫斯特伍德使他們兩人都開心。這時嘉莉心中深深感到：這是個了不起的人。她本能地覺得，他更強更高，而且平易近人。第三幕演完時，她已經明白，德魯埃只不過是個好心人，可是其他方面是有缺陷的。在鮮明的對比下，他在她心中的價值愈降愈低了。

　　"我過得高興極了。"散場後，他們走出來的時候，嘉莉說。

　　"是啊，真的。"德魯埃補充了一句，他一點也沒有察覺到，一場較量已經進行了，他的防禦力量已經削弱了。他像中國的皇帝，坐在那裏妄自尊大，最好的省份正在被人奪走，還麻木不仁。

　　"好吧，你們讓我避過了一個沉悶的夜晚，"赫斯特伍德回答，"再見。"

　　他拿起嘉莉的一隻小手，感情的暖流便從一人傳到另一人身上。

　　　　　　　　　　　　　（美）德萊塞：《嘉莉妹妹》

33   She Was Different

And so it was that Roberta, after encountering Clyde and sensing the superior world in which she imagined he moved, and being so taken with the charm of his personality, was seized with the very virus of ambition and unrest that afflicted him. And every day that she went to the factory now she could not help but feel that his eyes were upon her in a quiet, seeking and yet doubtful way. Yet she also felt that he was too uncertain as to what she would think of any overture that he might make in her direction to risk a repulse or any offensive interpretation on her part. And yet at times, after the first two weeks of her stay here, she wishing that he would speak to her—that he would make some beginning— at other times that he must not dare—that it would be dreadful and impossible. The other girls there would see at once. And since they all plainly felt that he was too good or too remote for them, they would at once note that he was making an exception in her case and would put their own interpretation on it....

At the same time in so far as Clyde and his leaning toward her was concerned there was that rule laid down by Gilbert[1].

---

1. Gilbert（吉爾伯特）：廠主的兒子，協助他父親管理工廠。

三十三　與眾不同

　　羅伯塔與克萊德相遇，察覺到她想像他活動於其中的上流社會，被他頗有魅力的性格所吸引，於是，他受感染的奢望和不安本分的病毒現在也傳染給了她。現在，她每天到工廠上班的時候，不由自主地就感到他默默地看著她，目光含有尋求和懷疑的神情。可是，她也感到他沒有足夠的信心對她採取主動的一步，因為他不知道她會有什麼想法，怕遭到她的拒絕，引起她的誤會。不過，她來工廠過了兩週以後，有時候，她很想他能跟她攀談 —— 他能打開話題 —— 有時候，她又認為他不應該這樣冒失，這是可怕的，不可能的。別的姑娘會馬上發現的。她們很清楚地感到，他太好了，是高不可攀的，所以假如他對她態度特殊，她們會立即注意到的，對此她們會有各自的猜測。……

　　與此同時，對於克萊德和他對她偏愛這個問題上，已經有吉爾伯特定下的規矩了。正因為這樣，到目前為止，

And although, because of it, he had hitherto appeared not to notice or to give any more attention to one girl than another, still, once Roberta arrived, he was almost unconsciously inclined to drift by her table and pause in her vicinity to see how she was progressing. And, as he saw from the first, she was a quick and intelligent worker, soon mastering without much advice of any kind all the tricks of the work, and thereafter earning about as much as any of the others—fifteen dollars a week. And her manner was always that of one who enjoyed it and was happy to have the privilege of working here. And pleased to have him pay any little attention to her.

At the same time he noted to his surprise and especially since to him she seemed so refined and different, a certain exuberance and gayety that was not only emotional, but in a delicate poetic way, sensual.

Theodore Dreiser: <u>An American Tragedy</u>

儘管他在表面上不注意或不過多注意某一個姑娘，還是有那麼一次，當羅伯塔來上班時，他幾乎是下意識地逛到她的桌子旁邊，在她的周圍停下來看她工作進展的情況。正如他一開始就看到的那樣，她是個聰明伶俐的女工，不需多少指點就掌握了工作的全部技巧，後來掙的錢跟別的女工幾乎一樣多 —— 每週十五美元。她幹起來總是像一個樂於幹這工作的工人，為能有幸在這裏工作而感到高興。他只要對她有一點微小關注，她就心滿意足了。

　　與此同時，由於他一開始覺得她似乎很文雅，與眾不同，現在卻發現，她為人開朗快活，這不只是情感方面的，而且含有雅致的詩意，具有性感，這使他感到驚奇。

（美）德萊塞：《美國悲劇》

34 Your Daffodils Are Nearly Out

...Paul[1] she eyed rather wistfully. On the whole, she scorned the male sex. But here was a new specimen, quick, light, graceful, who could be gentle and who could be sad, and who was clever, and who knew a lot, and who had a death in the family. The boy's poor morsel of learning exalted him almost sky-high in her esteem. Yet she tried hard to scorn him, because he would not see in her the princess but only the swine-girl. And he scarcely observed her.

Then he was so ill, and she felt he would be weak. Then she would be stronger than he. Then she could love him. If she could be mistress of him in his weakness, take care of him, if he could depend on her, if she could, as it were, have him in her arms, how she would love him!

...

Miriam, peeping through the kitchen window, saw the horse walk through the big white gate into the farmyard that was backed by the oak-wood, still bare. Then a youth in a heavy overcoat climbed down. He put up his hands for the

---

1. Paul：保羅受到母親的寵愛。但當他與米麗亞姆（Miriam）相愛時，卻得不到母親的支持。米麗亞姆靦腆，寡言，是個虔誠的教徒。

三十四　水仙花

……她以相當渴望的心情看保羅。總的說來，她是藐視男性的。可是，眼前是一個從沒見過的人，機智、靈巧、文雅；能溫柔，也能悲傷；他聰明，見多識廣，家裏有過喪事。這男孩的一點知識就把她心中對他的尊敬捧上了天。不過她還盡力蔑視他，因為他總不把她看作公主，只把她看作卑賤的女孩。而且他幾乎沒注視過她。

後來他病得很厲害，所以她覺得他身體會虛弱的。這時，她就比他強了。這樣她可以愛他了。如果她能在他體弱的時候做他的情人，照料他，如果他能依靠她，如果可以說把他摟在懷中，那她不知多麼愛他呢！

……

米麗亞姆透過廚房的窗戶在窺探，看到馬兒走過白色的大門，進入了背靠着未長樹葉的橡樹林的院子。然後一個穿厚大衣的年輕人爬下車來。他舉起雙手去接那個相貌

whip and the rug that the good-looking, ruddy farmer handed down to him.

Miriam appeared in the doorway. She was nearly sixteen, very beautiful, with her warm colouring, her gravity, her eyes dilating suddenly like an ecstasy.

"I say," said Paul, turning shyly aside, "your daffodils are nearly out. Isn't it early? But don't they look cold?"

"Cold!" said Miriam, in her musical, caressing voice.

"The green on their buds—" and he faltered into silence timidly.

D. H. Lawrence: _Sons and Lovers_

好、紅光滿面的農民給他的鞭子和毯子。

米麗亞姆在門口出現。她快十六歲了，長得很漂亮，面色紅潤，端莊大方。她的眼睛突然睜得大大的，欣喜若狂。

"喂，"保羅靦腆地轉向一邊説，"你們的水仙花就要開花了。是不是太早了點兒？不過這些花看上去是不是怪冷的？"

"冷！"米麗亞姆以音樂般、充滿柔情的聲音説。

"花蕾上的綠色 ——"他害羞得支支吾吾就不往下説了。

(英) 勞倫斯：《兒子與情人》

35   They Were of the Same

Gudrun[1] reached out the sketch-book, Gerald[2] stretched
from the boat to take it. And as he did so, he remembered
Gudrun's last words to him, and her face lifted up to him as
he sat on the swerving horse. An intensification of pride went
over his nerves, because he felt in some way she was
compelled by him. The exchange of feeling between them
was strong and apart from their consciousness....

She looked back at him, with her fine blue eyes, and
signalled full into his spirit, as she said, her voice ringing
with intimacy almost caressive now it was addressed to him:

"Of course, it doesn't matter[3] in the *least*."

The bond was established between them, in that look, in
her tone. In her tone, she made the understanding clear—
they were of the same kind, he and she,... Henceforward,
she knew, she had her power over him. Wherever they met,
they would be secretly associated. And he would be helpless
in the association with her. Her soul exulted.

---

1. Gudrun（古德倫）：是個畫家。
2. Gerald（杰拉爾德）：煤礦主。
3. it doesn't matter：指 Gerald 不慎把寫生簿落入水中。

三十五　他們同類

　　古德倫把寫生簿遞過去，杰拉爾德從船上伸出手來接的時候，想起了他騎在突然轉向的馬上，古德倫對他說過的最後幾句話和她向他仰起的臉。一陣強烈的自豪感通過他的神經，因為他感到，在某種程度上，她被他制服了。他們之間的感情交流是強烈的，獨立於他們的意識。……

　　她用那明亮的藍眼睛看他一眼，把意思直接傳遞到他的心靈中。她的說話聲十分親熱，幾乎是愛撫地，對他說：

　　"當然，這一點也沒關係。"

　　她的目光和語氣使他們聯結起來了。她的語氣清楚地說明她的理解：他們——他和她——是同一類的人。……此後，她知道，她對他已經有了控制力。無論他們在什麼地方遇見，他們會秘而不宣地聯繫在一起。在這聯繫中他是無能為力的。她的心靈歡欣鼓舞。

"Good-bye! I'm so glad you forgive me[4]. Gooood-bye!"

... Gerald automatically took the oar and pushed off. But he was looking all the time, with a glimmering, subtly-smiling admiration in his eyes, at Gudrun, who stood on the shoal shaking the wet book in her hand. She turned away and ignored the receding boat. But Gerald looked back as he rowed, beholding her, forgetting what he was doing.

D. H. Lawrence: <u>Women in Love</u>

---

4. you forgive me：指 Gudrun 對於 Gerald 把寫生簿弄濕的事並不介意。

"再見！你能原諒我，我真高興，再——見！"

……杰拉爾德無意識地拿起槳把船推開了，可是他還一直看着古德倫，目光中泛出帶着含蓄喜悅的愛慕之情。她站在淺灘上，揮動着手裏濕漉漉的寫生簿。她轉身走開了，沒看漸漸離去的小船。可是杰拉爾德一邊划着船，一邊回頭盼望，注視着她，忘記自己在做什麼。

（英）勞倫斯：《戀愛中的女人》

36　A Bull-fighter

"Do you still love me[1], Jake?"

"Yes," I said. ...

"... I'm mad about the Romero boy, I'm in love with him, I think."...

"What do you want me to do?"

"Come on," Brett said. "Let's go and find him."

...

Pedro Romero was in the café. He was at a table with other bull-fighters and bull-fight critics. ...

... He came over to our table. I stood up and we shook hands.

"Won't you have a drink?"

"You must have a drink with me," he said. He seated himself, asking Brett's permission without saying anything. ...

... I saw he was watching Brett. He felt there was something between them. He must have felt it when Brett gave him her hand. ...

1.　me：三十四歲的勃萊特（Brett），一直和杰克（Jake）很要好，但她
出於一時的狂熱，開始愛慕年僅十九歲的鬥牛士羅梅羅（Romero）。
不過，不久之後，她結束了和羅梅羅的來往。

三十六　鬥牛士

"你還愛我嗎，杰克？"

"還愛你。"我說。……

"……那小伙子羅梅羅迷住我了。我想，我是愛上他了。"……

"你要我做什麼？"

"走，"勃萊特說，"我們去找他吧。"

……

佩德羅・羅梅羅在咖啡店裏。他跟別的鬥牛士和鬥牛評論員同桌共飲。……

……他走到我們桌旁。我站起來和他握手。

"你不喝一杯嗎？"

"你們應該陪我喝一杯。"他說。他坐下來，用表情徵求勃萊特的許可。……

……我看見他注視着勃萊特。他感到他們之間已經有點什麼。勃萊特跟他握手的時候，他一定感到這點了。……

I stood up. Romero rose, too.

"Sit down," I said. "I must go and find our friends and bring them here."

He looked at me. It was a final look to ask if it were understood. It was understood all right.

"Sit down," Brett said to him. "You must teach me Spanish."

He sat down and looked at her across the table. I went out. The hard-eyed people at the bull-fighter table watched me go. It was not pleasant. When I came back and looked in the cafe, twenty minutes later, Brett and Pedro Romero were gone. The coffee-glasses and our three empty cognac-glasses were on the table.

Ernest Hemingway: The Sun Also Rises

我站起身來。羅梅羅也站了起來。

"坐下吧，"我說，"我該去找我們的朋友，把他們帶到這兒來。"

他看看我。這是最後一眼，為的是詢問這一切是否明白。這一切很明白。

"坐下吧，"勃萊特對他說，"你該教我西班牙語。"

他坐下來，隔着餐桌看着她。我走出去了。坐着鬥牛士那桌的人冷眼地看着我走出門。這讓人不好受。二十分鐘後，我回到咖啡店往裏看看，這時，勃萊特和佩德羅·羅梅羅已經走了。咖啡杯和我們用過的三個空酒杯還留在桌上。

（美）海明威：《太陽照常升起》

37   Playing the Schoolboy

He would be there, in the driver's seat, reading a paper while he waited, and when he saw me[1] he would smile, and toss it behind him in the back seat, and open the door, saying, "Well, how is the friend-of-the-bosom this morning, and where does she want to go?" If he had driven round in circles it would not have mattered to me, for I was in that first flushed stage when to climb into the seat beside him, and lean forward to the wind-screen hugging my knees, was almost too much to bear. I was like a little scrubby schoolboy with a passion for a sixth-form prefect, and he kinder, and far more inaccessible.

"There's a cold wind this morning, you had better put on my coat."

I remember that, for I was young enough to win happiness in the wearing of his clothes, playing the schoolboy again who carries his hero's sweater and ties it about his throat choking with pride, and this borrowing of his coat, wearing it around my shoulders for even a few minutes at a time, was a triumph in itself, and made a glow about my morning.

------

1. me：書中的 "我" 與喪妻的邁克西姆・德溫特（Maxim de Winter）
   邂逅相識。

三十七　像個小學生

　　他坐在駕駛座上等着，讀着報，看到我的時候總是微微一笑，然後把報紙扔到他身後的後座上，打開車門説："啊，知心朋友，早上好啊，要想上哪兒去呀？"要是他開着車來回打圈子，我也不在乎，因為我還處於最初的興奮階段，上了車坐在他身邊，抱着雙膝朝擋風玻璃曲身坐着，這已經足夠我消受的了。我像個卑微的小學生愛上了一個中學六年級的班長。而他比班長雖然和藹些，可是要接近他卻難得多。

　　"今天早上風很冷，你最好穿上我的大衣。"

　　這情景我還記得，因為我還幼稚，穿了他的衣服就覺得甜滋滋的，就像一個小學生那樣拿着他崇拜的人的運動衣，把它扎在自己脖子上，威風得説不出話來。他借給我大衣穿，即使每次披在肩上只有幾分鐘，這本身就是勝利，為我上午的光陰增添了光彩。

Not for me the languor and the subtlety I had read about in books, ... The art of provocation was unknown to me, and I would sit with his map upon my lap, the wind blowing my dull, lanky hair, happy in his silence yet eager for his words. Whether he talked or not made little difference to my mood. My only enemy was the clock on the dashboard, whose hands would move relentlessly to one o'clock. We drove east, we drove west, amidst the myriad villages that cling like limpets[2] to the Mediterranean shore, and today I remember none of them.

Daphne du Maurier: Rebecca

---

2. like limpets：形容黏貼得很緊很牢。

我可不會做出像在書裏讀到的那種悠然矜持的樣子。……我不會挑逗異性那一套。我坐在那裏，膝上放着他的地圖，風吹拂着我稀疏難看的頭髮。他沉默不語我感到高興，可是又渴望他說話。他說話還是不說話我都不在乎。我唯一的敵人是儀表板上的鐘，指針無情地走到一點鐘。我們一會兒東，一會兒西，在無數的村子中穿行。這些村子像帽貝那樣緊貼在地中海沿岸，如今我一個也記不清了。

　　　　　(英) 達夫妮‧杜穆里埃：《蝴蝶夢》

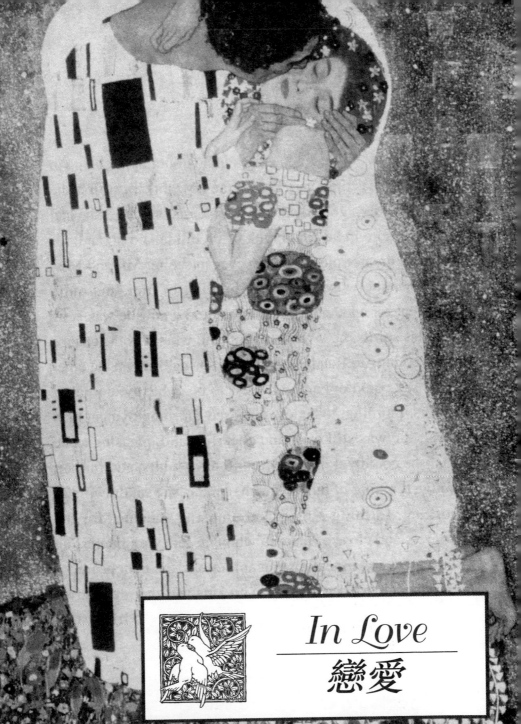

In Love
戀愛

Painting by Gustav Klimt (1862-1918)

38　A Good Thing Over

... Emma continued to entertain no doubt of her being in love. Her ideas only varied as to the how much. At first she thought it was a good deal; and afterwards but little. She had great pleasure in hearing Frank Churchill talked of; and, for his sake, greater pleasure than ever in seeing Mr. and Mrs. Weston[1]; she was very often thinking of him, and quite impatient for a letter, that she might know how he was, how were his spirits, how was his aunt, and what was the chance of his coming to Randalls again this spring. But, on the other hand, she could not admit herself to be unhappy, nor, after the first morning, to be less disposed for[2] employment than usual; she was still busy and cheerful; and, pleasing as he was, she could yet imagine him to have faults; and further, though thinking of him so much, and, as she sat drawing or working, forming a thousand amusing schemes for the progress and close of their attachment, fancying interesting dialogues, and inventing elegant letters; the conclusion of every imaginary declaration on his side was that she refused him. Their affection was always to subside into friendship.

1.　Mr. and Mrs. Weston：弗蘭克・邱吉爾（Frank Churchill）的父母。
2.　disposed for：有意於。

三十八　事過境遷

　　……愛瑪仍然一點兒也不懷疑自己在戀愛了。只是對愛得多深這個問題，想法有些不同。起初，她認為愛得很深，後來，又覺得只有一點兒。她聽到大家談論弗蘭克‧邱吉爾，心裏就很高興。正是為了他的緣故，她比以往更樂意去看望威斯頓夫婦了。她經常想念他，不耐煩地等着他的信，好知道他身體怎樣，精神怎樣，他舅媽身體怎樣，今年春天他有無可能再來蘭得爾斯。但是，另一方面，她不能承認自己不愉快，也不能承認，第一個早晨後，她不如平常那樣願意做事了。她仍舊忙碌，很樂觀的。他雖然討人喜歡，她還是能想像出他有缺點。而且，她雖然很想念他，坐下來畫畫或者工作的時候，為他倆戀愛的過程和結果制定了上千個有趣的計劃，設想了有意思的對話，構思了風雅的情書；但是，在想像中，他每次的愛情表白，她都拒絕了。他們的愛情總是降溫，止於友

...When she became sensible of this, it struck her that she could not be very much in love; ...

"... I do suspect that he is not really necessary to my happiness. So much the better. I certainly will not persuade myself to feel more than I do. I am quite enough in love. I should be sorry to be more."

Upon the whole, she was equally contented with her view of his feelings.

"He is undoubtedly very much in love—everything denotes it—very much in love indeed! ... His feelings are warm, but I can imagine them rather changeable. Every consideration of the subject, in short, makes me thankful that my happiness is not more deeply involved. I shall do very well again after a little while—and then, it will be a good thing over; for they say everybody is in love once in their lives, and I shall have been let off[3] easily."

Jane Austen: <u>Emma</u>

---

3. let off：從輕處置。

誼。……當她感覺到這一點的時候，她就想，她不可能愛
得很深。……

"……我認為我的幸福並不真是非他不可。這就更好
了。我是肯定不會讓自己在感情上增進。我現在已經相當
鍾情了。若再增進，我就會感到遺憾了。"

總的說來，她也是滿意自己怎樣看他的感情的。

"他無疑非常鍾情 —— 一切都說明這一點 —— 的確
是非常鍾情！……他的感情很熱烈，但是我能想像，他的
感情是相當易變的。對這個問題，我的一切想法都使我慶
幸，我的幸福沒有受到更深的牽涉。過一陣子，我會恢復
如常的。這將是一件事過境遷的好事。大家都說，每個人
在一生中總要戀愛一次，而我會順利通過的。"

(英) 奧斯丁：《愛瑪》

39   I'm Your Slave

He flew up the ladder and tapped on the shutter. After a
few moments Mathilde[1] heard him; she tried to open the
shutters, but the ladder was in the way. He clung to one of
the iron hooks used to keep the shutters open and, gravely
risking a fall, shook the ladder violently, shifting it a little to
one side. Mathilde was able to open the shutter.

He rushed into the room more dead than alive.

"It's really you!" she said, throwing herself into his arms.

Who could describe the intensity of Julien's happiness?
Mathilde's was almost as great.

She spoke to him against herself, she accused herself to
him. "Punish me for my horrible pride," she said pressing
him so tightly in her arms that she nearly suffocated him.
"You're my master, I'm your slave: I must beg you on my
knees to forgive me for trying to rebel." She slipped from his
arms to fall at his feet. "Yes, you're my master," she went on,
still intoxicated with love and happiness. "Rule me forever,
punish your slave severely whenever she tries to rebel."

---

1. Mathilde：侯爵小姐瑪蒂爾德（Mathilde）深深地陷入情網，甚至請
   求她的侯爵父親允諾了這門第懸殊的親事。但勒那爾（Rênal）夫人
   向侯爵揭發了于連（Julien）的行徑。于連的野心破滅。

三十九　奴隸

他飛快地爬上梯子，敲敲百葉窗。過了一會兒，瑪蒂爾德聽見他在敲窗。她想打開百葉窗，可是梯子礙事。於是他緊緊抓住支撐開窗用的一個鐵鈎子，冒着摔下去的危險，用勁搖晃梯子，把它略略向一側移動了一下。瑪蒂爾德得以打開窗戶。

他衝進了房間，已經是半死不活了。

"真是你啊！"她說，便投入了他的懷抱。

誰能把于連極其快樂的程度描寫出來呢？瑪蒂爾德幾乎和他一樣快樂。

她對他講自己的不是，還責備自己。"我這樣傲慢，你就懲罰我吧。"她說，把他緊緊摟着，差點沒把他悶死。"你是我的主人，我是你的奴隸。我該跪着向你求饒，寬恕我的反抗。"她滑脫他的擁抱，倒在他的腳下。"對，你是我的主人，"她繼續說，仍舊陶醉在愛情和喜悅中，"永遠統治我吧。你的奴隸要是反抗，你就嚴懲她吧。"

At another moment she tore herself from his arms and lit a candle, and it was only with enormous difficulty that Julien prevented her from cutting off one side of her hair.

"I want to remind myself that I'm your servant," she said. "If I'm ever led astray by my detestable pride, point to my hair and say, "It's no longer a question of love, or whatever emotion your heart may be feeling; you've sworn to obey: obey in the name of honour."

But it is better not to describe such madness and ecstasy.

H. B. Stendhal: The Red and the Black

過了一會，她掙脫了他的擁抱，點上一支蠟燭。于連費了九牛二虎之力才沒讓她剪掉她自己的一側頭髮。

"我要提醒自己我是你的奴僕，"她說，"要是我那討厭的傲慢把我引入歧途，你就指指我的頭髮對我說：'現在不是什麼愛情問題了，也不是你的心可能有什麼感情的問題。你發過誓要服從我，那就為了名譽服從吧。'"

不過最好還是不去描寫這種痴情和狂喜了吧。

(法) 司湯達：《紅與黑》

40 She Sprang into His Arms

The count[1] shuddered at the tones of a voice which penetrated the inmost recesses of his heart; his eyes met those of the young girl, and he could not bear their brilliancy.

"Oh heavens!" exclaimed Monte Cristo, "can my suspicions be correct? Haydée, would it please you not to leave me?"

"I am young," gently replied Haydée, "I love the life you have made so sweet to me, and should regret to die."

"You mean, then, that if I leave you, Haydée—"

"I should die; yes, my lord."

"Do you then love me?"

...

The count felt his heart dilate and throb; he opened his arms, and Haydée, uttering a cry, sprang into them.

"Oh, yes," she cried, "I do love you! I love you as one loves a father, brother, husband! I love you as my life, for you are the best, the noblest of created beings!"

---

1. the count：指基督山伯爵（Monte Cristo）。唐泰斯遭陷害入獄。他歷盡艱難險阻，化名基督山伯爵，懲罰了仇人。最後，他懷着萌發的愛情，攜帶希臘公主海蒂（Haydée）漫遊天下。

四十　投入懷抱

　　有個人說話的聲音一直滲入伯爵的內心深處，他為之不寒而慄。他的目光和年輕姑娘的目光相遇，難以經受來自她眼中的光芒。

　　"天哪！"基督山伯爵喊道，"我的猜想難道都猜對了嗎？海蒂，你不離開我，這會使你高興嗎？"

　　"我正年輕，"海蒂溫柔地回答，"我愛你為我安排的這樣甜美的生活，所以我是捨不得死的。"

　　"那麼，你是說，要是我離開你，海蒂 ——"

　　"我會去死的，真的，大人。"

　　"那麼你是愛我的啦？"

　　……

　　伯爵覺得心在膨脹，在搏動。他張開雙臂，於是海蒂喊叫着，撲進他的懷抱。

　　"啊，是啊，"她喊道，"我真愛你！我愛你就像愛父親，愛兄弟，愛丈夫！我愛你就像愛我的生命，因為你是世上最好的、最高尚的人！"

"Let it be, then, as you wish, sweet angel; God has sustained me in my struggle with my enemies, and has given me this victory; he will not let me end my triumph with this penance; I wished to punish myself, but he has pardoned me! Love me then, Haydée! Who knows? perhaps your love will make me forget all I wish not to remember."

"What do you mean, my lord?"

"I mean that one word from you has enlightened me more than twenty years of slow experience; I have but you in the world, Haydée; through you I again connect myself with life, through you I shall suffer, through you rejoice."

A. Dumas: The Count of Monte Cristo

"那麼就如你所願吧，親愛的。天主支持我跟仇人搏鬥，賜予我勝利。他在我取得勝利以後，並沒讓我以苦行贖罪。我曾經想懲罰自己，可是他寬恕了我！那就愛我吧，海蒂！誰知道？也許你的愛將使我忘掉我不願回憶的一切。"

"你想說些什麼呀，大人？"

"我是說，我二十年漫長的經歷不如你的一句話，你的話使我心裏開了竅。這世界上，我只有你了，海蒂。你使我重新和生活聯繫，你使我感受痛苦，也感受歡樂。"

（法）大仲馬：《基督山伯爵》

41　Love Has Come Quickly

"You come quickly to love, sir," said the young woman[1], shaking her head.

"It is because love has come quickly on me, and for the first time; and I am not yet twenty years of age."

The young woman stole a glance at him. ...

"Ah! I was convinced that you were an honourable man!" exclaimed Madame Bonancieux, offering one of her hands to him, as she placed the other on the knocker of a small door, which was well-nigh concealed in a recess.

D'Artagnan seized the hand which was offered to him, and kissed it eagerly.

"Alas!" exclaimed d'Artagnan, with that unpolished simplicity which women sometimes prefer to the delicacies of politeness, because it illuminates the depths of thought, and proves that feeling is more powerful than reason, "I wish I had never seen you!"

"Well!" said Madame Bonancieux, in a tone almost affectionate, and pressing the hand which held hers, "well! I will not say the same as you do; that which is lost today may

---

1. the young woman：指 Madame Bonancieux。

四十一　愛情來得快

"您很快就談到了愛情，先生。"這位年輕女子搖搖頭說。

"因為我的愛情來得快，而且是第一次。我還不滿二十歲呢。"

年輕女子偷看了他一下。……

"啊！我早就相信您是個誠實的人！"波那雪夫人大聲說道，向他伸出一隻手，另一隻手放在小門的門環上，這門幾乎是隱藏在壁龕裏。

達達尼昂抓住伸過來的手，熱切地吻着。

"哎呀！"達達尼昂以其不加修飾的純真驚呼一聲，有時候女人更喜歡這種沒有修飾的純真，而不喜歡高雅的禮貌，因為它表露了思想的深處，而且說明感情強於理智，"我真願意從來沒見過您！"

"好吧！"波那雪夫人說，她的聲音充滿深情，同時緊按着那隻握着她的手，"好吧！我不說您說的這樣的話。

not be lost for ever. Who knows whether, when I am freed from my present embarrassments, I may not satisfy your curiosity?"

"And do you make the same promise regarding my love?" asked the overjoyed d'Artagnan.

"Oh! I dare give no promises in that respect. It must depend upon the sentiments with which you may inspire me."

"But, at present, madame?"

"At present, sir, I have not got beyond gratitude."

"Alas! you are too charming; and only take advantage of my love."

"No, I take advantage of your generosity, that's all. But, believe me, with some people, nothing can be wholly lost."

"You make me the happiest of men. Oh! do not forget this evening, and this promise?"

A. Dumas: _The Three Musketeers_

今天失去的可能不會永久失去。誰知道，當我走出目前窘境的時候，是不是不能滿足您的好奇心呢？"

"您對我的愛能作出同樣的承諾嗎？"狂喜的達達尼昂問道。

"噢！這個問題我不敢向您承諾。這要看您把我的感情激起到什麼程度了。"

"可是現在呢，夫人？"

"現在，先生，我還沒有超過感激之情。"

"哎呀！您太迷人了。您在利用我的愛情。"

"不，我是利用您的慷慨大度，如此而已。不過，請相信我，對於有些人，不會什麼都全失去的。"

"您使我成為一個最幸福的人。噢！別忘了今天的夜晚和您的承諾。"

(法）大仲馬：《三個火槍手》

42   An Amorous Conversation

... An amorous conversation is a rather commonplace thing. It is essentially a perpetual "I love you," an extremely bare and insipid phrase for a disinterested listener. But Dom Claude[1] was not a disinterested listener. ...

La Esmeralda was silent for a moment, then a tear welled up in her eye, a sigh escaped from her lips and she said, "Oh, Captain Phoebus, I love you so!"

There was such an aura of chastity and charming virtue around her that Phoebus did not feel entirely at ease. Her last words emboldened him, however. "You love me!" he cried ecstatically and put his arm around her waist. This was what he had been waiting for. ...

"Phoebus," said the girl, gently removing the captain's tenacious hands from her waist, "you're kind, noble and handsome. You saved my life, even though I'm only a poor gypsy girl. For years I dreamed of an officer who would save my life. I was dreaming of you before I ever saw you, my Phoebus. ... I love your name and I love your sword. Draw

---

1. Dom Claude（堂・克羅德）：巴黎聖母院副主教，是個偽君子。他想佔有愛斯美臘達（La Esmeralda），在她與費比斯（Phoebus）幽會時，刺傷了費比斯，嫁禍於她，她被判了死刑。

四十二　綿綿情話

　　……綿綿情話是相當平凡的東西。其實也就是沒完沒了的"我愛你"。對於無關的旁聽者來說，這是一句空泛乏味的話。但是堂·克羅德並不是無關的旁聽者。……

　　愛斯美臘達沉默了一會兒，然後眼裏冒出淚水，嘴裏嘆出口氣，說："啊！費比斯長官，我多麼愛您！"

　　她周身散發着純潔的氣質和童貞的魅力，費比斯感到多少有些不自在。可是她最後的幾句話壯了他的膽。"你愛我！"他欣喜若狂地喊道，便伸出一個胳臂摟住了她的腰。這正是他一直等待着的。……

　　"費比斯，"姑娘輕輕地把隊長緊抱她腰肢的雙手挪開，說道，"您善良，高尚，英俊。雖然我只不過是一個吉卜賽窮女孩，您還是救了我的性命。我夢想了好幾年，希望有一位軍官救我的性命。費比斯，我見到您以前就已經夢見過您了。……我愛您的名字，也愛您的長劍。費比

your sword, Phoebus, and let me see it."

...

As she bent over it, Phoebus took advantage of the opportunity to kiss her on the neck. She looked up and blushed to the roots of her hair. ...

"Listen to me, darling..." he began but she put her lovely hand over his lips in a gesture of playful grace.

"No," she said, "I won't listen to you. Do you love me? I want you to tell me if you love me."

"Do I love you, angel of my life!" cried the captain, half-kneeling before her. "My body, my blood, my soul, everything is yours, everything is for you! Yes, I love you and I've never loved anyone but you!"

He had repeated this little speech on so many other similar occasions that he delivered it all in one breath, without making a single mistake.

Victor Hugo: The Hunchback of Notre Dame

斯，拔出您的長劍給我看看。"

……

當她俯身看劍時，費比斯乘機在她脖子上吻了一下。
她抬起頭來，臉漲得通紅，紅到了髮根。……

"聽我説，親愛的……"費比斯開口説，但她用她可愛
的手蒙住他的嘴，姿勢頑皮而優美。

"不嘛，"她説，"我不想聽您説。您愛我嗎？我要您
告訴我，您愛不愛我。"

"我愛不愛您？我終生的天使！"隊長半跪在她面前，
叫嚷道，"我的軀體，我的鮮血，我的靈魂，一切都屬於
您，一切都為了您！是啊，我愛您，除了您我從沒愛過別
人！"

他在許多其他類似的場合，把這小段演辭已經説過好
多遍，所以他一口氣就説完了，一個錯誤也沒有。

（法）雨果：《巴黎聖母院》

43　Vacant Place

"When I loved her[1]—even then, my love would have been incomplete, without your sympathy. I had it, and it was perfected. And when I lost her, Agnes, what should I have been without you, still!"

Closer in my arms, nearer to my heart, her trembling hand upon my shoulder, her sweet eyes shining through her tears, on mine!

"I went away, dear Agnes, loving you. I stayed away, loving you. I returned home, loving you!" ...

"I am so blest, Trotwood—my heart is so overcharged—but there is one thing I must say."

"Dearest, what?"

She laid her gentle hands upon my shoulders, and looked calmly in my face.

"Do you know, yet, what it is?"

"I am afraid to speculate on what it is. Tell me, my dear."

"I have loved you all my life!" ...

We were married within a fortnight. ...

---

1. her：指大衛‧科波菲爾的愛妻朵拉（Dora）。朵拉病故，舊友艾尼斯（Agnes）一直與他保持着聯繫，有情人終成眷屬。

四十三　誰補空缺

"當我愛她的時候 —— 即使在那時，沒有你的同情，我的愛是不會圓滿的。我得到了愛，而且很完美。後來失去她時，艾尼斯，我仍然覺得，要是沒有你，我不知道會怎麼樣！"

我把她摟得更緊了，她更貼近我的心了，她顫抖的手放在我的肩上，她溫柔的眼睛透過淚水對着我閃亮！

"我到國外去，艾尼斯，愛着你。我不在國內，也愛着你。我回國了，還愛着你！"……

"我真有福氣，特洛烏德，我心裏的事情太多了，不過有一件事必須對你說。"

"最親愛的，什麼事？"

她把柔軟的雙手放在我的肩上，平靜地正面看着我。

"你知道是什麼嗎？"

"我害怕猜測這件事。告訴我吧，親愛的。"

"我這一生一直在愛着你。"……

我們在兩週內結了婚。……

"Dearest husband!" said Agnes. "Now that I may call you by that name, I have one thing more to tell you."

"Let me hear it, love."

"It grows out of the night when Dora died. She sent you for me."

"She did."

"She told me that she left me something. Can you think what it was?"

I believed I could. I drew the wife who had so long loved me, closer to my side.

"She told me that she made a last request to me, and left me a last charge."

"And it was—"

"That only I would occupy this vacant place."

And Agnes laid her head upon my breast, and wept; and I wept with her, though we were so happy.

Charles Dickens: <u>David Copperfield</u>

“最親愛的丈夫！”艾尼斯説，“既然我可以這樣稱呼你，還有一件事情要告訴你。”

“我聽你説，親愛的。”

“這是在朵拉去世的那個晚上。她讓你來找我去。”

“對呀，她讓我找你了。”

“她對我説，她給我留下一件事情。你能猜出來是什麼嗎？”

我想我能猜出來。我把早就愛我的這位妻子拉得更近我些。

“她告訴我，她對我有最後一個要求，給我留下最後的任務。”

“這任務是 ——”

“只有我來填補這個空缺。”

艾尼斯便把她的頭靠在我的胸前，哭了起來，我也跟她一塊兒哭了，當然我們是很快樂的。

（英）狄更斯：《大衛·科波菲爾》

44 My Great Thought in Living

"... and you love Edgar, and Edgar loves you. All seems smooth and easy—where is the obstacle?"

"Here! and here!" replied Catherine, striking one hand on her forehead, and the other on her breast. "In whichever place the soul lives—in my soul, and in my heart, I'm convinced I'm wrong!" ...

"... I've no more business to[1] marry Edgar Linton than I have to be in heaven; and if the wicked man in there[2] had not brought Heathcliff so low, I shouldn't have thought of it. It would degrade me to marry Heathcliff, now; so he shall never know how I love him; and that, not because he's handsome, Nelly[3], but because he's more myself than I am. Whatever our souls are made of, his and mine are the same, and Linton's is as different as a moonbeam from lightning, or frost from fire." ...

"... My great miseries in this world have been Heathcliff's miseries, and I watched and felt each from the beginning; my great thought in living is himself. If all else perished, and

---

1. have no business to (do something)：沒有權力（做某事）。
2. the wicked man in there：指呼嘯山莊的主人，他虐待 Heathcliff，把他貶為僕人。
3. Nelly：女管家。

四十四　思念

"……你愛埃德加，埃德加也愛你。一切都好像穩當順利。那麼，障礙在哪兒呢？"

"在這兒！還在這兒！"凱瑟琳回答，一隻手拍打着前額，另一隻手拍打着胸脯，"有靈魂的地方 —— 在我的靈魂裏，還在我的心裏，我相信我做錯了。"……

"……我沒資格進天堂，我也配不上埃德加·林頓。要是那兒的那個壞蛋沒把希斯克利夫貶得這樣卑賤，我是不會考慮和埃德加結婚的。而現在，如果嫁給希斯克利夫，就有失我的身份。所以他絕不會知道我愛着他。我愛他，倒不是因為他長得英俊，耐莉，而是因為他比我更像我自己。不管我們的靈魂是什麼造的，他和我的靈魂是一樣的。可是林頓的靈魂和我們的不同，就像月光和閃電，冰霜和火焰那樣截然不同。"……

"……這世界上我最大的苦難都是希斯克利夫的苦難，每一次苦難我都從頭注視着，都感受到。我生活中最強的思念就是他。如果其他一切都消失了，而他還在，那麼，

he remained, I should still continue to be; and, if all else remained, and he were annihilated, the Universe would turn to a mighty stranger. I should not seem a part of it. My love for Linton is like the foliage in the woods. Time will change it, I'm well aware, as winter changes the trees—my love for Heathcliff resembles the eternal rocks beneath—a source of little visible delight, but necessary. Nelly, I am Heathcliff— he's always, always in my mind— ..."

Emily Brontë: <u>Wuthering Heights</u>

我也會繼續存在。可是，如果其他一切還在，而他被消滅了，那麼，這宇宙就會變成巨大的陌生人了。我不像是宇宙的一部分了。我對林頓的愛就像樹林中的葉子。我很清楚，時光會改變這愛，正如冬天改變着樹木。我對希斯克利夫的愛就像腳下永恒不變的岩石，是快樂的來源，雖然能見到的不多，但卻是必不可少的。耐莉，我就是希斯克利夫，他時時刻刻都在我的心間 ——……"

(英) 艾米莉·勃朗特：《呼嘯山莊》

45 I Love You Stupidly

Anna Sergeevna gave him a questioning look.

"As you wish," she went on, "but something tells me that it's not just luck that's made us get on so well, that we'll be good friends. I'm sure that your—how can I put it?—your tenseness, your self-control will vanish eventually, won't it?"

"So you've noticed my self-control, my—as you put it—tenseness?"

"Yes."

Bazarov stood up and went to the window.

"And would you like to know the cause of this self-control, would you like to know what is occurring inside me?"

"Yes," repeated Odintsova[1] with a certain apprehension that was as yet unclear to her.

"And you won't be angry?"

"No."

"No?" Bazarov stood with his back to her. "Then you should know that I love you, stupidly, madly ... So now you've got what you wanted."

---

1. Odintsova（奧金佐娃）：安娜‧謝爾蓋耶夫娜（Anna Sergeevna）
出嫁後隨丈夫的姓。

四十五　傻愛瘋愛

安娜·謝爾蓋耶夫娜疑惑地看着他。

"隨您尊便吧，"她接着說，"有情況對我表明，並不只是幸運使我們相處得很好的，使我們會成為好朋友的。我相信您的這種——讓我怎麼說呢？——緊張、矜持終究會消失的，是吧？"

"那我的矜持、我的——照您的說法——緊張，您已經發現了？"

"是的。"

巴扎羅夫起身走到窗前。

"您想知道這矜持的原因嗎？您想知道我心裏發生了什麼嗎？"

"是的，"奧金佐娃以當時還不清楚的憂慮心情重說了一遍。

"那您不會生氣嗎？"

"不會。"

"不會？"巴扎羅夫背對着她問，"那麼我該告訴您，我愛您，傻乎乎地愛，瘋狂地愛……現在您終於達到您的目的了。"

Odintsova stretched out both hands in front of her, but Bazarov pressed his forehead to the glass of the window. He took in deep breaths. His whole body was visibly quivering. But it was not the quivering of boyish shyness, nor was it the sweet horror of first confession that possessed him. It was passion that beat within him, strong and laboured, passion that resembled anger and was probably akin to it. Odintsova grew both alarmed and sorry for him.

"Evgeny Vasilich[2]," she said and, despite herself, her voice resounded with tenderness.

He quickly turned round, cast a devouring look at her and, seizing both her hands, drew her suddenly to him.

Ivan Turgenev: <u>Fathers and Sons</u>

---

2. Evgeny Vasilich（葉夫蓋尼‧瓦西里伊奇）：巴扎羅夫（Bazarov）的名和父稱。

奧金佐娃向前伸出雙手，可是巴扎羅夫把前額緊靠在窗玻璃上。他深深地吸了幾口氣。看得出，他渾身在顫抖。但這種顫抖不是由於孩子似的膽怯，也不是由於第一次表白愛情時甜蜜的慌張。這是他心中跳動的激情，既強烈又吃力，這激情很像憤怒，也可能類似憤怒。奧金佐娃開始驚慌起來，同時也為他感到不安。

"葉夫蓋尼·瓦西里伊奇。"她說，說話的聲音裏有一種情不自禁的溫柔。

他很快地轉過身來，貪婪地看了看她，抓住她的雙手，便突然把她拉到自己的懷抱。

(俄) 屠格涅夫：《父與子》

46 What's That Word Mean?

Arkady turned to Katya[1]. She was sitting in the very same position, except that she had dropped her head even lower.

"Katerina Sergeevna[2]," he said in a trembling voice, his hands clasped tightly together, "I love you eternally and irrevocably and I love no one but you. I wanted to tell you this, discover what your own thoughts were and ask for your hand, because I'm not a rich man and I feel I'm ready to make any kind of sacrifice ... Why don't you say something? Don't you believe me? Do you think I'm not being serious? But just think of these last few days! Haven't you become convinced long ago that everything else—you know what I mean—everything, everything else has long ago vanished without trace? Look at me, say just one word to me... I love... I love you... Believe me now!"

Katya turned on Arkady a solemn and bright look and, after a long pause for thought, with hardly a smile, said: "Yes."

Arkady jumped up from the seat.

1.　Katya（卡佳）：安娜・謝爾蓋耶夫娜的妹妹，十八歲。
2.　Katerina Sergeevna（卡捷琳娜・謝爾蓋夫娜）：即卡佳（Katya）。

四十六 一字千金

　　阿爾卡季轉向卡佳。她還是保持原來的姿勢坐着，不過她把頭埋得更低了。

　　"卡捷琳娜·謝爾蓋耶夫娜，"他聲音發顫地說，兩手緊緊地捏在一起，"我永遠愛您，永不變心，除了您我誰也不愛。我想告訴您這個，想知道您有什麼想法，還想向您求婚，因為我不是一個有錢的人，我覺得我準備為您作出任何犧牲……您怎麼什麼也不說呢？您不相信我嗎？您以為我不是當真的嗎？您只要想想最近幾天的情形吧！難道您不是早就相信，其他的一切 —— 您知道我指的是什麼 —— 其他的一切，一切早已消失得毫無蹤跡了？看着我，對我只要說一句……我愛……我愛您……相信我！"

　　卡佳用莊嚴、明亮的目光朝阿爾卡季看看，思索了好一會兒才幾乎沒有笑意地說："是。"

　　阿爾卡季從坐位上跳起來。

"Yes! You've said yes, Katerina Sergeevna! What's that word mean? Is it that I love you and that you believe me... or... or... I daren't say more ..."

"Yes," repeated Katya and this time he understood her. He took hold of her large beautiful hands and, sighing with joy, pressing them to his heart. He could scarcely remain on his feet and went on repeating "Katya... Katya..." while she quite innocently started crying, laughing quietly to herself at her own tears. He who has not seen such tears in the eyes of a loved one has not yet experienced to what extent, though totally consumed by gratitude and shame, a man can be happy on this earth.

Ivan Turgenev: <u>Fathers and Sons</u>

"是！您説了'是'，卡捷琳娜・謝爾蓋耶夫娜！這個詞什麼意思？意思是我愛您，而您相信我……還是……還是……我不敢再多説了……"

　　"是，"卡佳又説了一遍，這一次他懂她説的意思了。他握住她那雙漂亮的大手，放到他自己的心旁，高興地嘆了口氣。他差點兒站不住了，只是重覆地説"卡佳……卡佳……"。這時她卻天真地哭起來，又小聲地笑自己的眼淚。誰要是沒有看到所愛的人眼中這樣含着淚，誰就還體會不到，在這個世界上一個人儘管被感激和害羞弄得筋疲力竭的時候，卻還能夠快樂到什麼樣的程度。

（俄）屠格涅夫：《父與子》

47   They Were Renewed by Love

How it happened he[1] did not know. But all at once
something seemed to seize him and fling him at her feet. He
wept and threw his arms round her knees. For the first instant
she was terribly frightened and she turned pale. She jumped
up and looked at him trembling. But at the same moment she
understood, and a light of infinite happiness came into her
eyes. She knew and had no doubt that he loved her beyond
everything and that at last the moment had come. ...

They wanted to speak, but could not; tears stood in their
eyes. They were both pale and thin; but those sick pale faces
were bright with the dawn of a new future, of a full resurrection
into a new life. They were renewed by love; the heart of each
held infinite sources of life for the heart of the other.

They resolved to wait and be patient. They had another
seven years to wait, and what terrible suffering and what
infinite happiness before them! But he had risen again and
he knew it and felt in it all his being, while she—she only
lived in his life.

---

1. he：指窮大學生拉斯柯尼科夫（Raskolnikov）。他殺死了放高利貸
   的老嫗。索尼亞(Sonia)為貧窮所困，淪為妓女。拉斯柯尼科夫在索
   尼亞 "愛" 的感召下投案自首，被判刑投獄。他被她 "為全人類自覺
   地受苦受難" 的基督教思想所感動，決心 "等待和忍耐"。

四十七　新生

　　這是怎麼發生的，他不知道。可是轉眼之間，好像有什麼東西抓住了他，又把他扔在她的腳旁。他哭了，抱着她的膝頭。起初，她大驚失色，跳了起來，哆嗦地看着他。不過，就在這一瞬間，她明白了，無限幸福的光芒在她眼裏出現。她明白了，而且深信不疑，他愛她超乎一切，這一時刻終於來臨了……

　　他們想說說話，可是說不出來；兩人噙着眼淚，面色蒼白憔悴；但是在他們帶病容的蒼白的臉上泛起新前途的曙光，新生命完全復活的曙光。愛情使他們更生了，他們倆的心裏彼此為對方的心田保存着無窮無盡的生命泉源。

　　他們決定等待和忍耐。他們還要再等待七年，他們將要經受多麼深重的苦難，享受多少無限的幸福！但是他重新站起來了，他知道這一點，在這新生中他感覺到自己整個的身心。而她 —— 她只是活在他的生命中。

On the evening of the same day, when the barracks were locked, Raskolnikov lay on his plank bed and thought of her. He had even fancied that day that all the convicts who had been his enemies looked at him differently; he had even entered into talk with them and they answered him in a friendly way. He remembered that now, and thought it was bound to be so. Wasn't everything now bound to be changed?

He thought of her. He remembered how continually he had tormented her and wounded her heart. He remembered her pale and thin little face. But these recollections scarcely troubled him now; he knew with what infinite love he would now repay all her sufferings. And what were all, *all* the agonies of the past! Everything, even his crime, his sentence and imprisonment, seemed to him now in the first rush of feeling an external, strange fact with which he had no concern.

Fyodor Dostoyevsky: <u>Crime and Punishment</u>

當天晚上，牢房上鎖以後，拉斯柯尼科夫躺在木板牀上，想着她。這天，他甚至覺得，所有對他有過敵意的囚犯對他刮目相看了。他甚至和他們攀談起來，他們也友好地和他說話。他現在回想起這一切，認為這一切都是必然的。現在一切不是應該改變了嗎？

　　他想着她。他還記得，他常使她痛苦，使她傷心。他想起了她那蒼白瘦削的面孔。但是這些回憶現在不怎麼使他煩惱了。他知道，他現在要用無限的愛情去補償她受過的一切痛苦。過去的一切，一切痛苦算得了什麼！這一切，甚至他的罪行、判刑和囚禁，現在對於他，這第一次感情衝動時，好像都是與他無關的身外陌生的事了。

　　　　　　　　　　(俄) 陀思妥耶夫斯基：《罪與罰》

48　The Future Was Free of Clouds

The countryside has always been associated with love, and rightly so. Nothing creates a more fitting backdrop to the woman you love than the blue sky, the fragrances, the flowers, the breezes, the solitary splendour of fields and woods. However much you love a woman, however much you trust her, however sure of the future her past life makes you, you are always jealous to some degree. If you have ever been in love, really in love, you must have experienced this need to shut out the world and isolate the person through whom you wished to live your whole life. It is as though the woman you love, however indifferent she may be to her surroundings, loses something of her savour and consistency when she comes into contact with men and things. Now I experienced this more intensely than any other man. Mine was no ordinary love; I was as much in love as mortal creature can be. But I loved Marguerite Gautier, which is to say that in Paris, at every turn, I might stumble across some man who had already been her lover, or would be the next day. Whereas, in the country, surrounded by people we had never seen before who paid no attention to us, ... I could shelter my love from prying eyes, and love without shame or fear.

四十八　未來一片光明

　　人們總是把鄉村和愛情聯想在一起，這種聯想很有道理。藍天、芳香、鮮花、微風、田野和樹林僻靜的光輝，再也沒有比些更適合於襯托你心愛的人兒了。無論你多麼愛她，多麼信任她，無論你對她舊日的生活為你塑造的未來是多麼確信無疑，你總是還有些妒意。如果你戀愛過，而且是真正戀愛過，你很想與世隔絕，不讓你未來的終生伴侶與人來往。對這種要求你一定有切身的感受。好像你所愛的女人，只要接觸了別的男人和事物，不管她對周圍的一切是多麼不關心，她也會失去一些魅力，感情不再專一。現在我對這方面的體驗比任何別的男人都要深刻。我的戀愛絕不普通，我像常人一樣戀愛，但我愛的卻是瑪格麗特·戈蒂埃，就是説，在巴黎我隨時隨地都可能偶然碰見她的某個情人，或許是明日的情人。而在鄉間，我們周圍都是素不相識的人，他們不會注意我們，……我可以讓我的愛情避開好奇的眼光，不必害羞，不必害怕。

There, the courtesan faded imperceptibly. At my side, I had a young and beautiful woman whom I loved, by whom I was loved and whose name was Marguerite; the shapes of the past dissolved and the future was free of clouds. The sun shone on my mistress as brightly as it would have shone on the purest fiancée. ... Marguerite was wearing a white dress. She leaned on my arm. Beneath the starry evening sky, she repeated the words she had said to me the previous night, and in the distance the world went on turning without casting its staining shadow over the happy picture of our youth and love.

Such was the dream which that day's burning sun brought me through the leafy trees...

A. Dumas fils: <u>La Dame aux Camélias</u>

在這裏，娼家女子的形象在不知不覺中消失。我的身旁是位年輕美貌的女子，她就叫瑪格麗特，我們彼此相愛。她過去的一切已經蕩然無存，而未來卻是一片光明。陽光照在我的情人身上，就像照着一個最純潔的未婚妻一樣光輝燦爛。……瑪格麗特穿着白色衣裙。她偎依在我的手臂上。在點點繁星的夜空下，她反覆傾訴着昨夜對我説過的話。在遠處，城市生活依然如舊，但是在我們青春和愛情的幸福美景上，沒有城市污迹的陰影。

這就是那天熾熱的陽光穿過葉茂的樹林給我帶來的夢境。……

(法) 小仲馬：《茶花女》

49　I'll Say Goodbye to the Old Life

"My life is yours, Marguerite. You don't need this man[1]: am I not here? How could I ever desert you? How could I ever repay the happiness you give me? Away with all constraints, dearest Marguerite! We love each other! What does the rest matter?"

"Oh yes! I do love you, my Armand!" she murmured, circling my neck with both arms, "I love you as I never believed I could love anybody. We will be happy, we'll live in peace, and I'll say goodbye forever to the old life I'm so ashamed of now. You'll never hold my past against me, will you?"

The tears dimmed my voice. The only answer I could give was to clasp Marguerite to my heart.

"Come," she said, turning to Prudence[2], her voice tinged with emotion, "you can go and report this scene to the Duke and, while you're at it, tell him we don't need him.'

From that day on, the Duke was never mentioned again. Marguerite was no longer the girl I had met. She avoided anything which might have reminded me of the life she had

---

1.　this man：指一位資助瑪格麗特（Marguerite）生活的年老公爵。
2.　Prudence（普律當絲）：瑪格麗特的知心女友。

四十九　告別舊生活

"我的生命是屬於你的，瑪格麗特。你不需要那個人了，我不是在這兒了嗎？我怎麼能拋棄你呢？我怎麼能報答你給我的幸福呢？一切的約束都不要了，親愛的瑪格麗特！我們相親相愛！其餘的事有什麼要緊呢？

"啊，是啊！我確實愛你，我的阿爾芒！"她雙臂摟着我的脖子，低聲説道，"我愛你，我從來都沒想到我會這樣愛一個人。我們會幸福的，我們會安靜地生活。我要永遠告別那我現在感到羞恥的舊生活。你不會拿我的過去責怪我，不會吧？"

淚水使我的聲音模糊了。我唯一能夠回答的是，把瑪格麗特緊緊地摟在懷裏。

"去吧，"她聲音激動，轉身對普律當絲説，"你可以去把這情景講給公爵聽。講的時候，還對他説，我們用不着他了。"

從那天以後，再也沒提到過公爵。瑪格麗特不再是我以前見到的那個姑娘了。任何可能引起我想起初次認識她

been leading when I first made her acquaintance. Never did wife or sister show husband or brother such love, such consideration as she showed me. Her state of health left her open to sensation, and made her vulnerable to her feelings. She had broken with her women friends just as she had broken with her old ways; she controlled her language just as she curbed the old extravagance. Had you observed us leave the house for an outing in a delightful little boat I had bought, you would never have thought that this woman in a white dress, wearing a large straw hat and carrying on her arm a simple fur-lined silk coat which would protect her against the chill of the water, was the same Marguerite Gautier who, four months before, had attracted such attention with her extravagant ways and scandalous conduct.

A. *Dumas fils: La Dame aux Camélias*

時她所過的生活的事情，她都回避不提。她對我的愛和關心，是任何的妻子對丈夫或姐姐對弟弟從來沒做到過的。她的健康狀況不好，容易激動，感情脆弱。她斷絕了和女友們的來往，也改變了過去的生活方式。她改變了談吐，也不再奢侈揮霍。要是你看到我們走出家門，乘着我買的那隻可愛的小船去遊玩，你怎麼也不會想到，這個穿白長裙、戴大草帽、手臂上搭着一件抵禦水上寒氣的綢面皮裏的普通外套的女人就是瑪格麗特‧戈蒂埃。四個月前，就是她，以其揮金如土的生活，醜惡可恥的行為曾經引人注目過。

(法) 小仲馬：《茶花女》

50   Not What She Wished to Say

He[1] looked at her[2] and was struck by the new, spiritual beauty of her face.

"What do you want of me?" he asked, simply and seriously.

"I want you to go to Moscow and beg Kitty's pardon," said she.

"You don't want that," he replied.

He saw that she was saying what she forced herself to utter and not what she wished to say.

"If you love me as you say you do," she whispered, "behave so that I may be at peace ."

His face brightened.

"Don't you know that you are all my life to me ?... But peace I do not know, and can't give to you. My whole being, my love ... yes! I cannot think about you and about myself separately. You and I are one to me. And I do not see before us the possibility of peace either for me or for you. I see the possibility of despair, misfortune ... or of happiness—what happiness! ... Is it impossible?" he added with his lips only, but she heard.

---

1. He：指 Vronsky，他認識 Anna 時，正追求着吉蒂（Kitty）。
2. her：指 Anna。

200

五十　言不由衷

他望着她，被她臉上出現的新的靈性的美所打動。

"您要我做什麼？"他簡單而認真地問了一句。

"我要您到莫斯科去，請求吉蒂的寬恕。"她說。

"您並不要我這樣做。"他回答。

他看得出來，她說的是硬逼着自己說的話，不是她願意說的話。

"要是您像您說的那樣愛我，"她低聲說，"那您所做的就該讓我得到安寧。"

他喜形於色。

"難道您不知道您就是我的整個生命嗎？……可是安寧，我體驗不到，也不能給您。我整個的人，我的愛情……是啊！在我的思想裏，您和我是不能分開的。我想，您和我是一個整體。我看，今後您和我都不會有安寧。我看可能有絕望，有不幸……或者有幸福 —— 無限的幸福！……難道這不可能嗎？"他只是動動嘴唇補充說道，但是她聽見了。

She exerted all the powers of her mind to say what she ought; but instead she fixed on him her eyes filled with love and did not answer at all.

"This is it!" he thought with rapture. "Just as I was beginning to despair, and when it seemed as though the end would never come ... here it is! She loves me! She acknowledges it!"

"Do this for me: never say such words to me, and let us be good friends." These were her words, but her eyes said something very different.

Lev Tolstoy: <u>Anna Karenina</u>

她想方設法説她應該説的話，可是她沒説，只是凝視着他，眼裏充滿着愛，什麼也沒回答。

　　"正是這樣！"他欣喜若狂地想，"我剛開始絕望，好像永遠不會有什麼結果，……可是這不就是嘛！她愛我，她承認了！"

　　"我求您為我做到：永遠不要對我説這樣的話，讓我們做個好朋友吧。"她説的是這些話，可是她眼神裏表示的完全是另一回事。

　　　　（俄）列夫·托爾斯泰：《安娜·卡列尼娜》

51 The Easter Kiss

She had come out into the porch with Matriona Pavlovna[1] and stopped, distributing alms to the beggars. A beggar with a red scar in place of a nose went up to Katusha. She took something from her pocket-handkerchief, gave it to him and then drew nearer to him and without showing the least disgust—on the contrary, her eyes shone with joy as brightly as ever—kissed him three times. And while she was exchanging kisses with the beggar her eyes met Nekhlyudov's with a look as if she were asking, "Am I doing right?"

"Yes, yes, dear, everything is right, everything is just as it should be, and I love you."

They came down the steps of the porch and he walked over to her. He did not mean to exchange the Easter kiss[2] with her, he only wanted to be nearer to her. ...

He looked round at Katusha. She blushed and at once went up to him.

"Christ is risen, Dmitri Ivanovich!"

---

1. Matriona Pavlovna：老女僕。
2. the Easter kiss：復活節人們見面時一人說："基督復活了！"，對方回答："真的復活了！"並且互吻三下。

五十一　復活節的吻

她隨着瑪特寥娜·帕夫洛夫娜出來，走到門廊，停下，向乞丐一一給錢。一個沒有鼻子只有塊紅疤的乞丐走到卡秋莎跟前。她從袋中手帕裏拿出點什麼給了他，走近他吻了他三下，沒表現絲毫的嫌惡——相反，眼睛裏閃耀着慣常的歡樂的光芒。在她和乞丐互吻的時候，她的目光和聶赫留朵夫的目光相遇，好像她在問：“我這樣做對嗎？”

“對，對，親愛的，什麼都對，什麼都做得應該做的那樣，我愛你。”

她們走下門口的台階。他走到她身旁。他倒並沒打算和她作復活節的互吻，只是想靠她更近些。……

他轉過頭來看看卡秋莎。她臉上泛起紅暈，立刻向他挨過來。

“基督復活了，德米特里·伊凡內奇！”

"He is risen indeed!" he said. They kissed twice, then paused, as though considering whether a third kiss was necessary, and, having decided that it was, kissed a third time and smiled. ...

In the love between a man and a woman there is always a moment when that love reaches its zenith—a moment when their love is unconscious, unreasoning, and with nothing sensual about it. Such a moment came to Nekhlyudov on this joyful Easter night. Now when he thought of Katusha, this was the occasion which effaced all others. ...

He knew she had that love in her because that night and morning he was conscious of it in himself, and conscious that in this love he became one with her.

Lev Tolstoy: <u>Resurrection</u>

"真的復活了！"他説。他們互吻了兩次，便停了下來，好像在考慮，第三次吻還有沒有必要，考慮結果有必要，便吻了第三次，然後他們都笑了。……

男女間的愛情總有達到頂點的時候，這時他們的愛情是意識不到的，非理智的，也沒有肉慾的成份。在那個歡樂的復活節夜晚，聶赫留朵夫經歷着這樣的時刻。現在，每當他想起卡秋莎的時候，這天的經歷使其他的經歷消失泯滅了。……

他知道，她心中有這樣的愛，因為那天夜晚一直到清晨他自己心中意識到了這樣的愛，也意識到，正是在這種愛情中，他和她合二為一了。

（俄）列夫·托爾斯泰：《復活》

52　Triumphant Pleasure

Thereupon the contour of a man became dimly visible against the low-reaching sky over the valley, beyond the outer margin of the pool. He came round it and leapt upon the bank beside her. A low laugh escaped her—the third utterance which the girl had indulged in tonight. The first, when she stood upon Rainbarrow, had expressed anxiety; the second, on the ridge, had expressed impatience; the present was one of triumphant pleasure. She let her joyous eyes rest upon him without speaking, as upon some wondrous thing she had created out of chaos.

"I have come," said the man, who was Wildeve. "You give me no peace. Why do you not leave me alone? I have seen your bonfire all the evening."...

...

"I knew it was meant for me."

"How did you know it? I have had no word with you since you—you chose her[1], and walked about with her, and deserted me entirely, as if I had never been yours life and soul so irretrievably!"

---

1. her：指朵蓀（Thomasin）。當游苔莎（Eustacia）得知韋狄（Wildeve）拖延了與朵蓀結婚的婚期時，以篝火約他相會。

五十二　勝利的喜悅

這時，水塘的外邊緣以外，低空之下的山谷上面，一個男子的身形朦朧地顯現。他繞過水塘，跳上堤岸，站在她的身旁。她不禁低聲笑了——這是這個姑娘今晚抒發的第三種感情。當她站在雨山上的時候，她抒發的是第一種感情，表示焦慮。她在山脊上抒發的是第二種感情，表示不耐煩。現在第三種表示的是勝利的喜悅。她那歡樂的目光注視着他，一句話也不說，好像看着她從混沌之中創造出來的一件奇妙的東西。

"我來了，"這個男子說，他就是韋狄，"你使我不得安寧。你為什麼不放過我？整個晚上我總看到你點燃的篝火。"……

……

"我知道這火是為我點燃的。"

"你怎麼會知道的？你——你看中了她。跟她形影不離，你完全不理我了，好像我們從來沒有過山盟海誓的恩情似的，這以後，我沒跟你說過一句話！"

...

... The man who had begun by being merely her amusement, and would never have been more than her hobby but for his skill in deserting her at the right moments, was now again her desire. Cessation in his love-making had revivified her love. Such feeling as Eustacia had idly given to Wildeve was dammed into a flood by Thomasin.

Thomas Hardy: The Return of the Native

……

　　……　這個男子開始只不過是作為她的嘻笑逗趣的人而已。要不是他有適時丟掉她的本事，他至多也就是她的特別愛好罷了。現在，他又成為她渴求的人了。他停止了向她求愛，這卻使她的愛情復甦。游苔莎悠閒地給予韋狄的這種感情被朵蓀抑制而成為狂瀾。

　　　　　　　　　　　　（英）哈代：《還鄉》

53　A Half-public Meeting

For what or whom was she[1] waiting, in the silence,...

Then her charming face grew eager, and, glancing round, with almost a lover's jealousy, young Jolyon[2] saw Bosinney striding across the grass.

Curiously he watched the meeting, the look in their eyes, the long clasp of their hands. They sat down close together, linked for all their outward discretion. He heard the rapid murmur of their talk; but what they said he could not catch.

He had rowed in the galley[3] himself! He knew the long hours of waiting and the lean minutes of a half-public meeting; the tortures of suspense that haunt the unhallowed lover.

It required, however, but a glance at their two faces to see that this was none of those affairs of a season that distract men and women about town; ... This was the real thing! ...

---

1. she：指伊琳（Irene）。她想掙脫和索米斯（Soames）的不幸結合，與建築師波辛尼（Bosinney）相遇後，產生了愛情。顯然最後是悲劇的下場，但卻是對私有世界的控訴。

2. young Jolyon（小喬里恩）：索米斯（Soames）的堂兄，正在植物園中畫畫，看見了他們相遇的情景。

3. rowed in the galley：直譯為"在大帆船上划槳"，意指經歷某種處境。

五十三　半公開的幽會

　　她在等什麼，還是等誰，默不作聲……

　　後來她迷人的臉龐變得更加焦急了。小喬里恩四處張望，幾乎是懷着情人的妒忌，看見波辛尼穿過草地大步走來。

　　他好奇地注視着他們的見面，他們目光中的神情，長時間的握手。他們坐下，靠得很近，儘管外表矜持，但實際是聯繫在一起的。他聽到他們快速的低語，可是聽不清說些什麼。

　　他有過同樣的經歷！他能體會到半公開幽會的滋味，等待了幾個小時，而見面就不過幾分鐘。他能體會到不顧禮教的情人所感受的懸念折磨。

　　不過，只需對他們的臉看一眼就知道，這絕不是使那些情場上男女痴狂一時的戀情。……這是真正的愛情！……

Bosinney was pleading, and she so quiet, so soft, yet immovable in her passivity, sat looking over the grass.

Was the man to carry her off, that tender, passive being, who would never stir a step for herself? Who had given him all herself, and would die for him, but perhaps would never run away with him!

It seemed to young Jolyon that he could hear her saying: "But, darling, it would ruin you!" For he himself had experienced to the full the gnawing fear at the bottom of each woman's heart that she is a drag on the man she loves.

And he peeped at them no more; but their soft, rapid talk came to his ears, with the stuttering song of some bird that seemed trying to remember the notes of spring: Joy — tragedy? Which—which?

John Galsworthy: The Forsyte Saga

波辛尼在懇求，而她坐在那裏望着草地，神情是那樣平靜、溫柔，不過又是順從而毫不動搖。

　　他這個男人能把這樣一個從不為自己而挪動一步的柔弱被動的女子帶走嗎？她把整個身心奉獻給了他，甚至願為他而死，但是恐怕怎麼也不會跟他私奔的！

　　小喬里恩好像能聽見她在説："可是，親愛的，這會毀了你的！"因為他自己充分體驗過，每個女子的內心深處都懷着折磨人的懼怕，怕她拖累所愛的人。

　　他不再偷看他們了，但是他們輕聲快速的情話傳到他的耳中，伴隨着一隻鳥兒斷斷續續的鳴囀，鳥兒好像盡力地回憶着春天的調子：歡樂——悲劇？哪一樣——哪一樣？

　　　　　　　　　　　　（英）高爾斯華綏：《福爾賽世家》

54   A Budding Passion

... It was a flowering out of feelings which had been withering in dry and almost barren soil for many years. It is probable that Carrie[1] represented a better order of woman than had ever attracted him before. He had had no love affair since that which culminated in his marriage, and since then time and the world had taught him how raw and erroneous was his original judgment. Whenever he thought of it, he told himself that, if he had it to do over again, he would never marry such a woman. ...

Hurstwood had gone, at Drouet's invitation, to meet a new baggage of fine clothes and pretty features. He entered, expecting to indulge in an evening of lightsome frolic, and then lose track of[2] the newcomer forever. Instead he found a woman whose youth and beauty attracted him. In the mild light of Carrie's eye was nothing of the calculation of the mistress. In the diffident manner was nothing of the art of the courtesan. He saw at once that a mistake had been made, that some difficult conditions had pushed this troubled

---

1. Carrie（嘉莉）：嘉莉認識赫斯特伍德（Hurstwood）以後，深深地陷入情網，被他拐騙私奔。
2. lose track of：失去……的綫索。

五十四　愛情萌動

　　……這是多年埋在幾乎是寸草不長，乾燥土壤裏的枯萎了的感情又開了花。這可能是嘉莉這樣的女人比以前引起他興趣的任何女人更好。自從以結婚告終的那次戀愛以後，他再也沒有過什麼風流韻事。結婚以來，時間和人世使他懂得，他當初的判斷多麼不成熟，多麼錯誤。他每想到這件事情，總對自己說，要是重來一次，他是決不會娶這麼一個女人的。……

　　赫斯特伍德應德魯埃邀請作客，原想會見一位衣着華麗、容貌標致的陌生女子。他進門後打算縱情享受輕鬆歡樂的夜晚，然後把新朋友忘得一乾二淨。可是，他看到的是一個青春和美貌都吸引了他的女子。在嘉莉溫和的眼光中絲毫沒有情婦那種謀算，在完全不同的姿態中絲毫沒有名妓的伎倆。他立刻明白，這一定是弄錯了，一定是什麼困境把這個苦惱的女子推到了他的面前，這引起了他的興

creature into his presence, and his interest was enlisted. Here sympathy sprang to the rescue, but it was not unmixed with selfishness. He wanted to win Carrie because he thought her fate mingled with his was better than if it were united with Drouet's. He envied the drummer, his conquest as he had never envied any man in all the course of his experience....

... He had no definite plans regarding her, but he was determined to make her confess an affection for him. He thought he saw in her drooping eye, her unstable glance , her wavering manner, the symptoms of a budding passion. He wanted to stand near her and make her lay her hand in his— he wanted to find out what her next step would be —what the next sign of feeling for him would be. Such anxiety and enthusiasm had not affected him for years. He was a youth again in feeling—a cavalier in action.

Theodore Dreiser: <u>Sister Carrie</u>

趣。 他起了同情心，想去搭救她，不過也不是沒有混雜着私心。他想贏得嘉莉，因為他認為，她的命運和他的相融合比和德魯埃的相結合要更好些。他妒忌這個推銷員和他的收穫，在他的經歷中還從來沒有這樣妒忌過任何男人。……

　　……他對她並沒有明確的計劃，但是他下了決心要讓她承認對他的愛情。他認為在她低垂的眼睛中，不穩定的目光中，裊娜的體態中，他看到了愛情萌動的徵兆。他想要站在她身旁， 讓她把手放在他的手裏──他想了解她下一步做什麼──對他感情的新標誌是什麼。他這樣的渴望和熱情已經有很多年沒出現了。他在感情上又成了青年，在行動上成了殷勤的男士了。

　　　　　　　　　　(美) 德萊塞：《嘉莉妹妹》

55 Our First Love in Each Other

"When did you love me?" she whispered.

"From the first, the very first, the first moment I laid eyes on you. I was mad for love of you then, and in all the time that has passed since then I have only grown the madder. I am maddest, now, dear. I am almost a lunatic, my head is so turned with joy."

"I am glad I am a woman, Martin—dear," she said, after a long sigh.... "... How did you make me love you?"

"I don't know," he laughed, "unless just by loving you, for I loved you hard enough to melt the heart of a stone, much less the heart of the living, breathing woman you are ."...

"Do you know, Martin, you sometimes frighten me. I am frightened now, when I think of you and of what you have been. You must be very, very good to me. Remember, after all, that I am only a child. I never loved before."

"Nor I. We are both children together. And we are fortunate above most, for we have found our first love in each other." ...

They sat on through the passing glory of the day, talking as lovers are prone to talk, marveling at the wonder of love and at destiny that had flung them so strangely together, and dogmatically believing that they loved to a degree never

五十五　初戀

"你什麼時候愛上我的？"她悄聲問。

"從我第一眼看到你的那一刻，第一眼，就是第一眼。那時我就瘋狂地愛你。那時以來我愛得愈加瘋狂。而到現在，親愛的，我愛得最瘋狂了。我差不多是個瘋子了，高興沖昏了我的頭腦。"

"我真高興我是個女人，馬丁——親愛的。"她長長地嘆息一聲說。…… "……你是怎麼讓我愛上你的？"

"我不知道，"他笑着說，"反正我就是一個勁兒地愛你。我對你的愛足夠使鐵石心腸也熔化，更不用說你這樣一個活生生女人的心了。"……

"馬丁，你知道，有時候你讓我害怕。現在一想到你，一想到你是怎麼一個人，我就害怕。你應該對我非常，非常好。記住，不管怎樣，我還是個孩子呢。我從來沒戀愛過。"

"我也沒有。我們倆都是孩子。而且我們最幸運，因為我們彼此都是初戀。"……

他們坐在那裏，度過白天光輝漸漸消逝的時光，談着情人們的綿綿情語，讚嘆着愛情的奇妙，讚嘆着把他們神奇地湊在一起的命運，武斷地認為他們相愛的程度是任何

attained by lovers before. And they returned insistently, again and again, to a rehearsal of their first impressions of each other and to hopeless attempts to analyze just precisely what they felt for each other and how much there was of it.

The cloud-masses on the western horizon received the descending sun, and the circle of the sky turned to rose, while the zenith glowed with the same warm color. The rosy light was all about them, flooding over them, as she sang, "Good-by, Sweet Day." She sang softly, leaning in the cradle of his arm, her hands in his, their hearts in each other's hands.

Jack London: <u>Martin Eden</u>

情人前所未有的。他們總是一遍又一遍地回憶彼此的初次印象，並且分析彼此到底是什麼樣的感情，有多少感情，儘管這樣分析是徒勞的。

西邊地平綫上的朵朵彩雲承接了下沉的落日，天邊一圈變成了玫瑰色，天頂也閃亮着同樣的溫暖色彩。當她唱起了"再見吧，甜蜜的一天"的時候，玫瑰色的光輝環繞着他們，充溢着他們。她唱得很輕柔，依偎在他雙臂的搖籃裏，她雙手放在他的手裏，他們的心也在彼此的手握之中。

(美) 杰克‧倫敦：《馬丁‧伊登》

56　We Do Love Each Other

"Isn't it strange," she said, suddenly putting her hand on his arm, with a loving impulse[1], "how we always talk like this! I suppose we do love each other in some way."

"Oh yes," he said; "too much."

She laughed almost gaily.

"You'd have to have it your own way, wouldn't you?" she teased. "You could never take it on trust[2]."

He changed, laughed softly, and turned and took her in his arms, in the middle of the road.

"Yes," he said softly.

And he kissed her face and brow, slowly, gently, with a sort of delicate happiness which surprised her extremely, and to which she could not respond. They were soft, blind kisses, perfect in their stillness. Yet she held back from them. It was like strange moths, very soft and silent, settling on her from the darkness of her soul. She was uneasy. She drew away.

"Isn't somebody coming?" she said.

---

1. ... a loving impulse：女教師厄秀拉（Ursula）與督學柏金（Birkin）經過衝突和波折尋覓着理想的愛情。

2. on trust：without proof or investigation。

五十六　我們相愛

"好不奇怪，"她説，在愛的衝動下，突然把一隻手放在他的臂上，"我們總是這樣談話！我想我們大概是彼此相愛了。"

"是啊，"他説，"深得很。"

她大笑起來，幾乎很開心。

"你得用你自己的方式，是嗎？"她逗笑説，"你永遠也不能輕易相信啊。"

他有了變化，溫柔地笑笑，轉過身來，就在路中央把她摟在懷裏。

"是啊。"他溫柔地説。

於是他慢慢地、輕柔地吻她的臉和額，有一種微妙的幸福感使她萬分驚奇，她不知怎樣應付。這是輕柔的吻，盲目的吻，寧靜無聲，盡善盡美。可是她掙脱了吻。這吻像怪飛蛾，軟軟的，靜靜的，從她的心靈暗處飛出來停落在她身上。她感到不自在。她掙脱了身。

"是不是有人來了？"她説。

So they looked down the dark road, then set off again walking towards Beldover. Then suddenly, to show him she was no shallow prude, she stopped and held him tight, hard against her, and covered his face with hard, fierce kisses of passion. In spite of his otherness, the old blood beat up in him.

"Not this, not this," he whimpered to himself, as the first perfect mood of softness and sleep-loveliness ebbed back away from the rushing of passion that came up to his limbs and over his face as she drew him.

D. H. Lawrence: Women in Love

於是他們朝暗暗的大路看看，又開始朝貝爾多佛走去。突然，她停下腳步，緊緊地抱住他，緊貼着自己，在他臉上蓋滿了猛烈的、狂暴的激情之吻，要向他表明，她完全不是淺薄的假裝正經的女人。儘管他的特點不同，熱血還是在全身沸騰。

"不是這樣，不是這樣。"他抱怨地對自己說，當她把他拉過去的時候，湧向他四肢和臉上的激情，使最初輕柔的、寂靜美妙的完美情緒如潮退般消失。

（英）勞倫斯：《戀愛中的女人》

57   She Blossomed for Him

... One autumn night, five years before, they had been walking down the street when the leaves were falling, and they came to a place where there were no trees and the sidewalk was white with moonlight. They stopped here and turned toward each other. Now it was a cool night with that mysterious excitement in it which comes at the two changes of the year. The quiet lights in the houses were humming out into the darkness and there was a stir and bustle among the stars. Out of the corner of his eye Gatsby saw that the blocks of the sidewalks really formed a ladder and mounted to a secret place above the trees—he could climb to it, if he climbed alone, and once there he could suck on the pap of life, gulp down the incomparable milk of wonder.

His heart beat faster and faster as Daisy's white face came up to his own. He knew that when he kissed this girl, and forever wed his unutterable visions to her perishable breath, his mind would never romp again like the mind of God. So he waited, listening for a moment longer to the tuning-fork that had been struck upon a star. Then he kissed her. At his lips' touch she blossomed for him like a flower and the incarnation was complete.

F. S. Fitzgerald: <u>The Great Gatsby</u>[1]

五十七　花苞綻開

　　……五年前的一個秋夜，落葉紛飛，他們在大街上漫步。他們走到一塊地方，那裏沒有樹木，人行道上灑滿銀白色的月光。他們止步轉身，相對而立。這是處於季節交替時節的一個涼爽的夜晚，神秘而令人興奮。各家靜謐的燈光投射到黑夜中，天空的繁星在忙碌流動。蓋茨比從眼角看見，一段段的人行道確實形成了一架梯子，它通向樹上方一個秘密的地方——　要是他獨自攀登，他能攀登到那個地方。一旦到了那裏，他就能吮吸生命的汁液，吞咽無與倫比奇妙的乳汁。

　　黛西抬起白皙的臉靠近他的臉，他的心跳得愈來愈快了。他知道只要他親吻了她，把他說不明白的夢幻和她短暫的呼吸永遠結合在一起，那時，他的心就不能再像上帝的心那樣自由自在了。所以，他等着，再多聆聽一會兒在一顆星星上敲響的音叉。然後他吻了她一下。她一碰到他的嘴唇，就像朵鮮花為他綻開，他的夢幻變成了現實。

　　　　　　　　　　　　（美）菲茨杰拉德：《大亨小傳》

---

1. 這是一部當代思想很深刻的美國小說，揭露了金錢第一的社會是虛情寡義的。蓋茨比（Gatsby）年輕時並不富有，愛上黛西（Daisy）。她對蓋茨比也情有所鍾。

58   Talking's All Bilge

"What's the matter, darling? Do you feel rocky?"

She kissed me[1] coolly on the forehead.

"Oh, Brett, I love you so much."

...

"Couldn't we live together, Brett? Couldn't we just live together?"

"I don't think so. I'd just *tromper*[2] you with everybody. You couldn't stand it."

"I stand it now."

"That would be different. It's my fault, Jake. It's the way I'm made."

"Couldn't we go off in the country for a while?"

"It wouldn't be any good. I'll go if you like. But I couldn't live quietly in the country. Not with my own true love."

"I know."

----

1. me：本篇主人公杰克（Jake）熱戀着失去了丈夫的勃萊特（Brett），但他由於殘疾，對性愛可望而不可及，不能與鍾情的人結合。本書中的人物經過戰爭，身心受到摧殘，心靈空虛，想用愛情和尋歡作樂來解脫痛苦。
2. *tromper*：[法語] 欺騙；引申義為對丈夫或妻子不忠。

230

五十八　空談無用

“怎麼啦，親愛的？你覺得頭暈嗎？”

她冷漠地吻了一下我的前額。

“哦，勃萊特，我多麼愛你。”

……

“我們不能一起生活嗎，勃萊特？我們就不能一起生活嗎？”

“我看不能。我和誰都來往，會對你不忠的。你會受不了的。”

“我現在忍受着呢。”

“這情況不一樣。這是我的錯，杰克。我這個人就是這個樣。”

“我們不能到鄉下去住一陣子嗎？”

“這不會有什麼好處。你要，我就去。不過我住在鄉下也是待不住的。即使和我真正心愛的人也不行。”

“我知道。”

"Isn't it rotten? There isn't any use my telling you I love you."

"You know I love you."

"Let's not talk. Talking's all bilge. I'm going away from you, and then Michael's[3] coming back."

"Why are you going away?"

"Better for you. Better for me." ...

"Can't we go together?"

"No. That would be a hell of an[4] idea after we'd just talked it out."

"We never agreed."

"Oh, you know as well as I do. Don't be obstinate, darling."

"Oh, sure," I said. "I know you're right. I'm just low, and when I'm low I talk like a fool."

Ernest Hemingway: <u>The Sun Also Rises</u>

---

3. Michael（邁克爾）：另一個追求勃萊特（Brett）的男子。
4. a hell of an...：很好的；很糟的。

「這不很糟糕嗎？我對你說我愛你，嘴上說說是沒什麼用處的。」

「你知道我愛你。」

「我們別談了。空談都是無聊的。我要離開你了，邁克爾也要回來了。」

「為什麼你要走？」

「對你更好。對我更好。」……

「我們不能一塊去嗎？」

「不行。我們方才談明白了，這個主意就不妥當了。」

「我們意見總是不一致。」

「哦，你心裏和我一樣明白。別固執了，親愛的。」

「哦，當然，」我說，「我也明白你說得對。我只是情緒不好，而情緒不好的時候，就說傻話。

(美) 海明威：《太陽照常升起》

59 Where Do the Noses Go?

"I love thee[1], Maria."

"No. It is not true," she said. Then as a last thing pitifully and hopefully.

"But I have never kissed any man."

"Then kiss me now."

"I wanted to," she said. "But I know not how. Where things were done to me I fought until I could not see. I fought until—until—until one sat upon my head—and I bit him—and then they tied my mouth and held my arms behind my head—and others did things to me ."

"I love thee, Maria," he said. "And no one has done anything to thee. Thee, they cannot touch. No one has touched thee, little rabbit[2]."

"You believe that?"

"I know it."

"And you can love me?" warm again against him now.

"I can love thee more."

"I will try to kiss thee very well."

---

1. thee：[古] thou（你）的賓格。
2. rabbit：[俚] 姑娘。

234

五十九　吻你，鼻子往哪放？

"我愛你，瑪麗亞。"

"不，不是真的。"她說。然後可憐地、抱有希望地，好像是最後的一句話，說：

"可是我從來沒吻過男人。"

"那現在就吻我吧。"

"我倒是想吻你，"她說，"可是我不會吻。我被糟蹋的時候，我拼命反抗，直到什麼也看不見。我反抗到——到——到有個傢伙坐在我頭上，我就咬他——後來他們蒙上我的嘴，把我的手捆在腦袋後面——另外幾個傢伙就糟蹋我。"

"我愛你，瑪麗亞，"他說，"誰也沒把你怎麼樣。你，他們碰不着。誰也沒碰過你，小姑娘。"

"你相信是那樣的？"

"我知道是那樣。"

"那你還愛我嗎？"又熱烈地緊偎着他。

"我會更愛你。"

"我要想法好好吻你。"

"Kiss me a little."

"I do not know how."

"Just kiss me."

She kissed him on the cheek.

"No."

"Where do the noses go? I always wondered where the noses would go."

"Look, turn thy[3] head," and then their mouths were tight together and she lay close pressed against him and her mouth opened a little gradually and then, suddenly, holding her against him, he was happier than he had ever been, ...

Ernest Hemingway: <u>For Whom the Bell Tolls</u>

---

3. thy：[古] thou（你）的所有格，你的。

"吻吻我。"

"我不會吻。"

"你就吻我。"

她在他的臉頰上吻了一下。

"不對。"

"鼻子往哪放？我總也弄不明白鼻子往哪放。"

"你看，把頭轉過來。"他們的嘴就貼在一起了。她躺在他的身旁，緊偎着他。她的嘴慢慢地微微張開。接着，他突然把她摟住，他感到從未有過的快樂，……

（美）海明威：《戰地鐘聲》

60　Sublime Youth

Youth, sublime youth, when passion, as yet unknown, is only dimly felt in a quickening of the pulse; when your hand coming in chance contact with your sweetheart's breast trembles as if affrighted and falters, and when the sacred friendship of youth guards you from the final step! What can be sweeter than to feel her arm about your neck and her burning kiss on your lips!

It was the second kiss they had exchanged throughout their friendship[1]. Pavel, who had experienced many a beating but never a caress except from his mother, was stirred to the depths of his being. Hitherto life had shown him its most brutal side, and he had not known it could be such a glorious thing; now this girl had taught him what happiness could mean.

He breathed the perfume of her hair and seemed to see her eyes in the darkness.

"I love you so, Tonya, I can't tell you how much, for I don't know how to say it."

His brain was in a whirl. How responsive her supple body.... But youth's friendship is a sacred trust.

1.　their friendship：此篇描述保爾（Pavel）少年時代和女友冬妮亞（Tonya）的初戀。

六十　美好的青春

　　當陌生的激情只是在急促的心跳中朦朧地感到，當你的手無意碰到心愛人兒的胸部而顫抖，好像因受驚而躊躇，青春的聖潔友情沒讓你走最後的一步，青春啊，多美好的青春！你撫摸着摟着你脖子的胳膊，還有她印在你唇上的熱吻，還有什麼比這些更甜蜜的嗎？

　　這是他們交朋友以來的第二次互吻。保爾以前只是挨打受罵，除了母親，誰也沒有撫愛過他，現在他從內心深處激動起來。在此之前，他只見到生活殘酷的一面，他不知道生活竟還會這樣美好。現在這個少女讓他懂得了幸福的含義。

　　黑暗中他聞到了她頭髮的香味，好像還看到了她的眼神。

　　"冬妮亞，我多麼愛你，我說不清楚愛你愛得多深，因為我不知道怎麼說才好。"

　　他的思緒一陣迷亂。她柔軟的胴體是多麼柔順……但是青春的友情是一種聖潔的信任。

"Tonya, when all this mess is over I'm bound to get a job as a mechanic, and if you really want me, if you're really serious and not just playing with me, I'll be a good husband to you. I'll never beat you, never do anything to hurt you, I swear it."

Fearing to fall asleep in each other's arms—lest Tonya's mother find them and think ill of them—they separated.

Day was breaking when they fell asleep after having made a solemn compact never to forget one another.

N. Ostrovsky: How the Steel Was Tempered

"冬妮亞，等外面不再亂的時候，我準備找個當機修工的工作。要是你真的需要我，當真愛我，不是和我鬧着玩的，我要做你的好丈夫。我永遠不打你，永遠不做傷害你的事情，我向你保證。"

他們恐怕在擁抱中睡着了，讓冬妮亞的母親看到，對他們產生壞想法，只好分開，各睡各的了。

他們盟誓約定，永不背棄，待到睡着的時候，已經開始天亮了。

（俄）奧斯特洛夫斯基：《鋼鐵是怎樣煉成的》

Disappointment
失戀

Painting by Francis Danby (1793-1861)

61   An Agony of Impatience

"Good heavens!" she[1] exclaimed, "he is there—He is there—Oh! why does he not look at me? Why cannot I speak to him?"

"Pray, pray be composed," cried Elinor, ...

... She sat in an agony of impatience which affected every feature.

At last he turned round again and regarded them both; she started up, and pronouncing his name in a tone of affection, held out her hand to him. He approached, and addressing himself rather to Elinor than Marianne, as if wishing to avoid her eye, and determined not to observe her attitude, inquired in a hurried manner after Mrs. Dashwood[2], and asked how long they had been in town[3]. Elinor was robbed of all presence of mind by such an address and was unable to say a word. But the feelings of her sister were instantly expressed. Her face was crimsoned over, and she

---

1. she：指瑪麗安（Marianne）。在一次聚會上瑪麗安見到她終日思慕的威洛比（Willoughby）先生。
2. Mrs. Dashwood（達希伍德夫人）：埃莉諾（Elinor）等三姐妹的母親。
3. town：指倫敦市。

六十一　情感之苦

"天哪！"她大喊道，"他在那兒——他在那兒。啊！他為什麼不看看我？我為什麼不能和他說話？"

"請，請鎮靜，"埃莉諾喊道，……

……她坐在那裏焦急得痛苦萬狀，臉上的每個部分都表現出來。

他到底又轉過身來了，看看她們姐妹倆。她突然起身，用親昵的聲音喚着他的名字，一隻手向他伸去。他走過來，不是對着瑪麗安，而是對着埃莉諾講話，好像要避開她的目光，決心不觀察她的態度，匆忙地問一下達希伍德夫人的身體狀況，還問她們來本市有多久了。他這幾句話使埃莉諾心慌意亂，弄得她一句話也說不出來。可是她妹妹的感情卻立刻表現了出來。她漲紅着臉，情緒極度激

exclaimed in a voice of the greatest emotion, "Good God! Willoughby, what is the meaning of this? Have you not received my letters? Will you not shake hands with me?"

He could not then avoid it, but her touch seemed painful to him, and he held her hand only for a moment. ...

Marianne, now looking dreadfully white and unable to stand, sank into her chair, and Elinor, expecting every moment to see her faint, tried to screen her from the observation of others while reviving her with lavender water.

"Go to him, Elinor," she cried as soon as she could speak, "and force him to come to me. Tell him I must see him again—must speak to him instantly. I cannot rest—I shall not have a moment's peace till this is explained—some dreadful misapprehension or other. Oh, go to him this moment."

Jane Austen: <u>Sense and Sensibility</u>

動，高聲喊道：“天哪！威洛比，你這是什麼意思？我的信你都沒收到？你不想和我握手了？”

這時他躲不開了，可是碰到她好像會使他感到疼痛，所以把她的手只握了很短的時間。……

這時瑪麗安的臉色極度蒼白，站不住，癱倒在椅子上。埃莉諾隨時防備着她暈倒，設法遮擋着她不讓別人看見，用燻衣草香水使她清醒過來。

“埃莉諾，到他那裏去，”她剛恢復過來能說話就喊起來，“強迫他到我這裏來。跟他說我必須再見到他 —— 必須馬上跟他說話。我不能休息 —— 這事不說明白，我一分鐘也不會安寧 —— 可怕的誤會還是什麼。啊，你現在就到他那裏去吧。”

（英）奧斯丁：《理智與情感》

62 To Be Her Preserving Angel

Mary[1] loved another! That idea would rise uppermost in his mind, and had to be combated in all its forms of pain....

Then uprose the guilty longing for blood!—The frenzy of jealousy!—Some one should die. He would rather Mary were dead, cold in her grave, than that she were another's.... What had she done to deserve such cruel treatment from him? She had been wooed by one whom Jem knew to be handsome, gay, and bright, and she had given him her love. That was all! It was the wooer who should die. Yes, die, knowing the cause of his death. ... How he had left his own rank, and dared to love a maiden of low degree; and oh! stinging agony of all—how she, in return, had loved him! Then the other nature spoke up, and bade him remember the anguish he should so prepare for Mary! ...

No! he could not, said the still small voice. It would be worse, far worse, to have caused such woe, than it was now to bear his present heavy burden.

But it was too heavy, too grievous to be borne, and live. He would slay himself, and the lovers should love on, and

---

1. Mary（瑪麗）：她幼稚天真，夢想做闊太太，看上了工廠老板的兒子，拒絕了杰姆（Jem）的求愛。

248

六十二　守護天使

　　瑪麗愛上了別人！這是他腦子裏浮現的最主要的想法，不得不和這帶來萬分苦惱的想法搏鬥。……

　　這時出現了想兇殺的犯罪念頭！—— 嫉妒的狂熱！—— 應該死一個人。他寧願讓瑪麗死掉，冰冷地躺在墳墓裏，不甘心她屬於別人。……她幹了什麼錯事要受到他這樣殘酷的對待？她被一個人追求着。杰姆知道這個人相貌英俊，又聰明活潑。她以愛情回報。僅此而已！這個追求者才應該死。對，該死，而且讓他知道為什麼死。……他居然離開了自己的地位，竟敢愛一個地位低的姑娘。啊！最刺人的痛苦是，她竟然給他回報，愛起他來了！這時，他另一個本性説話了，叮囑他不要忘記，這樣會給瑪麗釀成痛苦！……

　　不！他不可以這樣做，説這話的聲音仍舊很小。比起承受他現在的沉重負擔，造成這樣的災禍會更壞，壞得多。

　　但是這個負擔實在太沉重、太傷心，簡直難以承受，活不下去。他想自殺，這一對情人會繼續相愛。陽光燦

the sun shine bright, and he with his burning, woeful heart would be at rest....

... Should he shrink from the duties of life, into the cowardliness of death? Who would then guard Mary, with her love and her innocence? Would it not be a goodly thing to serve her, although she loved him not; to be her preserving angel, through the perils of life; and she, unconscious all the while?

He braced up his soul, and said to himself, that with God's help he would be that earthly keeper.

Mrs. Gaskell: <u>Mary Barton</u>

爛，而他懷着一顆熾熱的、悲哀的心得以安息。⋯⋯

　　⋯⋯難道他應該逃避人生的責任，畏縮不前，膽小地死去嗎？那麼誰來保護瑪麗，保護她的愛情和清白？雖然她不愛他，可是為她服務，做她的守護天使，陪她走過人生的艱難險阻，而她可以對此毫不察覺，這豈不是一件大好的事情嗎？

　　他精神振作起來了，對自己說，他願靠上帝的幫助，做這樣一個人世間的保護人。

　　　　　　　　　　（英）蓋斯凱爾夫人：《瑪麗·巴頓》

63　All Done, All Gone!

"It seems," said Estella, very calmly, "that there are sentiments, fancies—I don't know how to call them—which I am not able to comprehend. When you say you love me, I know what you mean, as a form of words; but nothing more. You address nothing in my breast, you touch nothing there. I don't care for what you say at all. I have tried to warn you of this; now, have I not?"

I said in a miserable manner, "Yes."

"Yes. But you would not be warned, for you thought I did not mean it. Now, did you not think so?"

"I thought and hoped you could not mean it. ..."

...

"...You are part of my existence, part of myself. You have been in every line I have ever read, since I first came here, the rough common boy whose poor heart you wounded even then. You have been in every prospect I have ever seen since—on the river, on the sails of the ships, on the marshes, in the clouds, in the light, in the darkness, in the wind, in the woods, in the sea, in the streets. You have been the embodiment of every graceful fancy that my mind has ever become acquainted with. ..."

252

六十三　全都完了

　　埃斯特拉非常平靜地說：“好像存着在一些我不理解的感情、幻想——我也不知道它們叫什麼。你說你愛我的時候，我知道你說這些話字面上指的是什麼，再也沒有更多的意思了。你什麼也沒說到我的心裏，你沒有觸動我的心。你說什麼我根本不感興趣，這點我已經警告過你了。喂，我警告過沒有？”

　　我可憐兮兮地說：“警告過。”

　　“是啊，可是你不聽警告，因為你以為我說的不算數。喂，你不是這麼想的嗎？”

　　“我想，也希望，你說的不算數。……”

　　……

　　“……你是我存在的一部分，我的一部分。自從我到這裏，你一開始就傷了我這普通野孩子的可憐的心。我只要讀書，每一行字裏都有你的身影。我看到的每一個景象裏也有你的身影 —— 大河邊、船帆上、沼澤地裏、彩雲中、在亮處、在黑處、在風裏、森林裏、大海裏、大街上，哪兒沒有！你是我心中每一個美妙幻想的化身。……”

In what ecstasy of unhappiness I got these broken words out of myself, I don't know. The rhapsody welled up within me, like blood from an inward wound, and gushed out. I held her hand to my lips some lingering moments, and so I left her. ...

All done, all gone! So much was done and gone, that when I went out at the gate, the light of the day seemed of a darker colour than when I went in.

Charles Dickens: <u>Great Expectations</u>

我是何等傷心若狂，才説出這些語無倫次的話來，自己也不知道。這一番狂熱的話湧上心頭，從我內心的創傷處，猶如鮮血噴湧出來。我把她的一隻手放到我的嘴邊，放了好長一會。就這樣我離開了她。……

什麼都完了，什麼都沒了。完得徹底，沒得徹底。我走出大門的時候，白天的亮光比我進門的時候暗淡了。

（英）狄更斯：《遠大前程》

64　He Lost the Best

He[1] came back from France when Tom and Daisy were still on their wedding trip, and made a miserable but irresistible journey to Louisville on the last of his army pay. He stayed there a week, walking the streets where their footsteps had clicked together through the November night and revisiting the out-of-the-way places to which they had driven in her white car. Just as Daisy's house had always seemed to him more mysterious and gay than other houses, so his idea of the city itself, even though she was gone from it, was pervaded with a melancholy beauty.

He left feeling that if he had searched harder, he might have found her—that he was leaving her behind. The day-coach—he was penniless now—was hot. He went out to the open vestibule and sat down on a folding-chair, and the station slid away and the backs of unfamiliar buildings moved by. Then out into the spring fields, where a yellow trolley raced them for a minute with people in it who might once have seen the pale magic of her face along the casual street.

---

1. He：蓋茨比（Gatsby）。第一次世界大戰時，蓋茨比被調往歐洲，與黛西（Daisy）分手。待他回國時，金錢已使她背叛了心靈的貞潔，嫁給了富有的湯姆（Tom）。

六十四　最美好的

　　湯姆和黛西還在作新婚旅遊的時候，蓋茨比從法國回來。他用最後剩餘的一點軍隊津貼去了一次路易斯維爾。這次旅行雖然是痛苦的，但又是忍不住不去的。他在那裏逗留了一個多星期，徘徊於留有他們十一月夜晚情影足跡的街頭，重訪了那些停過她白色轎車的偏僻地區。黛西的房子在他看來比別的房子更神秘，更華麗。同樣，儘管她已離開這座城市，他仍覺得這裏充滿了傷感的美。

　　他離開這城市的時候覺得，要是再好好地找一下，也可能找到她 —— 覺得是棄她而走。硬席車廂裏很熱 —— 他這時已身無分文。他走出車廂，來到無頂篷的通廊，在一把折疊椅上坐下。站台緩緩滑走，陌生的大樓背面也移動而過。列車來到春天的田野。這時，一輛黃色有軌電車跟着他們跑了一會兒，車裏面的乘客也許在某條街上無意中見過她迷人的蒼白的面孔。

The track curved and now it was going away from the sun, which, as it sank lower, seemed to spread itself in benediction over the vanishing city where she had drawn her breath. He stretched out his hand desperately as if to snatch only a wisp of air, to save a fragment of the spot that she had made lovely for him. But it was all going by too fast now for his blurred eyes and he knew that he had lost that part of it, the freshest and the best, forever.

F. S. Fitzgerald: The Great Gatsby

鐵軌拐了彎，現在背離着西下的夕陽而東去。落日的餘輝灑遍了漸漸消失的城市，好像在向她呼吸過的地方祝福。他失望地伸出一隻手去，好像想只抓一把空氣，就可以把她為他變得美好的地方留下一小塊。但是，一切都飛速地閃過，他那模糊的雙眼來不及看清楚了。他明白了，他永遠失去了這一切中最鮮艷、最美好的部分。

（美）菲茨杰拉德：《大亨小傳》

65   She Slapped Him Across the Face

... She[1] tried to remember just exactly what she had planned last night to say to Ashley, but she couldn't recall anything. ...

All she could think of was that she loved him—everything about him, ...

At the touch of his hand, she began to tremble. It was going to happen now, just as she had dreamed it. A thousand incoherent thoughts shot through her mind, and she could not catch a single one to mould into a word. She could only shake and look up into his face. Why didn't he speak?

"What is it?" he repeated. "A secret to tell me?" ...

"Yes—a secret. I love you." ...

"Scarlett," he said, "can't we go away and forget that we have ever said these things ?"

"No," she whispered. "I can't. What do you mean? Don't you want to—to marry me?"

He replied, "I'm going to marry Melanie." ...

---

1. She：指斯卡雷特（Scarlett）。此篇描述斯卡雷特一直愛着阿什利（Ashley），在他與梅萊尼（Melanie）結婚前傾吐真情，遭回絕後又羞又惱，氣急敗壞。

六十五　一個耳光

　　……她努力把昨晚想好要對阿什利説的話完整地想一遍，可是什麼也想不起來了。……

　　她能想起來的只是她愛他 —— 有關他的一切……

　　她碰到了他的手，就顫抖起來。事情即將像她夢想的那樣發生。她思緒萬千，卻抓不住一條能説成一句話的。她只能打顫，仰頭望着他的臉。他為什麼沉默不語？

　　"怎麼啦？"他又説了一遍，"有秘密對我説？"……

　　"是的 —— 一個秘密。我愛你。"……

　　"斯卡雷特，"他説，"難道我們不能走開，忘掉我們曾經説過這些話嗎？"

　　"不，"她低聲説，"我可不能。你想説什麼意思？難道你不想 —— 不想和我結婚嗎？"

　　他回答説："我就要和梅萊尼結婚了。"

He had never once crossed the borders of friendliness with her and, when she thought of this, fresh anger rose, the anger of hurt pride and feminine vanity. She had run after him and he would have none of her. He preferred a whey-faced little fool like Melanie to her. ...

He put out his hand toward her and, as he did, she slapped him across the face with all the strength she had. The noise cracked like a whip in the still room and suddenly her rage was gone, and there was desolation in her heart.

The red mark of her hand showed plainly on his white tired face. He said nothing, but lifted her limp hand to his lips and kissed it. Then he was gone before she could speak again, closing the door softly behind him.

She sat down again very suddenly, the reaction from her rage making her knees feel weak. He was gone and the memory of his stricken face would haunt her till she died.

Margaret Mitchell: <u>Gone with the Wind</u>

……他一次也沒超越和她交往的友誼界綫，她想到這裏，新的怒火湧上心頭，這種怒火出自受損的自尊心和女人的虛榮心。她一直在追求他，而他卻對她沒有反應。他不喜歡她，寧可喜歡梅萊尼這個臉色蒼白的小蠢人。……

他向她伸出手，就在這時，她用盡全身力量打了他一個耳光。在寂靜的房間裏猶如鞭子啪響了一聲，她的怒火立即化為烏有，心中一片孤寂。

他那白淨疲憊的臉上清晰地留下了她手掌的紅印。他沒吭一聲，把她疲軟的手抬到唇邊，吻了一下。不等她開口，他已經走了，輕輕地隨手關上了門。

她很突然地又坐了下來。盛怒以後，她的兩膝發軟。他走了，他被打耳光的臉將終生縈繞在她的記憶中。

（美）米切爾：《飄》

Proposal
求婚

Painting by Edouard Manet (1832-1883)

66　I Am Thus Rejected

"In vain have I[1] struggled. It will not do. My feelings will not be repressed. You must allow me to tell you how ardently I admire and love you."

Elizabeth's astonishment was beyond expression. She stared, coloured, doubted, and was silent. This he considered sufficient encouragement, and the avowal of all that he felt and had long felt for her, immediately followed. He spoke well, but there were feelings besides those of the heart to be detailed, and he was not more eloquent on the subject of tenderness than of pride. ...

In spite of her deeply-rooted dislike, she could not be insensible to the compliment of such a man's affection, and though her intentions did not vary for an instant, she was at first sorry for the pain he was to receive; till, roused to resentment by his subsequent language, she lost all compassion in anger. She tried, however, to compose herself to answer him with patience, when he should have done. He concluded with representing to her the strength of that attachment which, in spite of all his endeavours, he had found

---

1. I：指達西（Darcy），他向伊麗莎白（Elizabeth）求婚時仍持傲慢的態度，而她也抱有偏見。求婚以失敗告終。

六十六　如此被拒

"我的努力徒勞無益，實在沒辦法。我的感情再也抑制不住了。請允許我告訴你，我是多麼熱烈地愛慕你，愛你。"

伊麗莎白的驚訝無法表達。她目瞪口呆，紅着臉，疑惑不解，默不作聲。他把這種情形當作了充分的鼓勵，接着便立刻把他現在和以前對她的感想和盤托出。他說得頭頭是道，不過除了愛情外，還一一細說了別的想法。而且，他的口才既善於傾訴柔情，也善於表達傲慢。……

儘管她對他的忿恨是根深蒂固的，終究對一個男人如此盛情的讚美不能無動於衷。雖然她的意圖一會兒也沒動搖過，可是起初她也感到過意不去，因為他將會受到痛苦。他後來說的話使她心頭火起，於是她的憐憫心在怒火中化為烏有。不過，她還是努力保持鎮靜，等他把話說完，耐心地給他一個答覆。最後，他講述了對她的愛情是那麼強烈，無論他怎麼努力，也不可能遏制。同時，他表

impossible to conquer; and with expressing his hope that it would now be rewarded by her acceptance of his hand. As he said this, she could easily see that he had no doubt of a favourable answer. He spoke of apprehension and anxiety, but his countenance expressed real security. Such a circumstance could only exasperate farther, and when he ceased, the colour rose into her cheeks, and she said, "... I have never desired your good opinion, and you have certainly bestowed it most unwillingly.... The feelings which, you tell me, have long prevented the acknowledgment of your regard, can have little difficulty in overcoming it after this explanation."

... He was struggling for the appearance of composure, and would not open his lips, till he believed himself to have attained it. ...

"And this is all the reply which I am to have the honour of expecting! I might, perhaps, wish to be informed why, with so little endeavour at civility, I am thus rejected. But it is of small importance."

Jane Austen: <u>Pride and Prejudice</u>

示希望，他的愛情能得到她的回報——接受他的求婚。他說這話的時候，她一下子就看出，他絲毫不懷疑，他會得到有利的答覆。他嘴裏說着擔心和憂慮，可是面部的表情卻是萬無一失。這情況只能使她的怒火更加旺盛。等他說完，她漲紅了臉說：“……我從來沒想得到你的誇獎，何況你給我的誇獎極為勉強。……你對我說，一些別的想法長時間妨礙了你向我表明對我的好感，那麼，在我這次說明以後，這些想法遏制你的好感，也就不會很困難了吧。”

　　……他竭力要做到外表的鎮靜，等到認為已經做到了才開口。……

　　“這就是我有幸期望得到的回答！也許我能希望知道，為什麼我遭到不講禮貌的拒絕。不過這也沒什麼關係。”

　　　　　　　　　　　　（英）奧斯丁：《傲慢與偏見》

67   Her Attention Demanded

... Emma[1] found, on being escorted and followed into
the second carriage by Mr. Elton, that the door was to be
lawfully shut on them, and that they were to have a tête-à-
tête drive. ... She believed he had been drinking too much of
Mr. Weston's good wine , and felt sure that he would want
to be talking nonsense.

... her hand seized—her attention demanded, and Mr.
Elton actually making violent love to her: availing himself
of the precious opportunity, declaring sentiments which must
be already well known, hoping—fearing—adoring—ready
to die if she refused him; but flattering himself that his ardent
attachment and unequalled love and unexampled passion
could not fail of having some effect, and, in short, very much
resolved on being seriously accepted as soon as possible. It
really was so. Without scruple—without apology—without
much apparent diffidence, Mr. Elton, the lover of Harriet[2],
was professing himself *her* lover. She tried to stop him; but

---

1. Emma（愛瑪）：愛瑪和埃爾頓（Elton）參加了威斯頓（Weston）家
   的宴會以後，乘車回各自的家。
2. Harriet：Harriet Smith（哈麗特·史密斯）是愛瑪的女友。愛瑪原先
   計劃促成她和埃爾頓相愛。

六十七　洗耳恭聽

　　……愛瑪發現埃爾頓先生跟在後面陪伴着她，上了第
二輛馬車，車門把他們合法地關在裏面，他們就要開始面
對面的行程了。……她想他把威斯頓先生的好酒喝得太多
了。她感到他要胡說八道了。

　　……她的手被抓住了 —— 她被要求洗耳恭聽，埃爾頓
先生實際上在向她熱烈地求愛：利用這次寶貴的機會宣布
那些大家一定知道的感情，希望啦，害怕啦，崇拜啦，要
是她不答應他，就準備死啦。但是他滿以為他那熱烈的依
戀，無與倫比的愛情，沒有先例的激情，都不會沒有一定
的效果。總之一句話，他決意要對方盡快地認真地接受求
愛。當時情況真是這樣。埃爾頓先生，這位哈麗特的情
人，不猶豫，不道歉，看不出有什麼膽怯，現在竟聲稱自
己是愛瑪的情人。她竭力止住他說下去，可是白費勁。他

vainly; he would go on, and say it all. Angry as she was, the thought of the moment made her resolve to restrain herself when she did speak. She felt that half this folly must be drunkenness, and therefore could hope that it might belong only to the passing hour. Accordingly, with a mixture of the serious and the playful, which she hoped would best suit his half-and-half state, she replied:

"I am much astonished, Mr. Elton. This to me! You forget yourself; you take me for my friend; any message to Miss Smith I shall be happy to deliver; but no more of this to me, if you please."

Jane Austen: <u>Emma</u>

還是不斷地説，直到説完為止。她雖然很生氣，但是她當時的想法使她決心在説話的時候控制住自己。她覺得這番蠢話，有一半原因要歸咎於喝醉了酒。所以，可以指望這一切只是轉瞬即逝的事情。她便似認真又似玩笑地 ── 她希望這樣最合適他半真半假的情況 ── 回答説：

"我感到萬分的驚奇，埃爾頓先生。這樣的話對我説！你忘乎所以了。你把我當作我的那位女友了。有什麼信要給史密斯小姐，我很樂意轉交。不過請不要再對我説這種話了。"

(英) 奧斯丁：《愛瑪》

68   My Love Can't Be Put in Words

He had been absent and abstracted all day long with the thought of the coming event of the evening. He almost smiled at himself for his care in washing and dressing in preparation for his visit to Mary; as if one waistcoat or another could decide his fate in so passionately a momentous thing. ...

Jem entered, looking more awkward and abashed than he had ever done before. Yet here was Mary all alone, just as he had hoped to find her. ...

"Is your father at home, Mary?" said he, by way of making an opening, for she seemed determined to keep silence, and went on stitching away.

"No, he's gone to his union[1], I suppose." Another silence. It was no use waiting, thought Jem. The subject would never be led to by any talk he could think of in his anxious, fluttered state. He had better begin at once. ...

"Dear Mary! (for how dear you are, I cannot rightly tell you in words). It's no new story I'm going to speak about. You must ha'[2] seen and known it long; for since we were

---

1. gone to his union：瑪麗（Mary）的父親是當時工人運動的積極
   分子。
2. ha'：= have

六十八　說不完的愛

　　他整天想着晚上的大事，精神恍惚。為了去見瑪麗作好準備，他細心梳洗打扮，自己幾乎也好笑起來。好像穿這件背心或那件背心就會決定他戀愛大事的成敗。……

　　杰姆進了門，看上去那笨拙窘迫樣是前所未有的。不過只有瑪麗一個人在那兒，這正是他所希望看到的。……

　　"你父親在家嗎，瑪麗？"他問了一句作為談話的開頭，因為她好像決意保持沉默，繼續做着針綫活。

　　"不在，我猜想，他到工會去了。"又沉默了。杰姆想，等着不是個辦法。他在這樣焦急不安的狀態下是想不出什麼話來談到正題上來的。他還是開門見山吧。……

　　"親愛的瑪麗！（因為我不能準確地用語言表達你是多麼的可愛）我要說的並不是什麼新鮮事。你一定早就看到，早就知道了。我們從小是青梅竹馬，那時我愛你就勝

boy and girl, I ha' loved you above father and mother and all; and all I've thought on by day and dreamt on by night, has been something in which you've had a share. I'd no way of keeping you for long, and I scorned to try and tie you down; and I lived in terror lest some one else should take you to himself. But now, Mary, I'm foreman in th'[3] works, and, dear Mary! listen," as she, in her unbearable agitation, stood up and turned away from him. He rose too, and came nearer, trying to take hold of her hand; but this she would not allow. She was bracing herself up to refuse him, for once and for all.

"And now, Mary, I've a home to offer you, and a heart as true as ever man had to love you and cherish you;... I cannot speak as I would like; my love won't let itself be put in words. But oh! darling, say you'll believe me, and that you'll be mine."

Mrs. Gaskell: <u>Mary Barton</u>

---

3. th' : = the

過愛我的父母和其他所有的人。我白天想的，晚上夢見的，都少不了你。我沒法長時間地守住你，我又嫌惡束縛你的行動。所以我提心吊膽，深怕別人把你奪走。可是現在，瑪麗，我是廠裏的領班了，親愛的瑪麗！請聽我說，"她按捺不住焦燥不安的心情，於是站了起來，轉過身去。他也站起來，挨近她，想要抓起她的一隻手，但是她不願意。她正鼓起勇氣徹底地拒絕他的求愛。

"而且現在，瑪麗，我能給你一個家，一顆愛你疼你的、誠摯的心。……我想要說的話說不好，我的愛不能用語言表達。可是，啊！親愛的，你快說呀，說你相信我，嫁給我。"

（英）蓋斯凱爾夫人：《瑪麗·巴頓》

69 My Eloquence

When I awoke next morning, I was resolute to declare my passion to Dora, and know my fate. Happiness or misery was now the question. There was no other question that I knew of in the world, and only Dora could give the answer to it. ...

I began to think I would put it off till to-morrow.

"I hope your poor horse was not tired, when he got home at night," said Dora, lifting up her beautiful eyes. "It was a long way for him."

I began to think I would do it to-day. ...

"Wasn't he fed, poor thing?" asked Dora.

I began to think I would put it off till to-morrow. ...

I don't know how I did it. I did it in a moment. I intercepted Jip. I had Dora in my arms. I was full of eloquence. I never stopped for a word. I told her how I loved her. I told her I should die without her. I told her that I idolised and worshipped her. Jip barked madly all the time.

When Dora hung her head and cried, and trembled, my eloquence increased so much the more. If she would like me to die for her, she had but to say the word, and I was ready. Life without Dora's love was not a thing to have on any

278

六十九　我的口才

我第二天早上醒來，決定向朵拉宣布我的愛情，看看我的命運怎樣。幸福還是苦難，是現在面臨的問題。我不知道世界上還有別的問題，而且只有朵拉能夠回答這個問題。……

我開始想，我要把它推到明天才提出。

"我希望你那可憐的馬兒昨晚到家的時候沒累着，"朵拉抬起漂亮的眼睛說，"這一回馬跑了很長的路啊。"

我開始想，我要今天提出。……

"給它喂食了嗎，這可憐的馬？"朵拉問。

我開始想，我要把它推到明天才提出。……

我不知道我是怎麼提的。才不用多久我就提出來了。我攔住吉普。我把朵拉摟在懷裏。我當時的口才好極了。從沒停下來斟酌用詞。我告訴她我多麼愛她。我告訴她要是沒有她我就要死。我告訴她，我把她當作偶像，我崇拜她。吉普一直吠叫不停。

朵拉低垂着頭哭，全身顫抖。這時，我的口才更好了。如果她要我為她去死，只要説個死字，我立即就去死。沒有朵拉愛情的生活決不是應該過的生活。我是受不

terms[1]. I couldn't bear it, and I wouldn't. I had loved her every minute, day and night, since I first saw her. I loved her at that minute to distraction. I should always love her, every minute, to distraction. Lovers had loved before, and lovers would love again; but no lover had ever loved, might, could, would, or should ever love, as I loved Dora. The more I raved, the more Jip barked. Each of us, in his own way, got more mad every moment.

Charles Dickens: David Copperfield

---

1. not...on any terms：決不。

了的，我也不願意忍受。自從我第一次見到她以後，我日日夜夜，每分每秒都愛着她。在那一刻我愛她愛得發狂。我將永遠時刻愛她至瘋狂。情人相愛過，情人還將會相愛。但是沒有那個情人像我愛朵拉那樣愛過、可能愛、能夠愛、將會愛。我說得愈激烈，吉普吠叫得愈厲害。我和它都以自己的方式變得愈來愈瘋狂。

（英）狄更斯：《大衛·科波菲爾》

70   Then I Will Marry You

A waft of wind came sweeping down the laurel-walk, and trembled through the boughs of the chestnut: it wandered away—away—to an indefinite distance—it died. The nightingale's song was then the only voice of the hour: in listening to it, I again wept. Mr. Rochester sat quiet, looking at me gently and seriously. Some time passed before he spoke; he at last said:—

"Come to my side, Jane[1], and let us explain, and understand one another."

"I will never again come to your side: I am torn away now, and cannot return."

"But, Jane, I summon you as my wife: it is you only I intend to marry."

I was silent: I thought he mocked me.

"Come, Jane—come hither."

"Your bride stands between us."

He rose, and with a stride reached me.

---

1. Jane（簡）：故事主角。作者塑造了一位敢於反抗、爭取自由和平等地位的婦女形象 —— 簡‧愛（Jane Eyre）。羅切斯特（Rochester）滿足了她在感情上不忘平等的要求，她才答應了他的求婚。

七十　我嫁給你

　　種着月桂的路上颳來一陣風，顫抖着穿過栗樹枝叢。風颳走了 —— 颳到遠遠的地方去了 —— 消失了。此刻，只有夜鶯的歌聲：我聽着，又哭了。羅切斯特先生坐着沉默不語，溫柔而嚴肅地看着我。過了一會兒才開口，他終於說：

　　"簡，到我身邊來，讓我們說說清楚，互相理解吧。"

　　"我再也不到你身邊去了。現在我被拉走，不能回來了。"

　　"可是，簡，我是把你當作妻子叫你過來的，我想娶的只是你。"

　　我沒說話，心想他在嘲笑我。

　　"簡，來，到這兒來。"

　　"可是我們之間有你的新娘。"

　　他站起來，一步就走到了我面前。

"My bride is here," he said, again drawing me to him, "because my equal is here, and my likeness, Jane, will you marry me?"

Still I did not answer; and still I writhed myself from his grasp: for I was still incredulous.

...

His face was very much agitated and very much flushed, and there were strong workings[2] in the features[3], and strange gleams in the eyes.

...

"Are you in earnest?—Do you truly love me?—Do you sincerely wish me to be your wife?"

"I do; and if an oath is necessary to satisfy you, I swear it."

"Then, sir, I will marry you."

Charlotte Brontë: Jane Eyre

---

2. workings：活動。
3. features：臉的一部分，如眼、鼻等。

284

"我的新娘就在這兒，"他又把我拉到身邊說，"因為和我平等的人在這兒，也是和我相似的人。簡，你願意嫁給我嗎？"

我還是不回答，還是掙脫了他，因為我還是不相信他。

……

他的臉很激動，很紅，五官活動劇烈，眼裏發出奇異的閃光。

……

"你是當真的嗎？—— 你確實愛我嗎？—— 你是真心要我做你的妻子嗎？"

"是真心的。要是需要發誓你才滿意，那我就發誓吧。"

"那麼，先生，我願意嫁給你。"

（英）夏洛蒂·勃朗特：《簡·愛》

71   Merely a Question of Time

"... Rachel! will you honor me, will you bless me, by being my wife?"

...

"Godfrey!" she said, "you must be mad!"

"I never spoke more reasonably, dearest—in your interests, as well as in mine. ... Is your happiness to be sacrificed to a man who has never known how you feel toward him, and whom you are resolved never to see again? Is it not your duty to yourself to forget this ill-fated attachment? ... I don't ask for your love— I will be content with your affection and regard. Let the rest be left, confidently left, to your husband's devotion, and to Time, that heals even wounds as deep as yours."

She began to yield already. ...

"One question, Rachel. Have you any personal objection to me?"

"I! I always liked you. After what you have just said to me, I should be insensible indeed if I didn't respect and admire you as well."

"... At your age, and with your attractions, is it possible for you to sentence yourself to a single life? Trust my knowledge of the world—nothing is less possible. It is merely

七十一　女大當嫁

"……雷茜兒！承蒙賞識，托你的福，嫁給我好嗎？"

……"高孚利！"她說，"你一定是瘋了！"

"我的心上人啊，我從來沒有像今天說得這樣有理，這是考慮到你的利益，也考慮到我的利益。一個並不了解你對他那麼痴情的人，一個你再也不想見到的人，難道你的幸福就為這樣一個人犧牲嗎？難道你不該忘掉這倒霉的痴情嗎？……我不要求你愛我，只要你喜歡我，尊敬我，我就滿足了。其他一切你就可以放心地讓你丈夫的忠誠，讓時間來處理吧，即使像你這樣重的創傷也會醫治好的。"

她已經開始動心了。……

"雷茜兒，我問你。你討厭我嗎？"

"我！我是一向喜歡你的。聽了你方才對我說的一番話，要是我再不敬佩和愛慕你，那我就是冷漠無情的人了。"

"……像你這樣的年齡，又這樣多情，難道你可能宣判你自己過獨身的生活嗎？請你相信我的閱歷吧。什麼事情都可能發生。只不過是時間問題罷了。也許過不了幾年，

a question of time. You may marry some other man, some years hence. Or you may marry the man, dearest, who is now at your feet, and who prizes your respect and admiration above the love of any other woman on the face of the earth."

"...You are tempting me with a new prospect, when all my other prospects are closed before me. ... Take the warning, and go!"

"I won't even rise from my knees till you have said yes!"

...

"You won't ask me for more than I can give?"

"My angel! I only ask you to give me yourself."

"Take me!"

W. W. Collins: The Moonstone

你可能嫁給別的一個什麼男人。我的心上人啊，或許你可能嫁給現在跪在你腳跟前的男人，他把你的敬佩和愛慕看得高於世界上所有女人的愛情"

"……在我的其他指望都落空的時候，你又用新的希望來引誘我。……聽我的警告，走開吧！"

"你不答應我，我就跪着不起來！"

……

"你不會要我給你我不能給你的東西吧？"

"我的天使啊！我只要你嫁給我。"

"娶我吧。"

（英）科林斯：《月亮寶石》

72   It Cannot Be

She felt sure that he had come so early on purpose to see her alone and to propose to her. ...

"I don't think I've come at the right time, I'm too early," he said gazing round the empty drawing-room. When he saw that his expectation was fulfilled and that nothing prevented his speaking to her, his face clouded over.

"Not at all," said Kitty and sat down at the table.

"But all I wanted was to find you alone," he began, still standing and avoiding her face so as not to lose courage.

"Mama will be down in a minute. She was so tired yesterday ..." She spoke without knowing what she was saying, her eyes fixed on him with a caressing look full of entreaty.

He glanced at her; she blushed and was silent.

"I told you that I did not know how long I should stay ... that it depends on you."

Her head dropped lower and lower, knowing the answer she would give to what was coming.

"That it would depend on you," he repeated. "I want to say ... I want to say ... I came on purpose ... that ... to be my wife!" he uttered hardly knowing what he said; but feeling that the worst was out he stopped and looked at her.

七十二　這不可能

她敢斷定，他那麼早來，為的是和她單獨見面，向她求婚。……

"我想我沒按時來，來得太早，"他說，環視着空無一人的客廳。他看到他的期望已經實現，沒有什麼會阻擋他去對她說話，這時，他的臉便陰沉下來了。

"一點也不早。"吉蒂說完在桌旁坐下。

"我要的就是和您單獨見面。"他開口說，仍舊站在那裏，不看她的臉，怕失去勇氣。

"媽媽過一會就下樓。昨天她太累了……"她說，不知道自己在說些什麼，目不轉睛地看着他，撫愛的目光充滿懇求的心情。

他看了她一眼，她臉紅了，便不作聲了。

"我對您說過，我不知道要來住多久……這要看您了。"

她的頭垂得越來越低了，因為她知道對即將提出的問題，她要給的是什麼答覆。

"這要看您了，"他又說了一遍，"我是想說……我想說……我來的目的……是……做我的妻子！"他說，卻幾乎不知道說了什麼，不過他感到，最不好說的話已經說出去了，於是住了口看着她。

She was breathing heavily and not looking at him. She was filled with rapture. Her soul was overflowing with happiness. She had not at all expected that his declaration of love would make so strong an impression on her. But that lasted only for an instant. She remembered Vronsky, lifted her clear, truthful eyes to Levin's face, and noticing his despair she replied quickly:

"It cannot be[1]... forgive me."

How near to him she had been a minute ago, how important in his life! And how estranged and distant she seemed now!

Lev Tolstoy: Anna Karenina

---

1. It cannot be：吉蒂（Kitty）真心愛着列文（Levin），但伏倫斯基（Vronsky）追求着她，在彷徨中的吉蒂違心地拒絕了列文的求婚。但他們的愛情真誠純潔，終於得到了美滿幸福的婚姻。

她吃力地喘着氣，不看他。她欣喜若狂，心裏洋溢着幸福的感覺。她一點也沒想到，他的愛情表白對她會產生這樣強烈的印象。不過這只是一剎那的事情。她想起了伏倫斯基，於是她抬起那雙明亮、誠實的眼睛看着列文的臉，察覺到他的絕望神情，便很快地回答說：

　　"這不可能……請原諒。"

　　一分鐘之前她離他多麼近，在他的生活中多麼重要！可是現在覺得她多麼陌生、疏遠！

　　　　（俄）列夫·托爾斯泰：《安娜·卡列尼娜》

73　She Was Agitated

"I feel, Mr. Boldwood[1], that though I respect you much, I do not feel—what would justify me to—in accepting your offer," she stammered.

This giving back of dignity for dignity seemed to open the sluices of feeling that Boldwood had as yet kept closed.

"My life is a burden without you," he exclaimed, in a low voice. "I want you—I want you to let me say I love you again and again!"

...

"I wish I could say courteous flatteries to you," the farmer continued in an easier tone, "and put my rugged feeling into a graceful shape: but I have neither power nor patience to learn such things. I want you for my wife—so wildly that no other feeling can abide in me; but I should not have spoken out had I not been led to hope."

...

"Mr. Boldwood, it is painful to have to say I am surprised, so that I don't know how to answer you with propriety and respect—but am only just able to speak out

---

1.　Boldwood（博爾德伍德）：他是構成大幫瘋狂的追求者（madding crowd）之一，弄得巴絲謝葩（Bathsheba）不得安寧。

七十三　焦慮不安

　　"博爾德伍德先生，我覺得，雖然我很尊敬你，可是我感覺不到有什麼理由接受你的求婚。"她結結巴巴地說。

　　這種以莊嚴回應莊嚴的答話，打開了博爾德伍德從沒開啟過的感情閘門。

　　"沒有你，我活着就是個累贅，"他低聲地喊道，"我要你 —— 我要你允許我一遍又一遍地說我愛你！"

　　……

　　"我希望我能對你說些有禮貌的恭維話，"農場主以從容一些的聲調繼續說，"讓我粗魯的感情有文雅的表達形式。不過我沒有能力，也沒有耐心去學這種本領。我想要你嫁給我，這種願望那麼強烈，我心中再也沒有別的感情了。要是我這樣希望是無緣無故的，那我也不會說出來了。"

　　……

　　"博爾德伍德先生，令人痛苦的是，我不得不說我感到驚奇，因此，我不知道怎樣恰當地、尊敬地回答你，但是，我只能說出我的感情 —— 我是說我真正的意思：儘管

my feeling—I mean my meaning; that I am afraid I can't marry you, much as I respect you. You are too dignified for me to suit you, sir."

...

"But you will just think—in kindness and condescension think—if you cannot bear with me as a husband! ... I cannot say how far above every other idea and object on earth you seem to me—nobody knows—God only knows—how much you are to me!"

"Don't say it: don't! I cannot bear you to feel so much, and me to feel nothing.... O, I am wicked to have made you suffer so!" She was frightened as well as agitated at his vehemence.

Thomas Hardy: <u>Far from the Madding Crowd</u>

我非常尊敬你，可是恐怕我還是不能嫁給你。對我來說，你太尊貴了，我配不上你，先生。"

……

"可是請你想想 —— 請你仁慈地、屈尊地想想 —— 我做你的丈夫，你是不是受不了？……你高於世上的一切思想和事物，我說不清你有多高 —— 誰也不知道 —— 只有上帝才知道 —— 你對我多麼重要！"

"別說這些了，別說了！我真不忍心看到你這樣動情，而我卻無動於衷。……啊，我太壞了，讓你這麼痛苦！"他的強烈感情使她焦慮不安，也使她害怕。

（英）哈代：《遠離塵囂》

74 You Will

"I[1] mean, that it is only your wanting me very much, and being hardly able to keep alive without me, whatever my offences, that would make me feel I ought to say I will."

"You will—you do say it, I know. You will be mine for ever and ever." He clasped her close and kissed her.

"Yes." She had no sooner said it than she burst into a dry hard sobbing. ...

"Why do you cry dearest?"

"I can't tell—quite!—I am so glad to think—of being yours, and making you happy ."

"But this does not seem very much like gladness, my Tessy."

"I mean—I cry because I have broken down in my vow! I said I would die unmarried."

"But if you love me, you would like me to be your husband?"

"Yes, yes, yes! But O, I sometimes wish I had never been born!"

---

1. I：指苔絲（Tess）。她是個遭受欺凌的失身女子，倍受歧視。因此，在愛情面前躊躇不前，在內心矛盾中勉強答應了克萊（Clare）的求婚。但她仍隱藏着這段痛心的身世。

七十四 你答應了

"我是想說，只有當你很需要我，沒有我就不能活，不管我有什麼過錯，那才會讓我覺得該答應你。"

"你答應了 —— 我知道你是說答應了。你永遠，永遠是我的。"他緊緊地摟着她、吻她。

"是。"她剛說完就猛然無淚地抽噎起來，……

"最親愛的，你為什麼哭了？"

"我說不出 —— 說實在的！—— 想到我是你的人，又讓你幸福 —— 太高興了。"

"可是這不太像個高興樣，苔絲。"

"我是說 —— 我因為沒遵守我起過的誓！我說過終生不嫁人的。"

"不過要是你愛我，你要我做你的丈夫嗎？"

"要，要，要！不過，哦，有時我真想沒生我這個人！"

"Now, my dear Tess, if I did not know that you are very much excited, and very inexperienced, I should say that remark was not very complimentary. How came you to wish that if you care for me? Do you care for me? I wish you would prove it in some way ."

"How can I prove it more than I have done?" she cried in a distraction of tenderness . "Will this prove it more?" She clasped his neck, and for the first time Clare learnt what an impassioned woman's kisses were like upon the lips of one whom she loved with all her heart and soul, as Tess loved him. "There—now do you believe?" she asked, flushed, and wiping her eyes.

"Yes. I never really doubted—never, never!"

Thomas Hardy: <u>Tess of the d'Urbervilles</u>

"唉，我親愛的苔絲，要是我不知道你很激動，又沒有經驗，我會説你這話不太近人情啊。要是你喜歡我，怎麼會願意那樣呢？你喜歡我嗎？我希望你用一種方式證明你喜歡我。"

"我已經表示過了，叫我再用什麼辦法證明呢？"她一陣柔情，恍恍惚惚地説，"這樣能再證明嗎？"她摟住他的脖子，克萊第一次感受到，一個熱烈的女人吻她真心所愛的人，就像苔絲跟他那樣，是什麼滋味。"你看 —— 現在你該信我了吧？"她滿臉通紅地問，邊擦着眼淚。

"信了。其實我從來也沒懷疑過 —— 從來，從來沒有！"

(英) 哈代：《德伯家的苔絲》

75　Without the Usual Courting

"That is the situation[1]. Now for the most important thing. The storm[2] in this family is only beginning. We must get out of here into the fresh air and as far away from this hole[3] as possible. We must start life afresh. Once I have taken a hand in this fight I'm going to see it through. Our life, yours and mine, is none too happy at present. I have decided to breathe some warmth into it. Do you know what I mean? Will you be my life's companion, my wife?"

Taya was deeply moved by his confession, but these last words startled her.

"I am not asking you for an answer tonight," he went on. "You must think it over carefully. I suppose you cannot understand how such things can be put so bluntly without the usual courting. But you and I have no need of all that nonsense. I give you my hand, little girl, here it is. If you will put your trust in me you will not be mistaken. We can both give each other a great deal...."

---

1. the situation：此篇描述保爾（Pavel）向革命戰友達雅（Taya）求婚。
2. The storm：達雅的父親專橫暴虐，她哥哥是個浪蕩公子，姐姐因丈夫酗酒而離婚。保爾有心幫助達雅改變現狀，引起她父親的仇恨。
3. this hole：貶指達雅的家。

七十五　不落俗套

　　"情況就是這樣。現在講最重要的事吧。這家裏的風暴還只是開始。我們應該離開這裏，呼吸新鮮空氣，走得愈遠愈好。我們應該重新開始生活。既然我干預了這場糾紛，我就要把它進行到底。你我兩人的生活現在一點也不快活。我已經決定給它注入一些暖意。你明白我的意思嗎？你願意做我的人生伴侶，做我的妻子嗎？"

　　達雅聽了他的愛情表白，深受感動，但是這最後的一句話卻使她大吃一驚。

　　"我不要求你今天晚上就回答我，"他接着說，"你要好好考慮一下。我想你不能理解，沒有通常的談情說愛，怎麼就直接了當地提出這種事情。可是你和我都不需要這些無聊的老規矩。我把手給你，小姑娘，給你。要是你相信我，你錯不了。我們互補的東西很多很多。……"

He fell silent for a few moments, then he went on in a tender, caressing voice: "And for the present, I offer you my friendship and my love."

He held her fingers in his, feeling at peace, as if she had already given her consent.

"Do you promise never to leave me?"

"I can only give you my word, Taya. it is for you to believe that men like me do not betray their friends...."

"I can't give you an answer tonight. It is all very sudden," she replied.

N. Ostrovsky: How the Steel Was Tempered

他沉默了一會以後，親切溫柔地說：“至於現在，我向你提出我對你的友誼和愛情。”

　　他握住她的手，心情平靜，覺得好像她已經同意了。

　　“你能保證永遠不拋棄我嗎？”

　　“達雅，我只能向你保證。而你，你得相信我這樣的人不會背叛朋友。……”

　　“今晚我不能給你答覆。這事太突然了。”她回答說。

　　　　（俄）奧斯特洛夫斯基：《鋼鐵是怎樣煉成的》

76　It Shocked Me

"... You haven't answered my question. Are you going to marry me?"

... This sudden talk of marriage bewildered me, even shocked me I think. It was as though the King asked one. It did not ring true. And he[1] went on eating his marmalade as though everything were natural. In books men knelt to women, and it would be moonlight. Not at breakfast, not like this.

"My suggestion doesn't seem to have gone too well," he said. "I'm sorry. I rather thought you loved me. A fine blow to my conceit."

"I do love you," I said. "I love you dreadfully. You've made me very unhappy and I've been crying all night because I thought I should never see you again."

When I said this I remember he laughed, and stretched his hand to me across the breakfast table. "Bless you for that," he said; "one day, when you reach that exalted age of thirty-six which you told me was your ambition, I'll remind you of this moment. And you won't believe me. It's a pity you have to grow up."

1.　he：指 Maxim de Winter。

七十六　受寵若驚

"⋯⋯你還沒回答我的問題呢。你打算嫁給我嗎？"

⋯⋯突然談到婚姻使我很尷尬，我想甚至使我吃了一驚。好像是國王在求婚。這事聽起來不像是真的。他繼續吃着果醬，好像一切都很自然。在書裏，男人向女人下跪，而且是在月光下。不在吃早飯的時候，不像這樣。

"我的建議好像不怎麼受歡迎，"他說，"對不起！我還以為你愛我呢。這對我的傲慢是一次迎頭痛擊。"

"我確實是愛你的，"我說，"我愛你愛得要命。你弄得我很痛苦，我整夜都在哭，因為我想以後再也見不到你了。"

我記得，我說這些話的時候，他笑了，從吃早飯的餐桌對面向我伸過手來。"因為這個，願上帝保佑你，"他說，"你對我說過，活到三十六歲這樣成熟的年齡，是你的抱負。到了那一天，我會提醒你想起今天這個時刻。那時你一定不會相信我說的話了。你的年齡會增長，真可惜。"

I was ashamed already, and angry with him for laughing. So women did not make those confessions to men. I had a lot to learn.

"So that's settled, isn't it?" he said, going on with his toast and marmalade; "instead of being companion to Mrs. Van Hopper you become mine,..."

I drummed with my fingers on the table, uncertain of myself and of him. Was he still laughing at me, was it all a joke? He looked up, and saw the anxiety on my face, "I'm being rather a brute to you, aren't I?" he said; "this isn't your idea of a proposal. We ought to be in a conservatory, you in a white frock with a rose in your hand, and a violin playing a waltz in the distance. And I should make violent love to you behind a palm tree. You would feel then you were getting your money's worth. Poor darling, what a shame. Never mind, I'll take you to Venice for our honeymoon..."

Daphne du Maurier: Rebecca

308

這時我已經感到害羞，而且因為他笑，我對他生氣了。是啊，女人是不向男人作這樣的表白的。我還有許多事情要學習呢。

"那麼，就這樣決定了，是不是？"他說，繼續吃着烤麵包片和果醬，"你不用陪伴範·霍珀夫人，你是我的伴侶了。……"

我用手指敲打着桌子，我對我自己，對他，都弄不明白。他還在笑我嗎？這一切都是在開玩笑嗎？他抬起頭看我，看到我臉上焦慮的神情。"我對於你來說，是個狠心的人，是不是？"他說，"這不是你想像的求婚。我們應該在音樂學院裏，你穿着白禮服，手裏拿着玫瑰花，在遠處奏起華爾茲舞曲。而我在棕櫚樹後面向你熱烈地求愛。那樣，你就會感到你有身價了。可憐的小寶貝，多麼遺憾！不過不要緊，我帶你到威尼斯去度蜜月，……"

（英）達夫妮·杜穆里埃：《蝴蝶夢》

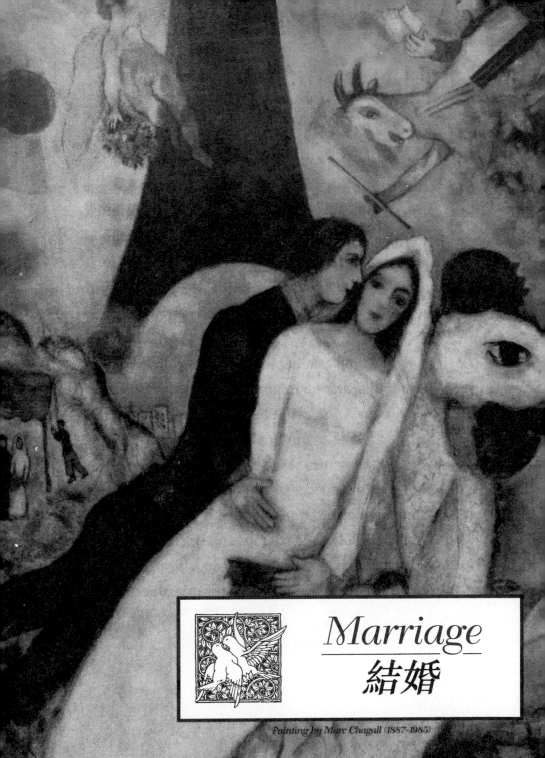

Marriage
結婚

Painting by Marc Chagall (1887-1985)

77 The Object of Her Choice

"Or in other words, you are determined to have him[1]. He is rich, to be sure, and you may have more fine clothes and fine carriages than Jane[2]. But will they make you happy?"

"Have you any other objection," said Elizabeth, "than your belief of my indifference?"

"None at all. We all know him to be a proud, unpleasant sort of man, but this would be nothing if you really liked him."

"I do, I do like him," she replied, with tears in her eyes, "I love him. Indeed he has no improper pride. He is perfectly amiable. You do not know what he really is; then pray do not pain me by speaking of him in such terms."

"Lizzy," said her father, "I have given him my consent. He is the kind of man, indeed, to whom I should never dare refuse any thing, which he condescended to ask. I now give it to you, if you are resolved on having him. But let me advise you to think better of it. I know your disposition, Lizzy. I know that you could be neither happy nor respectable, unless

---

1. him：指達西（Darcy）。他改變了最初的傲慢，使伊麗莎白（Elizabeth）克服了偏見，最終贏得了她的心。
2. Jane（珍妮）：伊麗莎白的大姐。

七十七　意中人

"換句話説，你決心嫁給他了？當然，他很有錢，你可以比珍妮有更好的衣服和更好的馬車。不過這些東西能讓你幸福嗎？"

伊麗莎白説："你認為我對這些毫無考慮。除了這一點，你還有別的反對意見嗎？"

"別的一點也沒有。我們都知道他是個傲慢的、不討人喜歡的人。不過你真要喜歡他，這也算不得什麼了。"

"我真的，真的喜歡他，"她含着眼淚回答説，"我愛他。其實，他並沒有不合理的傲慢。他非常可愛。你不了解他實際上是怎樣的人，所以我求你不要這樣説他，這樣會刺痛我的心。"

"麗莎，"她父親説，"我已經答應他了。他這樣的人，只要蒙他不棄，有所請求，我就不能拒絕。要是你決心嫁給他，現在我也答應你。不過我勸你還是慎重考慮。麗莎，我了解你的性情。要是你不真正尊重你的丈夫，要

you truly esteemed your husband; unless you looked up to him as a superior. Your lively talents would place you in the greatest danger in an unequal marriage. You could scarcely escape discredit and misery. My child, let me not have the grief of seeing you unable to respect your partner in life...."

Elizabeth, still more affected, was earnest and solemn in her reply; and at length, by repeated assurances that Mr. Darcy was really the object of her choice, by explaining the gradual change which her estimation of him had undergone, relating her absolute certainty that his affection was not the work of a day, but had stood the test of many months suspense, and numerating with energy all his good qualities, she did conquer her father's incredulity, and reconcile[3] him to the match.

Jane Austen: *Pride and Prejudice*

---

3. reconcile (sb. to sth.)：使甘心（於）。

是你不把他看作優勝於你的人，我知道你是不會覺得幸福和體面的。要是你的婚姻不相稱，你那充滿生機的天資會使你遇到最大的危險。丟臉和痛苦的事你是避免不了的。我的孩子，別讓我因為看到你不能尊重你的終身伴侶，而為你傷心。……"

伊麗莎白更加感動，回答的時候，神情認真而嚴肅。最後，她反覆地說，達西先生確實是她選中的人；她又說明了她對他的看法是怎樣逐漸改變了；她說她完全相信，他對她的情感不是一朝一夕的結果，而是經受了好多個月忐忑不安的考驗；她生動地歷數他的一切優良品德。這樣，她消除了她父親的疑慮，使他想通了這門親事。

（英）奧斯丁：《傲慢與偏見》

78 We Must Be Married Instantly

"Mr. Rochester, if ever I did a good deed in my life—if ever I thought a good thought—if ever I prayed a sincere and blameless prayer—if ever I wished a righteous wish, — I am rewarded now. To be your wife is, for me, to be happy as I can be on earth."

"Because you delight in sacrifice."

"Sacrifice! What do I sacrifice? Famine for food, expectation for content. To be privileged to put my arms round what I value—to press my lips to what I love—to repose on what I trust: is that to make a sacrifice? If so, then certainly I delight in sacrifice."

"And to bear with my infirmities, Jane: to overlook my deficiencies."

"Which are none, sir, to me. I love you better now, when I can really be useful to you, than I did in your state of proud independence, when you disdained every part but that of the giver and protector."

"Hitherto I have hated to be helped—to be led: henceforth, I feel, I shall hate it no more. I did not like to put my hand into a hireling's, but it is pleasant to feel it circled by Jane's

七十八　馬上結婚

"羅切斯特先生，如果我在一生中做過一件好事——如果我有過一個好的念頭 —— 如果我做過一次真誠的、無可指摘的祈禱 —— 如果我有過一個正當的願望，— 那我現在得到了回報。做你的妻子，對我來說，是我活在人間最大的幸福。"

"因為你以犧牲為樂。"

"犧牲！我有什麼犧牲的？犧牲饑餓而換取食物，犧牲期望而換取滿意。有特權摟抱我珍視的人 —— 親吻我鍾愛的人 —— 依靠我信賴的人。難道這些是作出犧牲嗎？如果這些是犧牲，那麼我肯定樂於作出犧牲。"

"還要忍受我的體弱病痛，簡，寬容我的缺陷。"

"先生，這對我來說不算什麼。我現在能更好地愛你了，比起你處於驕傲地不依靠人的狀況時，現在我可以對你真正有用了。那時你除了做賞賜人和保護人以外，不屑扮其他角色。"

"我一直討厭接受別人的幫助，討厭讓人領着走。可是我覺得從今以後，我再不討厭了。我不喜歡把手放到傭人的手裏，可是讓簡的小指頭握着我的手卻是很愉快的。過

little fingers. I preferred utter loneliness to the constant attendance of servants; but Jane's soft ministry will be a perpetual joy. Jane suits me: do I suit her?"

"To the finest fibre of my nature, sir."

"The case being so, we have nothing in the world[1] to wait for: we must be married instantly."

Charlotte Brontë: <u>Jane Eyre</u>

---

1. in the world：[用於加強語氣] 到底。

去，我寧可極端的孤獨，也不願總讓傭人侍候。可是簡溫柔的照料將會是永久的歡樂。簡適合我；我適合她嗎？"

"即使對我個性最細小的部分也合適，先生。"

"既然這樣，我們沒什麼可以等待的了：我們必須馬上結婚。"

(英) 夏洛蒂·勃朗特：《簡·愛》

79   His Unceasing Happiness

He[1] was happy, without a care in the world. A meal alone
with her, an evening stroll along the highway, the movement
of her hand as she smoothed her hair, the sight of her straw
hat hanging from a window hasp, and many other things
which he had never dreamed would give him pleasure—such
were the components of his unceasing happiness. Each
morning, lying in bed with his head beside hers on the pillow,
he watched the sunlight shining through the golden down on
her cheeks, half covered by the scalloped flaps of her
nightcap. Seen from so close, her eyes seemed larger than
usual, especially when she opened and shut them several
times on awakening; ... After he had gotten up, she would go
to the window to watch him leave; she would lean on her
elbows between two pots of geraniums, her dressing gown
hanging loosely around her. Outside in the street, Charles
would put his foot on the curbstone to buckle his spurs and
she would go on talking to him from above, occasionally
biting off a piece of a flower or a leaf and blowing it down to
him; it would flutter and seem to hover momentarily, making
little half-circles in the air like a bird, and finally, before

---

1. He：指 包法利先生（Charles Bovary）。

七十九　幸福無窮

　　他是幸福的，活在這世上無憂無慮。和她一起用餐、黃昏在大路上散步、她用手撫平頭髮的動作、看見窗搭扣上掛着她的草帽，還有許多他做夢也沒想到的事情，都給他帶來愉悅 —— 這些都構成他無窮的幸福。每天早上，他躺在牀上，和她在枕上頭靠頭，看着陽光射過她面頰上的金色汗毛，睡帽的扇形帽沿遮住了一半面頰。從這樣近處看，她的眼睛顯得比平時的大，特別是她剛醒來，眼睛幾次開合的時候，……他起牀以後，她總是走到窗前，看他離去。她雙肘撐在兩盆天竺葵之間的地方，梳妝衣寬鬆地披在身上。夏爾在外面，把一隻腳擱在道邊石上，以便扣緊靴刺。這時，她在上面還繼續和他說着話，有時候咬下一瓣花或者一片葉子朝他吹下去，它像隻鳥兒拍拍翅膀，作短暫的盤旋，又在空中轉了幾個小半圓圈，最後在靜靜

reaching the ground, it would catch in the tangled mane of the old white mare standing motionless in front of the door . Charles would throw her a kiss after climbing into the saddle; she would reply with a wave of her hand; he would set off. ... with the sun on his shoulders and the morning air in his nostrils, his heart full of the night's bliss, his mind at peace and his flesh content, he would ride along ruminating his happiness, like those who, after dinner, still savor the taste of the truffles they are digesting.

Gustave Flaubert: Madame Bovary

地站在門前的老白母馬蓬亂的鬃毛上掛住，再落到地上。夏爾上馬以後，送她一個吻；而她揮揮手回應；他就走了。……太陽照在他的肩上，清晨的空氣吸進他的鼻孔，他心裏充滿昨夜的歡樂，精神安詳，肉體滿足，他騎着馬，邊走邊想着他的幸福，就像人們飯後還在回味着在消化中的蘑菇一樣。

（法）福樓拜：《包法利夫人》

80　Not the Happiness She Had Dreamed of

Before her marriage she[1] had believed herself to be in love; but since the happiness which should have resulted from this love had not come to her, she felt that she must have been mistaken. And she tried to find out exactly what was meant in life by the words "bliss," "passion" and "rapture," which had seemed so beautiful to her in books.

Her anxiety over her new position in life, or perhaps the stimulation of this man's presence, had been enough to make her believe that she at last possessed that marvelous passion which, until then, had been like a great rosy-plumaged bird soaring in the splendors of poetic skies. And now she could not bring herself to believe that the calm in which she was living was the happiness she had dreamed of.

It sometimes occurred to her that these were nevertheless the best days of her life : the honeymoon days, as they were commonly called. To taste their sweetness, she and her husband would probably have had to go off to those countries with romantic names where newlyweds can savor their bliss in such delicious languor! They would have slowly climbed the steep slopes in a post chaise with blue silk curtains, listening to the

---

1.　she：指包法利夫人（Madame Bovary）。

八十　見異思遷

　　結婚以前，她以為自己在戀愛。但是，這愛情應該帶來的幸福並沒來到她這裏。於是，她覺得自己一定是想錯了。"歡樂"、"激情"、"銷魂"這幾個詞在書本裏似乎很美，而在實際生活中的意思是什麼，她想法要徹底弄明白。

　　她對自己在生活中所處的新地位的焦慮，或者也許是這個男人的存在而引起的刺激，足以使她相信：她終於得到了那種妙不可言的愛情。這以前，愛情像一隻玫瑰色羽毛的巨鳥，在燦爛的詩的世界中翱翔。而現在她卻不能相信，目前這種靜謐的生活就是她夢寐以求的幸福。

　　有時候她想，這樣的日子就是她有生以來最美好的日子：通常稱作蜜月的日子。要領略蜜月的滋味，她和丈夫也許本應該去那些有浪漫名稱的地方，新婚夫婦在那裏可以感受一下美妙閒散中的歡樂！他們可以坐在掛有藍色綢簾的驛站馬車裏，緩慢地爬着陡坡，聆聽着馬車夫的歌聲

postilion's song echoing among the mountains, along with the tinkling of goat bells and the muffled roar of waterfalls. At sunset they would have breathed in the fragrance of lemon trees on the shore of a bay; and at night, alone on the terrace of a villa with their fingers intertwined, they would have looked up at the stars and made plans for the future. It seemed to her that certain parts of the earth must produce happiness like a plant indigenous to that soil and unable to flourish anywhere else. If only she could lean over the balcony of a Swiss chalet, or enclose her melancholy in a Scottish cottage, ...

She might have liked to confide all these things to someone, but how can one describe an elusive malaise which continually changes form like a cloud and whirls like the wind? She could not find the words she needed, and she had neither the opportunity nor the courage to speak.

And yet it seemed to her that if Charles had made the slightest effort, if he had been at all perceptive, if his glance had only once penetrated her thoughts, an abundance of feeling would suddenly have been released from her heart, like ripe fruit falling from a tree at the touch of a hand. As their daily life became more and more intimate, she was separated from him by a growing feeling of inner detachment.

Gustav Flaubert: <u>Madame Bovary</u>

在群山間迴蕩，和山羊的鈴兒丁當聲、瀑布的低沉怒吼聲匯成一片。夕陽西下的時候，他們可以在海灣岸邊吸進檸檬樹的香味。晚上，別墅的露台上只有他們倆，手指交錯，仰望繁星，計劃着未來。她覺得世界上有些地方應該產生幸福，就像一種植物只生長在一種土壤裏，換了地方就長不好一樣。要是她能在瑞士農舍的陽台上憑欄遠眺，要是她能把憂鬱關在蘇格蘭小屋裏，……

她可能想把所有這些心思向誰傾吐，但是誰能說得明白這捉摸不定的心病？它像雲那樣變幻無常，像風那樣瞬息即逝。她找不到需要的詞句，也沒有說出來的機會和勇氣。

不過她覺得，要是夏爾稍加努力，要是他稍許敏感，要是他能有一次看穿她的心思，她心裏說不盡的感情就會突然吐泄出來，好比熟透了的果實，經手一碰就紛紛落地一樣。他們的日常生活愈來愈親密，可是她內心隔閡的感覺不斷增長，這使她和他疏離了。

（法）福樓拜：《包法利夫人》

81 I'm You

We said to each other that we were married the first day she had come to the hospital and we counted months from our wedding day. ...

I know one night we talked about it and Catherine[1] said, "But, darling, they'd send me away."

"Maybe they wouldn't."

"They would. They'd send me home and then we would be apart until after the war."

"I'd come on leave."

"You couldn't get to Scotland and back on a leave. Besides, I won't leave you. What good would it do to marry now? We're really married. I couldn't be any more married."

"I only wanted to for you."

"There isn't any me. I'm you. Don't make up a separate me."

"I thought girls always wanted to be married."

"They do. But, darling, I am married. I'm married to you. Don't I make you a good wife ?" ...

---

1. Catherine（凱瑟琳）：來自英國的護士，在意大利後方護理傷員。
文中的 "我" 是美國負傷軍人亨利（Henry）。 凱瑟琳是作者塑造的
一個最溫柔、最善良、最浪漫、最勇敢的女性形象。

八十一　我就是你

　　我們彼此說，她來醫院的第一天我們就結婚了。這樣，從結婚日算起，已經有好幾個月了。⋯⋯

　　我記得一天晚上，我們談到這個問題，凱瑟琳說："可是，親愛的，他們會把我調走的。"

　　"也許他們不會。"

　　"他們會的。他們會把我遣送回國，那我們就要到戰爭結束才能見面了。"

　　"休假時我可以去。"

　　"休假一次去蘇格蘭再回來，你是來不及的。再說，我也不願離開你。現在結婚有什麼好處呢？我們實際上已經結了婚。沒法叫我再結婚了。"

　　"我本來只是為了你才想結婚的。"

　　"沒有什麼我了。我就是你。別再分出一個獨自的我了。"

　　"我本來以為姑娘們總是想結婚的。"

　　"是這樣的。可是，親愛的，我已經結過婚了。我已經和你結婚。我不是你的好妻子嗎？"⋯⋯

"Couldn't we be married privately some way? Then if anything happened to me or if you had a child."

"There's no way to be married except by church or state. We are married privately. You see, darling, it would mean everything to me if I had any religion. But I haven't any religion." ...

"Then nothing worries you?"

"Only being sent away from you. You're my religion. You're all I've got."

"All right. But I'll marry you the day you say."

Ernest Hemingway: <u>A Farewell to Arms</u>

“我們能不能想個辦法私下結婚呢？這樣，要是我出了事，或者是你有了孩子，就不怕了。”

“只有通過教會或者國家才能結婚。我們已經在私下結婚了。你看，親愛的，要是我信教，結婚對我就很重要了。可是我什麼宗教信仰也沒有。”……

“那麼沒什麼讓你擔憂的嗎？”

“就是一件事：把我調走，和你分開。你就是我的宗教信仰。你是我的一切。”

“好吧。你說那天結婚，我就那天和你結婚。”

（美）海明威：《永別了，武器》

82 Won't It Be Fun?

... We went up in the lift to the first floor, and so along the passage. He took my hand and swung it as we went along. "Does forty-two seem very old to you?" he said.

"Oh, no," I[1] told him, quickly, too eagerly perhaps. "I don't like young men."

"You've never known any," he said.

We came to the door of the suite. "I think I had better deal with this alone," he said; "tell me something—do you mind how soon you marry me? You don't want a trousseau, do you, or any of that nonsense? Because the whole thing can be so easily arranged in a few days. Over a desk, with a licence, and then off in the car to Venice or anywhere you fancy."

"Not in a church?" I asked. "Not in white, with bridesmaids, and bells, and choir boys? What about your relations, and all your friends?"

---

1. I：書中的"我"和邁克西姆（Maxim）相愛結婚，但他的前妻麗貝卡（Rebecca）的陰魂不散，困擾着他們婚後的生活。

八十二　別有情趣

……我們乘電梯來到二樓，順着走廊往前走。他拉着我的手，邊走邊搖晃。"四十二歲你覺得太大了嗎？"他問道。

"噢，不大，"我對他說，說的很快，也許太急切了，"我不喜歡年輕人。"

"你從來也沒認識過什麼年輕人。"他說。

我們來到套房門口。"我看最好由我一個人來處理吧，"他說，"告訴我，再要過多久我們結婚，你有什麼想法嗎？你不要嫁妝，對嗎？也不要別的這一套無聊的東西吧？因為這件事在幾天之內很容易就能全部辦好。通過一個辦事機構、領到證書，然後坐車去威尼斯，或者哪個你想去的地方。"

"不在教堂？"我問，"不穿白禮服？沒有女儐相陪伴？沒有鐘聲？沒有唱詩班童子？你的親戚朋友請不請？"

"You forget," he said, "I had that sort of wedding before."

We went on standing in front of the door of the suite, and I noticed that the daily paper was still thrust through the letter-box. We had been too busy to read it at breakfast.

"Well?" he said, "What about it?"

"Of course," I answered, "I was thinking for the moment we would be married at home. Naturally I don't expect a church, or people, or anything like that."

And I smiled at him. I made a cheerful face. "Won't it be fun?" I said.

Daphne du Maurier: Rebecca

“你忘啦，”他說，“我以前已經舉行過這種婚禮了。”

我們還站在套房的門口，我注意到當天的報紙仍舊扔在信箱裏。吃早飯的時候，我們有事，沒空讀報紙。

“怎麼樣？”他說，“這樣辦行嗎？”

“當然行啦，”我回答，“剛才我還在想，我們就在家裏結婚。自然啦，我沒想去教堂，沒想請客人，反正沒想這一套。”

於是我對他莞爾一笑。我臉上顯出高興的表情。“這不很有意思嗎？”我說。

（英）達夫妮·杜穆里埃：《蝴蝶夢》

Fruit of Love

愛情之果

Painting by Joshua Reynolds (1723-1792)

83　The Tie That United Them

"Thou wilt[1] love her dearly," repeated Hester Prynne, as she and the minister sat watching little Pearl. "Dost thou[2] not think her beautiful? And see with what natural skill she has made those simple flowers adorn her! Had she gathered pearls, and diamonds , and rubies, in the wood, they could not have become her better. She is a splendid child! But I know whose brow she has!"

"Dost thou know, Hester," said Arthur Dimmesdale, with an unquiet smile, "that this dear child, tripping about always at thy[3] side, hath[4] caused me many an alarm? Methought[5]— O Hester, what a thought is that, and how terrible to dread it!—that my own features were partly repeated in her face, and so strikingly that the world might see them! But she is mostly thine[6]!"

"No, no! Not mostly!" answered the mother, with a tender smile. "A little longer, and thou needest not to be afraid to trace whose child she is. But how strangely beautiful she looks, with those wild-flowers in her hair! It is as if one

---

1. Thou wilt：[古] = You will。
2. Dost thou：[古] = Do you。
3. thy：[古] = your。

八十三　聯繫的紐帶

　　"你會非常愛她的，"海斯特·白蘭反覆説，這時她和牧師正坐在那兒看着珠兒，"你不認為她漂亮嗎？你看，她用這些普通的花兒打扮自己，她能做得這樣巧妙，真是天生的！要是她在樹林裏採集了珍珠、鑽石和紅寶石，也不見得能把她變得更漂亮了。她真是個頂呱呱的孩子！可我知道她的容貌像誰！"

　　"海斯特，"亞瑟·丁梅斯代爾不安地微微一笑説，"這個總在你身邊跳跳蹦蹦的可愛的孩子引起我多少擔驚受怕，你知道嗎？我想 —— 哦，海斯特，這個想法多麼可怕！—— 我想我的部分相貌特徵在她的臉上重現，明顯得人們一眼便看出來！好在她大部分像你！"

　　"不對，不對！不是大部分！"這母親溫柔地微笑着説，"再過不久，你就不必為看出她是誰的孩子而害怕了。她頭上戴着這些野花，真是漂亮得出奇！真像我們留

---

4. hath：[古] = has。
5. Methought：[古] methinks 的過去式, = it seems to me。
6. thine：[古] = yours。

of the fairies , whom we left in our dear old England, had decked her out to meet us."

It was with a feeling which neither of them had ever before experienced that they sat and watched Pearl's slow advance. In her was visible the tie that united them . She had been offered to the world, these seven years past, as the living hieroglyphic[7], in which was revealed the secret they so darkly sought to hide,—all written in this symbol,—all plainly manifest, —had there been a prophet or magician skilled to read the character of flame[8]! And Pearl was the oneness of their being. Be the foregone evil what it might, how could they doubt that their earthly lives and future destinies were conjoined, when they beheld at once the material union, and the spiritual idea, in whom they met, and were to dwell immortally together? Thoughts like these—and perhaps other thoughts, which they did not acknowledge or define—threw an awe about the child as she came onward.

Nathaniel Hawthorne: The Scarlet Letter

---

7. hieroglyphic：象形文字，猶指古埃及的象形文字；喻指隱藏了秘密，難解的字符。有夫之婦海斯特（Hester）反抗命運，與牧師亞瑟（Arthur）相愛，並生一女。她被判通奸罪後須佩帶的紅色A字標記，代表了Adultery（通奸）。但她相信自己愛的權利，便賦予它另外的含義，她情人亞瑟（Arthur）就是其中之一。

在可愛的英格蘭的一個仙女把她打扮起來迎接我們的。

　　他們倆坐在那兒，看着珠兒慢慢走過來，這時的感情以前他們誰也沒感受過。在珠兒身上可以看到聯繫他倆的紐帶。這七年來，她出現在世界上，像一個難解的活符號，這符號裏顯露了他們暗地設法隱藏的秘密，——一切都寫在這個符號裏，——一切都清楚明白，——只要有一位能讀這種火焰文字符號的預言家或魔術師。珠兒是他們倆的結合體。無論以前的罪過是怎麼樣的，只要他們一看到這個肉體的結合，心靈的理想，他倆在其中相遇，而且永遠共同生活下去，他們怎麼能懷疑，他們現世的生命和未來的命運已經結合在一起了？像這樣的想法——也許還有他們沒承認或沒弄明白的別的想法——使正在走過來的孩子帶有一種令人望而生畏的感覺。

（美）霍桑：《紅字》

---

8. the character of flame：指 the "scarlet letter"，即 海斯特（Hester）佩帶的 "火" 紅色的 A 字標記。

84　Love and Hope Woke

... A day came—of almost terrified delight and wonder—when the poor widowed girl[1] pressed a child upon her breast—a child, with the eyes of George who was gone—a little boy, as beautiful as a cherub. What a miracle it was to hear its first cry! How she laughed and wept over it—how love, and hope, and prayer woke again in her bosom as the baby nestled there. She was safe. ...

... To see Dobbin holding the infant, and to hear Amelia's laugh of triumph as she watched him, would have done any man good who had a sense of humour. William was the godfather[2] of the child, and exerted his ingenuity in the purchase of cups, spoons, papboats, and corals for this little Christian.

How his mother nursed him, and dressed him, and lived upon him; how she drove away all nurses, and would scarce allow any hand but her own to touch him; how she considered that the greatest favour she could confer upon his godfather, Major Dobbin, was to allow the Major occasionally to dandle

---

1. widowed girl：指愛米麗亞（Amelia）。丈夫喬治（George）在戰場陣亡，她哀傷成疾。喬治生前好友 William Dobbin 對她關懷備至。
2. godfather：教父，即孩子受洗禮時，擔保其宗教教育者。

八十四　愛情復甦

……有一天，可憐的年輕寡婦把一個孩子緊抱在懷裏，出現了使人驚喜詫異的一幕。孩子的眼睛像去世的喬治。這是個男孩，和小天使一樣漂亮。聽到孩子第一聲啼哭簡直是個奇蹟！她看着孩子又是笑又是哭；孩子靠在她胸前的時候，愛情、希望和頌禱在心中復甦，她感到安穩了。……

……看到都賓抱着這個小娃娃，聽到愛米麗亞發出得意的笑聲望着他，凡是有幽默感的人怎能不為此而高興？威廉‧都賓是這孩子的乾爹，為這個小信徒動足了腦筋，給他買了杯子、湯匙、奶瓶，還買了珊瑚玩具。做媽媽的給他餵奶，給他穿衣，為他而活着。她把保姆一個個都趕走了，幾乎不准別人的手碰他。偶爾讓都賓少校抱着哄一陣，她就看作是給予他乾爹莫大的好處。這些都不必在這

him, need not be told here. This child was her being. Her existence was a maternal caress. She enveloped the feeble and unconscious creature with love and worship. It was her life which the baby drank in from her bosom. ...

W. M. Thackeray: <u>Vanity Fair</u>

兒細說了。這孩子就是她的生命。她活着就是為了給他母親的撫愛。她給這個弱小無知的小生命無限的愛，對他無限崇拜。小娃娃從她乳中吸吮的是她的生命。……

(英) 薩克雷：《名利場》

85　An Exemplary Wife and Mother

In her face there was none of the ever-glowing animation that had formerly burned there and constituted its charm. Now her face and body were often all that one saw, and her soul was not visible at all. All that struck the eye was a strong, handsome and fertile woman. The old fire very rarely kindled in her face now. That happened only when, as was the case that day, her husband returned home, or a sick child was convalescent,... or on the rare occasions when something happened to induce her to sing, a practice she had quite abandoned since her marriage. At the rare moments when the old fire kindled in her handsome fully-developed body she was even more attractive than in former days.

... All who had known Natasha before her marriage wondered at the change in her as at something extraordinary. ... and her mother was now surprised by the surprise expressed by those who had never understood Natasha and kept saying that she had always known that Natasha would make an exemplary wife and mother.

"Only she lets her love of her husband and children overflow all bounds," said the countess[1], "so that it even becomes absurd."

1.　the countess：指娜塔莎（Natasha）的母親。

八十五　賢妻良母

　　她臉上昔日洋溢着構成其魅力的、光彩奪目的青春活力已經蕩然無存。她的臉和身軀還是人們常見的那樣，可是她的靈魂卻完全看不見了。看得見的是一個健壯、美麗、多生養的女人。往日火似的熱情現在不常在臉上出現了。只是在她丈夫回家的日子，生病的孩子恢復健康的日子，……偶爾有什麼事引起她唱歌的場合（結婚以來她不常唱歌了），只有在這些日子和場合，往日火似的熱情才重放光芒。而這種光芒難得在她美麗、豐滿的身軀上重放的時候，她甚至比以前更加迷人了。

　　……在娜塔莎婚前就認識她的人，對於她的變化，都看作是很不尋常的，都不理解。……她母親見到別人總不理解娜塔莎，對於他們的驚奇，她倒是很驚奇。她總是說她早就知道，娜塔莎會成為賢妻良母的。

　　“只有她才把全部的愛傾注在丈夫和孩子身上，”伯爵夫人說，“甚至到了可笑的程度。”

...

... When her next baby was born, despite the opposition of her mother, the doctors, and even of her husband himself—who were all vigorously opposed to her nursing her baby herself, a thing then unheard of and considered injurious—she insisted on having her own way, and after that nursed all her babies herself.

Lev Tolstoy: <u>War and Peace</u>

……

　　她生第二個孩子的時候，不顧她母親和醫生，甚至她丈夫本人的反對 —— 他們極力反對她自己哺乳，那時自己哺乳是聞所未聞的事，且認為是有害的 —— 她自己堅持自己的做法。自那以後，所生的孩子都由她自己哺乳了。

　　　　　　　　　（俄）列夫·托爾斯泰：《戰爭與和平》

86　It's a Natural Thing

She seemed upset and taut.

"What's the matter, Catherine?"

"Nothing. Nothing's the matter."

"Yes there is."

"No nothing. Really nothing."

"I know there is. Tell me, darling. You can tell me."

"It's nothing."

"Tell me."

"I don't want to. I'm afraid I'll make you unhappy or worry you."

"No it won't."

"You're sure? It doesn't worry me but I'm afraid to worry you."

It won't if it doesn't worry you."

"I don't want to tell."

"Tell it."

"Do I have to?"

"Yes."

"I'm going to have a baby, darling. It's almost three months along. You're not worried, are you? Please please don't. You mustn't worry."

"All right."

八十六　正常的事

她好像很煩躁緊張。

"凱瑟琳，你怎麼啦？"

"沒什麼。什麼事也沒有。"

"準有事。"

"沒事。真沒事。"

"我知道有事。告訴我，親愛的。你可以告訴我。"

"是沒什麼。"

"告訴我吧。"

"我不想告訴你。我怕我會讓你不高興，讓你擔心。"

"不會的。"

"真的不會？我不擔心，可是就怕讓你擔心。"

"你不擔心的事我也不擔心。"

"我不想告訴你。"

"説出來吧。"

"我非説不可嗎？"

"是的。"

"我要生孩子了，親愛的。差不多有三個月了，你不擔心吧？你一定，一定不要擔心。你不該擔心。"

"沒事。"

"Is it all right?"

"Of course."

"I did everything. I took everything but it didn't make any difference."

"I'm not worried."

"I couldn't help it, darling, and I haven't worried about it. You mustn't worry or feel badly."

"I only worry about you."

"That's it. That's what you mustn't do. People have babies all the time. Everybody has babies. It's a natural thing."

Ernest Hemingway: A Farewell to Arms

"真的沒事嗎？"

"當然啦。"

"我什麼辦法都用過。我什麼藥都吃過。可是不起任何作用。"

"我不擔心。"

"我真的沒有辦法，親愛的，我倒也不擔心。你不要擔心，也不要覺得不好受。"

"我只是為你擔心。"

"我說的就是這個。你就是不該為我擔心。時時刻刻都有人生孩子。人人都有孩子。這是正常的事。"

（美）海明威：《永別了，武器》

87   The Child of Her Father's Heart

From the first, the baby stirred in the young father a deep, strong emotion he dared scarcely acknowledge, it was so strong and came out of the dark of him. ...

The golden-brown eyes of the child gradually lit up and dilated at the sight of the dark-glowing face of the youth. It knew its mother better, it wanted its mother more. But the brightest, sharpest little ecstasy was for the father.

... Already it knew his strong hands, it exulted in his strong clasp, it laughed and crowed when he played with it.

And his heart grew red-hot with passionate feeling for the child. ...

So Ursula became the child of her father's heart. She was the little blossom, he was the sun. ...

At evening, towards six o'clock, Anna very often went across the lane to the stile, lifted Ursula over into the field, with a: "Go and meet Daddy." Then Brangwen, coming up the steep round of the hill would see before him on the brow of the path a tiny, tottering, wind-blown little mite with a dark head, who, as soon as she saw him, would come running in tiny, wild, windmill fashion, lifting her arms up and down to him, down the steep hill. His heart leapt up, he ran his fastest to her, to catch her, because he knew she would fall.

八十七 寶貝

　　從一開始，孩子就在年輕父親的身上激起了深深的、強烈的感情。這感情來自他朦朧的內心深處，是這樣的強烈，他幾乎不敢承認。……

　　孩子的金棕色眼睛漸漸地明亮起來，看到年輕爸爸黝黑閃亮的臉龐，就睜得大大的。孩子更認識媽媽，更需要媽媽。但她興高采烈的模樣是給爸爸看的。

　　……孩子已經知道爸爸有強壯的胳臂，在他有力的摟抱中歡躍。他逗得孩子開懷地大笑大叫。

　　他對孩子充滿熱烈的感情，心裏熱乎乎的。……

　　於是厄秀拉成為她父親心中的寶貝。她是小花兒，而他是太陽。……傍晚快到六點鐘的時候，安娜常常穿過小路走到籬笆階梯前，把厄秀拉抱起來跨過柵門放到田地裏，說："去接你爹。"這時，布朗溫正在走上小山的陡坡，便看見前面坡頂上有個黑腦袋小傢伙，在風中蹣跚。她一見到他，就像狂轉的小風車，上下擺動着胳臂，朝他跑下陡坡。他的心猛跳起來，以最快的速度向她跑來，要把她摟住，因為他知道，孩子會摔倒的。她揮舞四肢，狂

She came fluttering on, wildly, with her little limbs flying. And he was glad when he caught her up in his arms. Once she fell as she came flying to him, he saw her pitch forward suddenly as she was running with her hands lifted to him; and when he picked her up, her mouth was bleeding. He could never bear to think of it, he always wanted to cry, even when he was an old man and she had become a stranger to him. How he loved that little Ursula!

D. H. Lawrence: _The Rainbow_

飛般撲向前，向他跑去。然後他把她抱起來，好不高興。有一次，她朝他飛跑的時候，摔倒了。他看見正當她向他張開雙臂跑去的時候，突然她趴地栽倒了。待他把她抱起來，她的嘴正流着血。他想起這件事，心裏總不能忍受，總想哭，即使當他已經年老，對她感到陌生的時候，還是這樣。他是多麼愛這個小小的厄秀拉！

（英）勞倫斯：《虹》

Separation
離別

Painting by *Philip Wilson Steer (1860-1942)*

88　God Bless You

The child was asleep. "Hush!" said Amelia, annoyed, perhaps, at the creaking of the Major's boots; and she held out her hand; smiling because William[1] could not take it until he had rid himself of his cargo of toys. ...

"I am come to say good-bye, Amelia," said he, taking her slender little white hand gently.

"Good-bye? and where are you going?" she said, with a smile.

"Send the letters to the agents," he said; "they will forward them; for you will write to me, won't you? I shall be away a long time."

"I'll write to you about Georgy[2]," she said. "Dear William, how good you have been to him and to me. Look at him. Isn't he like an angel?"

The little pink hands of the child closed mechanically round the honest soldier's finger, and Amelia looked up in his face with bright maternal pleasure. The cruellest looks could not have wounded him more than that glance of

---

1. William：威廉・都賓（William Dobbin），是愛米麗亞（Amelia）已故丈夫的好友，一直關心着愛米麗亞。
2. Georgy：喬杰，是愛米麗亞的兒子。

八十八　上帝保佑你

孩子睡着了。"嘘！"愛米麗亞説，聽到少校靴子吱吱嘎嘎的響聲，她大概有點生氣了。她伸出一隻手去。看到威廉把一大堆玩具放掉才能跟她握手，她微笑起來。……

"愛米麗亞，我是來向你告別的。"他輕輕地拉着她纖細白白的小手説道。

"告別？上哪去？"她微微一笑説。

"把信件寄給我的代理人，"他説，"他們會轉送給我的。你一定會給我寫信的，是不是？我這一走要很長時間才回來。"

"我要把喬杰的情況寫信告訴你，"她説，"親愛的威廉，你對他、對我都太好了。瞧他！他是不是像個小天使？"

孩子粉紅色的小手機械地緊攥着這誠實的軍人的手指。愛米麗亞滿懷做母親的欣慰，抬頭望着威廉。她的眼神是親切的，但並不鍾情於他，這比最冷酷的表情還要使

hopeless kindness. He bent over the child and mother. He could not speak for a moment. And it was only with all his strength that he could force himself to say a God bless you. "God bless you," said Amelia , and held up her face and kissed him.

"Hush! Don't wake Georgy!" she added, as William Dobbin went to the door with heavy steps. She did not hear the noise of his cab-wheels as he drove away: she was looking at the child, who was laughing in his sleep.

W. M. Thackeray: *Vanity Fair*

他傷心。他向着孩子和媽媽俯身，一時説不出話來。他用盡全力才逼着自己説了一句"上帝保佑你"。"上帝也保佑你。"愛米麗亞回答道，接着仰起臉吻了他一下。

威廉‧都賓以沉重的腳步朝門走去的時候，她又追説了一句："噓！別吵醒了喬杰！"她沒聽到他馬車離開的聲音。她只顧看着孩子，孩子正在睡夢中笑呢。

（英）薩克雷：《名利場》

89　She Was Gone

And then it came over him[1], ...that to all of them he and Madame Olenska were lovers, lovers in the extreme sense peculiar to "foreign" vocabularies. He guessed himself to have been, for months, the centre of countless silently observing eyes and patiently listening ears, he understood that, by means as yet unknown to him, the separation between himself and the partner of his guilt[2] had been achieved, and that now the whole tribe had rallied about his wife on the tacit assumption that nobody knew anything, or had ever imagined anything, and that the occasion of the entertainment was simply May Archer's natural desire to take an affectionate leave of her friend and cousin.

...

... He caught the glitter of victory in his wife's eyes, and for the first time understood that she shared the belief. ...

At length he saw that Madame Olenska had risen and was saying good-bye. He understood that in a moment she would

---

1. him：指阿切爾（Archer）。他傾慕更富文化教養的奧蘭斯卡（Olenska），但未能衝破階級的傳統規範而與智力淺薄的梅（May）結了婚。奧蘭斯卡被迫離開紐約社會。作者運用含蓄克制的語言表達阿切爾對奧斯卡的感情。
2. the partner of his guilt：指奧蘭斯卡（Madame Olenska）。

八十九　餞別

　　那時，他突然感覺到，……在大家的心目中，他和奧蘭斯卡夫人是一對情人，而且是"外國"詞語中具有最特殊意義的情人。他猜想，幾個月來他是無數人默默注視、耐心傾聽的中心。他明白，人們用了他不知道的手段達到了把他和同犯分離的目的。現在整個宗族聚集在他妻子的週圍，心照不宣地假設，沒人知道什麼事，沒人想過什麼事，而這次宴請只不過是梅·阿切爾發自內心的願望，給她的朋友和表姐深情的餞行。

　　……

　　……他從妻子的目光中捕捉到勝利的閃光，而且第一次恍然大悟，原來她和大家的見解是一樣的。……

　　他終於看到奧蘭斯卡夫人站起來告別。他知道，再過

be gone, and tried to remember what he had said to her at dinner; but he could not recall a single word they had exchanged.

She went up to May, the rest of the company making a circle about her as she advanced. The two young women clasped hands; then May bent forward and kissed her cousin.

...

A moment later he was in the hall, putting Madame Olenska's cloak about her shoulders.

Through all his confusion of mind he had held fast to the resolve to say nothing that might startle or disturb her.... But as he followed Madame Olenska into the hall he thought with a sudden hunger of being for a moment alone with her at the door of her carriage.

...

Archer's heart gave a jerk, and Madame Olenska, clasping her cloak and fan with one hand, held out the other to him. "Good-bye," she said.

...

... For a moment, in the billowy darkness inside the big landau, he caught the dim oval of a face, eyes shining steadily—and she was gone.

Edith Wharton: <u>The Age of Innocence</u>

一會兒她就要走了。他極力回憶宴會時對她說過的話，可是他們談些什麼，他一句話也想不起來了。

她走到梅的身前，她走過的時候，其他的人圍着她成一圈。這兩位年青女子緊緊地握手。梅又俯身向前，吻別表姐。

……

過了一會，他來到門廳，為奧蘭斯卡夫人披上斗篷。

他在思緒混亂中始終堅守已下的決心，凡是可能驚嚇或困擾她的話，一句也不說。……但是當他隨奧蘭斯卡夫人來到門廳的時候，他渴望在她馬車門前單獨和她呆一會兒。

……

阿切爾的心猛地一跳。奧蘭斯卡夫人一隻手握着斗篷和扇子，另一隻手伸向他說：“再見。”

……

……一瞬間，在大馬車裏波浪般的黑暗中，他看到一個朦朧的橢圓臉龐，目光堅定 —— 她走了。

（美）依迪絲·華頓：《天真時代》

90　A Startled Voice

A startled voice suddenly came from the cart: "Darya Dmitrevna!"

Someone jumped on to the ground and started running. At the sound of this voice Dasha's[1] heart gave a jump, and her knees began to wobble. She turned. Telegin was running up to her, sunburnt, agitated, blue-eyed, and so unexpectedly dear that Dasha put her hands impetuously on his chest, pressed her face against him, and began to sob loudly like a child.

Telegin held her firmly round the shoulders. When Dasha attempted in a broken voice to falter out some explanation, he said:

"Never mind, Darya Dmitrevna, never mind ... afterwards. It doesn't matter."

The front of his linen jacket was wet with Dasha's tears. She felt much better now.

"Were you coming to us?" she asked.

"Yes, I've come to say goodbye, Darya Dmitrevna...."

"Goodbye?"

---

1. Dasha（達莎）：是達麗亞（Darya）的昵稱。

九十　一聲驚喊

從馬車上傳來一聲吃驚的叫喊："達麗亞‧德米特里耶芙娜！"

有個人跳下車，開始跑過來。達莎聽到這叫喊聲的時候，她的心怦怦地直跳，膝蓋也開始發軟搖晃。她轉過身來。捷列金跑到她跟前，臉曬得黑黝黝的，神情激動，眼睛碧藍，出乎意料的那麼親切，使得達莎情不自禁地把雙手攔在他的胸前，還把臉頰貼上去，像個孩子似的開始大聲抽噎起來。

捷列金緊緊地摟住她的雙肩。當達莎正要用斷續的聲音結巴地解釋些什麼的時候，他卻說：

"不要緊，達麗亞‧德米特里耶芙娜，沒什麼……以後再說吧。不要緊的。"

他那亞麻布上裝的前襟給達莎的淚水弄濕了。她現在感到好多了。

"你是來看我們的嗎？"她問。

"是的，我是來告別的，達麗亞‧德米特里耶芙娜。……"

"告別？"

"I've been called up—it can't be helped."

...

Towards evening,... Dasha and Telegin went for a long walk over the curving sands. They walked in silence, keeping step. And here Ivan Ilyich[2] began to think he ought, after all, to say something to Dasha. She must be expecting a passionate, above all, a clear, declaration. And what could he say? Could any words express the feelings which filled him? No, they could not be expressed.

...

"I'll love you ever so much, after you've gone, Ivan Ilyich." She placed her hand against his neck and, gazing into his face from her clear grey eyes — ... she sighed again, lightly this time.

"We'll be together there, too, won't we?"

Ivan Ilyich had drawn her gently towards him and kissed her on her delicate, trembling lips. Dasha closed her eyes....

*A. N. Tolstoy: **The Sisters***

---

2. Ivan Ilyich（伊凡·伊立奇）：捷列金（Telegin）的名和父名。

“我被徵召入伍了，毫無辦法。”

……

傍晚，……達莎和捷列金久久地在曲折的海邊沙灘上漫步。他們默不作聲，步伐一致。此時此地，伊凡・伊立奇開始想到，他畢竟應該對達莎說些什麼才是。她一定期待着熱情的，而首先是明確的表白。他能説些什麼呢？難道有什麼語言能表達他滿腔的感情嗎？不，這些感情是難以表達的。

……

“伊凡・伊立奇，你走後，我會非常愛你的。”

她把一隻手放到他的頸旁，用她清澈的灰眼睛注視着他的臉，……她又嘆了口氣，這回很輕。

“在那裏我們也將在一起，對嗎？”

伊凡・伊立奇輕輕地把她拉到身邊，吻着她那顫動着的嬌嫩嘴唇。達莎緊閉着雙眼。……

（俄）A. N. 托爾斯泰：《兩姊妹》

91 I'll Come and Stay with You Nights

The nurse opened the door and motioned with her finger for me to come. I followed her into the room. Catherine[1] did not look up when I came in. I went over to the side of the bed. The doctor was standing by the bed on the opposite side. Catherine looked at me and smiled. I bent down over the bed and started to cry.

"Poor darling," Catherine said very softly. She looked grey.

"You're all right, Cat[2]," I said. "You're going to be all right."

"I'm going to die," she said; then waited and said, "I hate it."

I took her hand.

"Don't touch me," she said. I let go of her hand. She smiled. "Poor darling. You touch me all you want."

"You'll be all right, Cat. I know you'll be all right."

"I meant to write you a letter to have if anything happened, but I didn't do it."

---

1. Catherine：此篇描寫凱瑟琳（Catherine）在與死神搏鬥的痛苦中，仍保持對亨利（Henry）的真摯感情。"我會夜夜來陪你的。"這句話象徵着愛情可能超越死亡。
2. Cat：凱瑟琳的昵稱。

九十一　夜夜陪伴你

　　護士開了門，用手指示意我進去。我跟她進入病房。我進來後，凱瑟琳沒抬眼看我。我走到牀邊。醫生站在牀的另一邊。凱瑟琳看看我，微微一笑。我俯伏在牀上哭了起來。

　　"可憐的寶貝。"凱瑟琳溫柔地説。她臉色灰白。

　　"你不要緊的，凱特，"我説，"你會好起來的。"

　　"我就要死了，"她説；等了一會兒，又説，"我不願意死。"

　　我拿起她的一隻手。

　　"別碰我。"她説。我放開她的手。她笑了。"可憐的寶貝。你要碰我就碰吧，隨你怎麼碰。"

　　"你會好的，凱特。我知道你會好的。"

　　"要是有什麼變化，我本來想寫封信留給你的，可是我沒寫。"

"Do you want me to get a priest or anyone to come and see you?"

"Just you," she said. Then a little later, "I'm not afraid. I just hate it."

"You must not talk so much," the doctor said.

"All right," Catherine said.

"Do you want me to do anything, Cat? Can I get you anything?"

Catherine smiled. "No." Then a little later, "You won't do our things with another girl, or say the same things, will you?"

"Never."

"I want you to have girls though."

"I don't want them."

"You are talking too much," the doctor said. "Mr. Henry must go out. He can come back later. You are not going to die. You must not be silly."

"All right," Catherine said. "I'll come and stay with you nights," she said. It was very hard for her to talk.

Ernest Hemingway: <u>A Farewell to Arms</u>

“你要我去找個牧師什麼的來看看你嗎？”

“我只要你。”她說。過了不一會兒又說，“我不怕死。我是不願意死。”

“你不可以說這麼多話。”醫生說。

“好的。”凱瑟琳說。

“你要我做點什麼事嗎，凱特？我能給你拿點什麼嗎？”

凱瑟琳笑笑。“不用，”過了不一會兒又說，“你不會把我們做的事、說的話，去和另一個女人再做再說吧，不會吧？”

“永遠不會。”

“可我要你另找女人。”

“我不需要她們。”

“你說得太多了，”醫生說，“亨利先生該出去了。他可以遲些再來。你不會死的。你別傻了。”

“好吧。”凱瑟琳說。“我會夜夜來陪你的。”她說。她說話很吃力。

(美) 海明威：《永別了，武器》

92　Let Me Stay

Maria was kneeling by him and saying, "Roberto[1], what hast thou[2]?"

He said, sweating heavily, "The left leg is broken, *guapa*[3]."...

Then she started to cry.

"No, *guapa*, don't," he said. "Listen. We will not go to Madrid now but I go always with thee wherever thou goest[4]. Understand?"

She said nothing and pushed her head against his cheek with her arms around him.

"Listen to this well, rabbit[5]," he said. He knew there was a great hurry and he was sweating very much, but this had to be said and understood. "Thou wilt go now, rabbit. But I go with thee. As long as there is one of us there is both of us. Do you understand?"

"Nay[6], I stay with thee." ...

---

1. Roberto：[西班牙語] = Robert。作者用了混雜英語（pidgin English），其中包含了西班牙語和古英語的詞彙，以烘托故事的環境氣氛。
2. hast thou：[古] = have you。
3. *guapa*：[西班牙語] 美人兒。

376

九十二　讓我留下

　　瑪麗亞跪在他身旁說："羅伯托，你怎麼啦？"

　　他大汗淋漓，說："左腿骨折斷了，美麗的姑娘。"……

　　後來她哭了起來。

　　"美麗的姑娘，別哭，"他說，"聽我說。現在我們不去馬德里了，可是不管你去哪，我總和你在一起。懂嗎？"

　　她沒說話，把頭靠在他的臉頰上，雙臂摟着他。

　　"好好聽着，姑娘。"他說。他知道時間緊迫，他汗出得很多，但是這話不得不說，讓她明白。"你現在要走了，姑娘。可是我是跟你一起走的。我們倆只要還有一個，那就是我們兩個。你懂嗎？"

　　"不，我和你一起留下。"……

---

4. goest：[古] = go。
5. rabbit：[俚] 姑娘。
6. Nay：[古] = No。

"There is no goodbye, *guapa*, because we are not apart. That it should be good in the Gredos. Go now. Go good. Nay," he spoke now still calmly and reasonably as Pilar[7] walked the girl along. "Do not turn around. Put thy foot in. Yes. Thy foot in. Help her up," he said to Pilar. "Get her in the saddle. Swing up now."

He turned his head, sweating, and looked down the slope, then back toward where the girl was in the saddle with Pilar by her and Pablo[8] just behind. "Now go," he said. "Go."

She started to look around. "Don't look around," Robert Jordan said. "Go." And Pablo hit the horse across the crupper with a hobbling strap and it looked as though Maria tried to slip from the saddle but Pilar and Pablo were riding close up against her and Pilar was holding her and the three horses were going up the draw.

"Roberto," Maria turned and shouted. "Let me stay! Let me stay!"

"I am with thee," Robert Jordan shouted. "I am with thee now. We are both there. Go!" Then they were out of sight around the corner of the draw and he was soaking wet with sweat and looking at nothing.

Ernest Hemingway: <u>For Whom the Bell Tolls</u>

---

7. Pilar：女游擊隊員名。

"我們不説再見，美麗的姑娘，因為我們不是離別。在格雷多斯這地方蠻不錯。走吧。走好。不。"他説得還是很平靜，很有道理，這時匹拉爾扶着姑娘走了。"別回頭。把你的腳踩進馬鐙。對。把腳踩進去。扶她上馬，"他對匹拉爾説，"扶她上馬鞍。跨上去。"

　　他轉過頭，還冒着汗，朝着山坡往下望，然後又回頭看看馬鞍上的姑娘，她身邊是匹拉爾，後邊緊跟着帕勃羅。"走吧，"他説，"走吧。"

　　她轉身回頭看望。"別回頭看，"羅伯特・喬丹説，"走吧。"帕勃羅用馬腿上的皮帶抽打了一下馬屁股，好像瑪麗亞設法從馬鞍上滑下來，可是匹拉爾和帕勃羅騎着馬緊靠着她，匹拉爾還扶着她，三匹馬正往吊橋走去。

　　"羅伯托，"瑪麗亞回過頭來喊道，"讓我留下！讓我留下！"

　　"我是和你在一起，"羅伯特・喬丹喊道，"現在我和你在一起。我倆都在那兒。走吧！"一會兒他們走過了橋的拐角，便看不見了。他全身都汗濕透了，什麼也不去看了。

　　　　　　　　　　　　　(美) 海明威：《戰地鐘聲》

---

8. Pablo：男游擊隊員名。

93 She Had Lost Them Both

"Oh, Rhett, I love you so, darling! I must have loved you for years and I was such a fool I didn't know it. Rhett, you must believe me!" ...

"... But, Scarlett, did it ever occur to you that even the most deathless love could wear out? ... It was so obvious that we were meant for each other[1]. So obvious that I was the only man of your acquaintance who could love you after knowing you as you really are—hard and greedy and unscrupulous, like me. I loved you and I took the chance. I thought Ashley would fade out of your mind. But," he shrugged, "I tried everything I knew and nothing worked. And I loved you so, Scarlett. If you had only let me, I could have loved you as gently and as tenderly as ever a man loved a woman. But I couldn't let you know, for I knew you'd think me weak and try to use my love against me. And always—always there was Ashley. It drove me crazy. I couldn't sit across the table from you every night, knowing you wished Ashley was sitting there in my place. And I couldn't hold you in my arms at night and know that— well, it doesn't matter now. ..."

---

1. we were meant for each other：瑞得(Rhett)對斯卡雷特(Scarlett)
    的愛是真誠的。他們可說是珠聯璧合。但當她覺悟該真心愛瑞得時，
    他已決心棄家出走了。這是《飄》這個愛情故事的結局。

九十三　一無所得

"哦，瑞得，我多麼愛你，親愛的！多年來我早已愛你了，可我太傻了，自己還不知道。瑞得，你該相信我啊！"……

"……可是，斯卡雷特，你想到過沒有，最永恆的愛也會磨光的？……很明顯，我倆是天生的一對。還有一點也很明顯：我是你相識中唯一了解你真實面貌而能愛你的人——你像我一樣，冷酷貪婪，不擇手段。我愛你，想碰碰運氣。我原以為阿什利會從你心裏淡忘。可是，"他聳聳肩，"我想盡辦法，卻毫無結果。斯卡雷特，我是多麼愛你。要是你讓我愛，我本來是能夠像一個男人愛女人那樣，愛你愛得溫柔，愛得體貼。不過我當時不能讓你知道，因為我明白，你會認為我軟弱可欺，要利用我對你的愛來算計我。阿什利無時不在，無刻不在。我快瘋了。每天晚飯我不能坐在你的對面，因為我知道你希望坐在我的位子上的是阿什利。晚上睡覺我不能摟着你，知道——呃，現在也無所謂了。……"

...

"Stop," she said suddenly. ...

"Well, you get my meaning, don't you?" he questioned, rising to his feet.

She threw out her hands to him, palms up, in the age-old gesture of appeal and her heart, again, was in her face.

"No," she cried. "All I know is that you do not love me and you are going away! Oh, my darling, if you go, what shall I do?" ...

"My dear, I don't give a damn[2]."

She silently watched him go up the stairs, feeling that she would strangle at the pain in her throat. With the sound of his feet dying away in the upper hall was dying the last thing in the world that mattered.

She had never understood either of the men she had loved and so she had lost them both.

Margaret Mitchell: Gone with the Wind

---

2. don't give a damn：毫不在乎。

⋯⋯

“你別説了，”她突然説。⋯⋯

“好吧，你懂我的意思了，是不是？”他邊問邊站起來。

她向他伸出雙手，手掌向上，擺出自古以來就有的求助姿勢，她心中的感情又表露在臉上了。

“不，”她喊道，“我只知道你不愛我了，你要走了！哦，親愛的，你要是走了，我怎麼辦呢？”⋯⋯

“親愛的，隨你的便吧。”

她默默地看他走上樓去，感到喉嚨很痛，使人窒息。隨着他的腳步聲在樓上門廳遠去消逝，最後一件對她至關重要的事情也不復存在了。⋯⋯

對於她愛過的兩個男人她一個也不理解，所以兩個都失去了。

（美）米切爾：《飄》

 *Reunion*

重逢

Painting by Pablo Picasso (1881-1973)

94 We Are Friends

The figure showed itself aware of me, as I advanced. It had been moving towards me, but it stood still. As I drew nearer, I saw it to be the figure of a woman. As I drew nearer yet, it was about to turn away, when it stopped, and let me come up with it. Then, it faltered as if much surprised, and uttered my name, and I cried out:

"Estella!"

"I am greatly changed. I wonder you know me."

The freshness of her beauty was indeed gone, but its indescribable majesty and its indescribable charm remained. Those attractions in it, I had seen before; what I had never seen before, was the saddened softened light of the once proud eyes; what I had never felt before, was the friendly touch of the once insensible hand.

We sat down on a bench that was near, and I said, "After so many years, it is strange that we should thus meet again, Estella, here where our first meeting was!..." ...

"I little thought," said Estella, "that I should take leave of you in taking leave of this spot. I am very glad to do so."

"... To me, the remembrance of our last parting has been ever mournful and painful."

九十四　我們是朋友

我向前走去，那人的動作表明已經看到了我。這人原先是向我走來的，現在卻站住了。等我走近些，我看到的是個女人身影。我再走近些，她正要轉身走開，又突然停了下來，等我走到她那裏。這時她好像大吃一驚，躊躇不前，喊出了我的名字，我也喊出：

"埃斯特拉！"

"我大變樣了。我想你不認識我了。"

她的美雖已不再鮮艷，可是那難以形容的端莊和難以形容的風韻依舊存在。美的魅力我過去已見過；可是那雙一度高傲的眼睛如今已透出悲傷而柔弱的光彩，這是我沒見過的；那隻一度冷淡的手如今已使人感到友情，這是我沒有感到過的。

我們在近旁的長凳上坐了下來，我開口說："埃斯特拉，過了這麼多年，我們這樣又一次相見，真沒想到，就在這兒我們第一次相見的地方！……"……

"當時我沒想到，"埃斯特拉說，"和這個地方告別的時候，居然也和你告別了。現在這樣我真高興。"

"……對我來說，想起上次和你分手，一直感到悲傷、痛苦。"

"But you said to me," returned Estella, very earnestly, "God bless you, God forgive you!" And if you could say that to me then, you will not hesitate to say that to me now—now, when suffering has been stronger than all other teaching, and has taught me to understand what your heart used to be. I have been bent and broken, but—I hope—into a better shape. Be as considerate and good to me as you were, and tell me we are friends."

"We are friends," said I, rising and bending over her, as she rose from the bench.

Charles Dickens: <u>Great Expectations</u>

"可是你對我說過，"埃斯特拉很認真地回答説，"'願上帝保佑你！願上帝寬恕你！' 既然你那時能對我説這話，那麼你現在也會毫不猶豫地對我説的。現在，我受的痛苦比任何説教的力量都大，痛苦教會我理解你當初的心。我屈從了，被挫敗了，可是，我希望，變得更好了。希望你像從前一樣對我體貼，對我好，對我説我們是朋友。"

　　她從長凳起來，我也站起來，俯身對她説："我們是朋友。"

　　　　　　　　　　(英) 狄更斯：《遠大前程》

95　You Are Come Back to Me Then?

... my arm was seized, my shoulder—neck—waist—I was entwined and gathered to him[1].

"Is it Jane? What is it? This is her shape—this is her size—"

"And this is her voice," I added. "She is all here: her heart, too. God bless you, sir ! I am glad to be so near you again."

"Jane Eyre!—Jane Eyre!" was all he said.

"My dear master," I answered, "I am Jane Eyre: I have found you out—I am come back to you."

"In truth?—in the flesh? My living Jane?"

"You touch me, sir—you hold me, and fast enough: I am not cold like a corpse, nor vacant like air, am I?"

"My living darling! These are certainly her limbs, and these her features: but I cannot be so blest after all my misery. It is a dream: such dreams as I have had at night when I have clasped her once more to my heart, as I do now; and kissed her, as thus—and felt that she loved me, and trusted that she would not leave me."

1.　him：羅切斯特(Rochester)在一次火災中受傷，雙目失明。正當他孤寂無援的時候，簡‧愛（Jane Eyre）找到了他。

九十五　你回來了？

　　……我的一隻胳臂給抓住了，我的肩膀——脖子——腰，我整個身子都被擁抱住了，和他合攏了。

　　"是簡嗎？這是什麼？這是她的模樣——這是她的身材——"

　　"這是她的說話聲，"我附和着說。"她整個人在這兒：她的心也在這兒。上帝保佑你，先生！又這麼近在你的身邊，我真高興。"

　　"簡‧愛！——簡‧愛！"這就是他所說的一切。

　　"我親愛的主人，"我回答，"我是簡‧愛：我找到你了，我回到你身邊來了。"

　　"是真的？——她本人嗎？我活生生的簡嗎？"

　　"你觸摸我，先生——你抱着我，抱得夠緊的：我不是冷得像屍體，也不是空得像空氣，是不是？"

　　"我活生生的心愛的人兒！這肯定是她的手和腳，這是她的鼻子、嘴、眼睛和耳朵；可是我遭受了所有的苦難之後，不可能會這樣幸福。這是一場夢，像晚上夢中，把她摟到我心中，就像我現在這樣緊緊地摟着她；像這樣吻她；感到她愛着我，相信她不會離開我。"

"Which I never will, sir, from this day." ...

I pressed my lips to his once brilliant and now rayless eyes. I swept his hair from his brow, and kissed that too. He suddenly seemed to rouse himself: the conviction of the reality of all this seized him.

"It is you—is it Jane? You are come back to me then?"

"I am."

Charlotte Brontë: <u>Jane Eyre</u>

"從今天開始，先生，我永遠不會離開你。"……

我把嘴唇壓在他那曾經閃亮過而現在卻無光的眼睛上。我把他的頭髮從眉梢上拂開，也吻了一下眉梢。他好像突然醒來：確信這一切都是真的了。

"是你 —— 是簡嗎？那麼你是回到我身邊來了？"

"我回到你身邊來了。"

(英) 夏洛蒂·勃朗特：《簡·愛》

96 The Revival of Love

... The worn and wasted look which had prematurely aged her face, was fast leaving it; and the expression which had been the first of its charms in past days, was the first of its beauties that now returned. ...

...

In all else, she was now so far on the way to recovery, that, on her best and brightest days, she sometimes looked and spoke like the Laura of old times. The happy change wrought its natural result in us[1] both. From their long slumber, on her side and on mine, those imperishable memories of our past life in Cumberland now awoke, which were one and all alike, the memories of our love.

...

The door opened; and Laura came in alone. So she had entered the breakfast-room at Limmeridge House, on the morning when we parted. Slowly and falteringly, in sorrow and in hesitation, she had once approached me. Now, she came with the haste of happiness in her feet, with the light of happiness radiant in her face. Of their own accord, those

---

1. us：勞拉（Laura）和家庭教師夏特賴特（Hartright）相愛，但勞拉早已許配他人，婚後蒙受奇冤。夏特賴特為她申雪，兩人終成眷屬。

九十六　愛情重熾

……憔悴消瘦曾使她的面容過早衰老，現在很快地在消失。往日她最具魅力的表情現在是她美貌最先恢復的部分。……

……

她在其他各方面也恢復得很好。在她最高興的日子裏，眼神和説話有時很像昔日的勞拉。這讓人高興的變化對我們兩個人的影響是可想而知的。我們過去在坎伯蘭一段生活不可磨滅的回憶，現在從長期的沉睡中甦醒。這些回憶對她對我全都是愛情的回憶。

……

門開了。勞拉獨自一人進來了。在利默里吉莊園，我們告別的那天早晨，她走進吃早飯的飯廳。那時，她神情憂鬱，遲疑不決，緩慢踉蹌地走到我的身旁。而現在，她樣子興高采烈，腳步輕鬆愉快，急促地走了過來。她親切

dear arms clasped themselves round me; of their own accord, the sweet lips came to meet mine. "My darling!" she whispered, "we may own we love each other, now!" Her head nestled with a tender contentedness on my bosom. "Oh," she said, innocently, "I am so happy at last!"s

W. W. Collins: <u>The Woman in White</u>

的雙臂情不自禁地把我摟抱住，甜蜜的雙唇情不自禁地貼着我的雙唇。"親愛的！"她輕聲說，"現在，我們可以承認我們相愛了！"她滿懷柔情，心滿意足地把頭依偎在我的胸前。她天真地說："哦！終究我是很幸福的！"

（英）科林斯：《白衣女人》

97   Repeating Our Marriage

... In a few moments he could discern a female figure creeping in by the great north gap or public gateway. They met in the middle of the arena. Neither spoke just at first—there was no necessity for speech—and the poor woman leant against Henchard, who supported her in his arms.

"I don't drink," he said in a low, halting, apologetic voice. "You hear, Susan?—I don't drink now—I haven't since that night[1]." Those was his first words.

He felt her bow her head in acknowledgement that she understood. After a minute or two he again began:

"If I had known you were living, Susan! But there was every reason to suppose you and the child were dead and gone. I took every possible step to find you—travelled—advertised— my opinion at last was that you had started for some colony with that man, and had been drowned on your voyage out. Why did you keep silent like this?"

---

1. since that night：《卡斯特橋市長》一書描寫打草工亨查德（Henchard）
    酒醉時把妻子蘇珊（Susan）和女兒伊麗莎白（Elizabeth Jane）賣給了
    水手紐森（Newson）。亨查德酒醒後後悔莫及，發誓不再喝酒，千辛萬
    苦尋找妻女。在他成為市長後，終於與蘇珊破鏡重圓。

九十七　破鏡重圓

　　……過了一會兒，他能看清有一個女人的身影從北面缺口或大門悄悄地走進來。他們在競技場的中央見面了。一開始，誰也沒説話 —— 沒有説話的必要 —— 這可憐的女人倚在亨查德的身上，亨查德用雙臂扶着她。

　　"我不喝酒了，"他帶着歉意，吞吞吐吐地小聲説，"蘇珊，你聽見了嗎？—— 我現在不喝酒了 —— 從那天晚上以後我沒喝過。"這就是他一開口説的話。

　　他感覺到女人在點頭表示她聽懂了。過了一兩分鐘，亨查德又説起話來：

　　"蘇珊，我要是早知道你還活着，該多好！認為你和孩子已經死去，這種猜測是完全合乎情理的。我想盡辦法尋找你們 —— 去過不同的地方 —— 登過廣告 —— 最後我想你們跟那個男人到什麼殖民地去了，在海路上溺水身亡。你為什麼一直這樣保持沉默呢？"

"O Michael—because of him—what other reason could there be? I thought I owed him faithfulness to the end of one of our lives—I foolishly believed there was something solemn and binding in the bargain; I thought that even in honour I dared not desert him when he had paid so much for me, in good faith. I meet you now only as his widow—I consider myself that, and that I have no claim upon you. Had he not died I should never have come—never. Of that you may be sure."

...

... "I have thought of this plan; that you and Elizabeth take a cottage in the town as the widow Mrs. Newson and her daughter; that I meet you, court you, and marry you, Elizabeth-Jane coming to my house as my stepdaughter. ... the secret would be yours and mine only; and I should have the pleasure of seeing my own only child under my roof, as well as my wife." ...

"I like the idea of repeating our marriage," said Mrs. Henchard after a pause.

Thomas Hardy: <u>The Mayor of Casterbridge</u>

"啊，邁克爾！……因為他……還會有別的什麼原因嗎？我想應該對他不變心，直到我們兩人當中有一個人死去……我真傻，還以為那次交易有點什麼莊嚴和約束的東西；我想，既然他誠意地為了買我付出了那麼多錢，在道義上我不敢拋開他。現在我來見你只是作為他的寡婦來的……我想我是這樣的，我沒有權力對你要求什麼。要不是他死了，我永遠不會來……永遠不會。這一點你是可以相信的。"

　　……

　　……"我想出這麼一個計劃：你和伊麗莎白以寡婦紐森太太和她女兒的身份在城裏租間小房子。我和你見面，向你求愛，再娶你。而伊麗莎白到我家來，是我的繼女。……這秘密只有你我兩個人知道；這樣我就能在家裏愉快地看到我的獨生女兒和我的妻子。"……

　　"我贊同我們重結一次婚的想法"亨查德太太沉默了一會兒說。

　　　　　　　　(英) 哈代：《卡斯特橋市長》

98　It Is Too Late

He[1] had held out his arms, but they had fallen again to his side; for she had not come forward, remaining still in the opening of the doorway. ...

"Tess!" he said huskily. "Can you forgive me for going away? Can't you—come to me? How do you get to be—like this?"

"It is too late!" said she, her voice sounding hard through the room, her eyes shining unnaturally. ...

"But don't you love me, my dear wife, because I have been so pulled down by illness? You are not so fickle—I am come on purpose for you—my mother and father will welcome you now."

"Yes—O yes, yes! But I say, I say, it is too late."

"I inquired here and there—and I found the way."

"I waited and waited for you," she went on, her tones suddenly resuming their old fluty pathos. "But you did not come. And I wrote to you; and you did not come. He[2] kept on saying you would never come any more, and that I was a

---

1.　He：指克萊（Angel Clare）。苔絲（Tess）在新婚之夜，向克萊把往事和盤托出。但克萊立即棄她而遠走。
2.　He：此處的他即誘奸苔絲的亞歷克（Alec）。

九十八　太晚了

　　他伸出了雙臂，可是又在身體兩旁放下，因為她沒有走上前來，仍舊一動也不動地站在門口。……

　　"苔絲！"他嗓子沙啞地説，"我拋下你出走，你能原諒我嗎？你能回到我身邊嗎？你怎麼會變得 —— 現在這樣的？"

　　"太晚了！"她説，她的聲音重重地響徹整個房間，她的眼睛不自然地閃亮。……

　　"我親愛的妻子，你不愛我，是因為我生病體弱嗎？你不是一個感情不專一的人 —— 我是專程來找你的 —— 我的母親和父親現在會歡迎你了。"

　　"對 —— 對啊，對！可是我説，我説了，太晚了。"

　　"我到處打聽 —— 終於找到這兒來了。"

　　"我左等右等，等着你，"她繼續説，聲音一下子又恢復到以前那樣清脆而哀婉。"可是你不來。我又給你寫信，你還是不來。他總是説你再也不會來了，還說我是個

foolish woman. He was very kind to me, and to mother, and to all of us after father's death. He—"

"I don't understand?"

"He has won me back—to him."...

She continued: "He is upstairs. I hate him now, because he told me a lie—that you would not come again; and you *have* come! These clothes are what he's put upon me: I didn't care what he did wi' me! The step back to him was not so great as it seems. He had been as husband to me: you never had! But—will you go away, Angel, please, and never come any more?"...

"Ah—it is my fault!" said Clare.

Thomas Hardy: <u>Tess of the d'Urbervilles</u>

傻女人。他對我很好，我父親去世以後，他對母親、對我家的人都不錯。他 ——"

"我不懂，你説什麼呀？"

"他把我弄回 —— 到他那裏去了。"……

她繼續説："他就在樓上。我現在恨他，因為他對我撒了個謊 —— 説你不會再回來；可你卻回來了！這身上的衣服就是他弄給我穿的。他怎麼對待我，我也不在乎了！回到他那裏的這一步看來並不大。他曾經做過我的丈夫，而你從來沒有做過！不過 —— 安杰爾，請你走開吧，再也不要來了，好嗎？"……

"唉 —— 這是我的錯！"克萊説。

(英) 哈代：《德伯家的苔絲》

99   He Had Not Loved Her

A knock at the door aroused him.

...

"Ruth!" he said, amazed and bewildered.

Her face was white and strained. She stood just inside the door, one hand against it for support, the other pressed to her side. She extended both hands toward him piteously, and started forward to meet him. As he caught her hands and led her to the Morris chair[1] he noticed how cold they were. He drew up another chair and sat down on the broad arm of it. He was too confused to speak. In his own mind his affair with Ruth was closed and sealed. ...

She came forward, out of her chair and over to him. She rested her hand on his shoulder a moment, breathing quickly, and then slipped into his arms. And in his large, easy way, desirous of not inflicting hurt, knowing that to repulse this offer of herself was to inflict the most grievous hurt a woman could receive, he folded his arms around her and held her close. But there was no warmth in the embrace, no caress in the contact. She had come into his arms, and he held her,

---

1.   Morris chair：William Morris 推廣的椅子，靠背可調節。

九十九　沒愛過她

敲門聲把他驚醒了。

……

"羅絲！"他説，既驚奇，又迷惑。

她的臉色慘白，神情緊張。她進門站在那裏，一隻手扶着門，另一隻手抵在腰間。她可憐地朝他伸着雙手，便開始向他迎來。他握住她的雙手，引她到安樂椅邊。這時，他覺察到這雙手是多麼的涼。他拖來另一把椅子，坐在寬闊的扶手上。他慌亂得説不出話。他心裏想，他和羅絲的那段戀愛已經結束，有了定論。……

她從椅子裏朝着他站起來，走到他跟前，把一隻手放在他的肩上一會兒，急促地喘着氣，然後滑入他的懷抱。他寬宏大量，平易近人，不願傷害人，知道現在拒絕她的獻身，就是給一個女人所能承受的最痛心的傷害，他才用雙臂抱着她，把她摟得緊緊的。但是這擁抱缺乏熱情，這接觸沒有撫愛。她投入他的懷抱，而他摟着她，如此而

that was all. She nestled against him, and then, with a change of position, her hands crept up and rested upon his neck. But his flesh was not fire beneath those hands, and he felt awkward and uncomfortable. ...

"And now you want to renew our love. You want us to be married. You want me. And yet, listen—if my books had not been noticed, I'd nevertheless have been just what I am now. And you would have stayed away. It is all those damned books[2]—"

... They sat in silence for a long time, she thinking desperately and he pondering upon his love which had departed. He knew, now, that he had not really loved her. It was an idealized Ruth he had loved, an ethereal creature of his own creating, the bright and luminous spirit of his love-poems.

Jack London: <u>Martin Eden</u>

---

2. those damned books：羅絲（Ruth）與馬丁‧伊登（Martin Eden）熱戀一陣後，終因社會地位的懸殊，未能結合。待馬丁寫作成名，羅絲卻主動來找他了。

已。她依偎着他，接着，換了個姿勢，雙手慢慢地往上移動，擱在他的脖子上。可是他的肌膚在這雙手下面並不火熱，他覺得尷尬，很不自在。……

"而現在你想重溫舊夢了。你想要我們結婚。你需要我了。可是，聽着 —— 如果我的書還沒有引起人的注意，那我還是現在這個樣子。而你呢，還是不會理睬我。都是因為這些該死的書 —— "

……他們默不作聲地坐了很長時間。她絕望地思量着，而他呢，默想着已經泯滅的愛情。現在他知道，他並沒有真正愛過她。他愛的是理想化的羅絲，是他臆造的天仙，是他愛情詩裏光輝燦爛的神靈。……

（美）杰克·倫敦：《馬丁·伊登》

100   A Thunderclap

Ivan Ilyich closed his eyes as if awaiting some celestial thunderclap, and trembled from head to foot when he heard a clear voice say rapidly: "For me? Who is it?"

There was a sound of footsteps in the intervening rooms. They were flying out of the abyss of two years of waiting[1]....

"Have you come to see me?"

Dasha faltered. Her features twitched, the brows flying upwards, and the lips falling apart, but the fleeting shade of alarm disappeared instantly from her face and her eyes lit up with joy and astonishment.

"Is it you?" she murmured, almost inaudibly, and she threw her arms violently round the neck of Ivan Ilyich, kissing him with tender, quivering lips. Then she stood back.

"Come with me, Ivan Ilyich!"

And Dasha ran into the drawing room, sat down in an armchair and, bending over her knees, covered her face with her hands.

"I know I'm being silly," she whispered, wiping her eyes hard.

---

1.   ...waiting：此篇描寫伊凡‧伊立奇（Ivan Ilyich）逃離前綫重見達莎（Dasha）。

一百　晴天霹靂

　　伊凡・伊立奇閉上眼睛，就像等待着一聲晴天霹靂。他聽到清晰急促的說話聲：“來找我的？誰呀？”他不由得從頭到腳哆嗦起來。

　　幾個中間房間裏響起了腳步聲。這聲音好像是從兩年期待的深淵裏傳來的。……

　　“你是來看我的嗎？”

　　達莎遲疑着，臉抽搐起來，眉毛揚起，嘴張着。可是這短暫的驚恐的陰影立即從臉上消失，眼神裏露出喜悅和驚奇。

　　“是你？”她低聲說，低得幾乎聽不見，便張開雙臂，猛地摟住伊凡・伊立奇的脖子，以她哆嗦着的嬌嫩嘴唇吻起他來。接着她又退開了。

　　“伊凡・伊立奇，跟我來！”

　　於是達莎跑進客廳，在扶手椅上坐下，彎着上身，用雙手把臉遮掩起來。

　　“我知道我真傻。”她一邊低語，一邊使勁擦着眼睛。

...

They went on talking thus for a short time longer. Gradually they both became trammelled by their shyness.

"Have you been here—in Moscow—long?" asked Dasha, lowering her eyes.

"I came here straight from the station."

...

"Will you come again this evening?" asked Dasha, almost inaudibly.

...

"Well, I'm off," he said, getting up. "I'll come back in the evening." Dasha extended her hand to him. He took her soft, firm hand, and the contact seemed to burn him up, and send the blood flying into his face. He squeezed her fingers and went into the passage, but looked back from the door. Her back to the light, Dasha was looking after him from beneath bent brows.

A. N. Tolstoy: The Sisters

……

　　他們就這樣談了不一會兒，由於不好意思，逐漸感到拘束起來。

　　"你來這兒 —— 莫斯科 —— 好久了嗎？"達莎低垂着眼睛問道。

　　"我從火車站直接來的。"

……

　　"你今天晚上還來嗎？"達莎問道，聲音幾乎聽不出來。

……

　　"嗯，我走了，"他起身説，"我晚上再來。"達莎伸出一隻手給他。他握住她柔軟堅定的手。這一接觸好像把他點燃，使他的血液湧到臉上。他緊捏了一下她的手指，便走進過道，在門口又回頭看看。達莎背對着光綫，攢起眉頭，目送着他。

　　　　　　　　　　（俄）A. N. 托爾斯泰：《兩姊妹》

一百叢書㉙

外國名著愛情描寫一百段

100 LOVE DESCRIPTIONS FROM GREAT NOVELS

主編者◆張信威

選譯者◆賀方

發行人◆王學哲

總編輯◆方鵬程

責編◆金堅

出版發行：臺灣商務印書館股份有限公司

台北市重慶南路一段三十七號

電話：(02)2371-3712

讀者服務專線：0800056196

郵撥：0000165-1

網路書店：www.cptw.com.tw

E-mail：cptw@cptw.com.tw

網址：www.cptw.com.tw

局版北市業字第 993 號

香港初版一刷：1998 年 7 月

臺灣初版一刷：1999 年 2 月

臺灣初版二刷：2006 年 6 月

定價：新台幣 380 元

本書經商務印書館（香港）有限公司授權出版

ISBN 957-05-1564-3

100臺北市重慶南路一段37號

臺灣商務印書館　收

對摺寄回，謝謝！

傳統現代　並翼而翔

Flying with the wings of tradition and modernity.